LONG GUN

Center Point
Large Print

Also by Les Savage, Jr. and available from Center Point Large Print:

Danger Rides the River
Wolves of the Sundown Trail

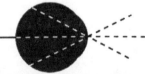

**This Large Print Book carries the
Seal of Approval of N.A.V.H.**

LONG GUN

— A Western Quartet —

Les Savage, Jr.

CENTER POINT LARGE PRINT
THORNDIKE, MAINE

This Center Point Large Print edition is published
in the year 2015 by arrangement with
Golden West Literary Agency.

Copyright © 2009 by Golden West Literary Agency.

Additional copyright information on page 301.

The text of this Large Print edition is unabridged.
In other aspects, this book may vary
from the original edition.
Printed in the United States of America
on permanent paper.
Set in 16-point Times New Roman type.

ISBN: 978-1-62899-447-6 (hardcover)
ISBN: 978-1-62899-452-0 (paperback)

Library of Congress Cataloging-in-Publication Data

Savage, Les.
[Short stories. Selections]
Long gun : a western quartet / Les Savage, Jr. —
    Center Point Large Print edition.
pages ; cm
Summary: "Four western stories of the struggles around Santa Fe
during New Mexico's transition from being a Mexican province to
becoming a United States territory"—Provided by publisher.
ISBN 978-1-62899-447-6 (hardcover : alk. paper)
ISBN 978-1-62899-452-0 (pbk. : alk. paper)
1. Large type books. I. Savage, Les. Long Gun.
    II. Savage, Les. Traitor town.
    III. Savage, Les. Blood star over Santa Fe.
    IV. Savage, Les. Death song of the Santa Fe rebels. V. Title.
PS3569.A826A6 2015
813′.54—dc23
                                                          2014041792

Table of Contents

Long Gun

The author's original title for this story was "Tall Man, Long Gun." It was completed in late October and sold to Fiction House on November 28, 1944. The author was paid $400.00 at the rate of 2¢ a word. Rather unusually, the short novel retained the author's title when it was published in *Frontier Stories* (Fall, 1945). For its first book appearance the title has been somewhat abbreviated.

— I —

They were camped in the cottonwoods down along the river south of Santa Fe, a motley collection of greasy, godless, cursing trappers, and the little girl was incongruous, somehow, moving through their outer circles toward the fire. The light caught her hair for a moment, the color of ripe chestnuts, done up in a high chignon above the delicate flush of her face. The milky line of her neck rose from the dark blue *capisayo* she had thrown over her shoulders, and one of her slim hands made a pale blot against the flowered crinoline of her skirt, holding it up out of the dirt.

One by one the men had stopped talking, and she reached the fire to stand a moment in the uncomfortable silence, looking around the circle of staring, bearded faces.

"I see you're ready to leave," she said. "I thought you'd be the last men Governor Armijo could frighten away."

One of them laughed. Little Tiswin was undoubtedly the biggest man she had ever seen, standing more than six and a half feet high in his quilled Ute moccasins. He claimed he had to wear his shirts till they rotted off him, because once having pulled them on over his head, he couldn't get them back off his gargantuan torso without ripping them to shreds, and no matter how big his Ute squaw sewed his buckskin leggings, they would invariably shrink in the wet season and split out at the seams with the pressure of his enormous thighs. He was a notoriously poor trapper, Little Tiswin, and the Indians attributed that to the hatred the beavers had for him, declaring that every time he laughed it collapsed all the beaver lodges within a radius of a hundred miles. He laughed now, and the girl wouldn't doubt it. "What's the use of staying around any more, Miss Arnaud? Governor Armijo's closed the Santa Fe Trail. Ain't going to be no more trade with the States. The fur business is through down this way as far as Yankees go."

The odor of sweat and leather and whiskey was growing stronger all the time, and Celia Arnaud couldn't keep her full low lip from curling faintly. Little Tiswin saw it, and the grin faded from his beefy face. The trappers began shifting restlessly.

"You all know I came from Saint Louis to take over Arnaud Furs when Dad died last month," said the girl. "I haven't been in Santa Fe for more than three weeks now, but from what little dealings I've had with you, I thought you were at least men. I'll grant you we're through down here . . . unless we can get our pelts through to Saint Louis this year. That's what I came to see you about. There's such a thing as running the blockade."

Little Tiswin ran thick, calloused fingers through a great beard that lay over his chest like curly yellow hoar frost. "I guess you ain't been here long enough to know how things stand, Miss Arnaud. Last year, Texas sent an expedition up here to start a revolution and throw off Mexico's rule over New Mexico, and help establish the Texas boundary claim to the east bank of the Río Grande. The whole Texas-Santa Fe expedition was arrested by Armijo, some of them shot, the rest sent to Mexico City. It made General Santa Anna so hopping mad he sent an order up here for Governor Armijo to close the Santa Fe Trail to further trade. Right now, Armijo has three thousand Mexican dragoons in the province, and, if you tried to run his blockade, you'd have every one of them down your neck. I don't see how you figure to get that beaver anyway, if Armijo's confiscated all your property. Did you think you could just go into his customhouse and ask him for your pelts back because your grandpa's old beaver hat's wearing out?"

"Oh, you fools!" Her *capisayo* rose across her bosom with her angry breath. "How many times did Dad give you a new outfit on credit when the beaver had run thin, Tiswin? How many times did he bail you out of Armijo's jail when you'd wrecked La Fonda on one of your corn brew sprees? You'd do this for him if he were alive. He was the best friend you had in Santa Fe, any of you. Half of you wouldn't be alive if it weren't for him. . . ."

"No." Little Tiswin shook his shaggy yellow head. "We wouldn't even attempt it for your father, Celia, because he wouldn't ask us to. He'd know it was suicide, trying to get those pelts out of Armijo's customhouse, and, even if we did succeed there, what chance would a handful of trappers have against three thousand Mexican dragoons? Me, I'm heading for Colter's Hell and brew me enough corn *tiswin* to last all winter and drink a buffalo-hide pail full of it for every Yellowstone beaver I trap, and even then I wouldn't be drunk enough to do what you ask. There ain't nobody drunk enough, or crazy enough to do it."

"Nobody but Washakie Winters."

Someone had said it from the group standing beyond the firelight. A sudden hush fell over the camp. A faggot snapping in the flames had a loud, startling sound. Celia Arnaud looked toward the one who had spoken, but couldn't distinguish his features. A strange, eerie sensation caught at her, and she turned swiftly back to Little Tiswin.

"Washakie Winters? What do you mean?"

Little Tiswin spoke reluctantly. "You don't know?"

"How could I?" she said. "Washakie Winters?"

The men had started shifting nervously again, and muttering, but as soon as she said the name, that strange hush fell once more. Little Tiswin licked his lips, avoiding her eyes.

"You don't want him to run your furs through."

"He could do it?" she said.

"He could do anything," answered Little Tiswin.

"Amen," said someone else.

"Where is he?" asked the girl.

"Nobody ever knows that," said the giant.

"Oh, someone must." Celia stamped her foot. "Will you stop all this mystery? If this Washakie Winters can get my furs through, I want to know who he is and where he is."

"Who might be easier to tell than where," said Little Tiswin. "Armijo has a price on Washakie's head of twenty thousand *pesos*. The British Crown wants him for poaching he did in the Territories a while back."

"You mean he's a thief?"

"He'd be insulted by such a common name," said Little Tiswin. "I've heard him called worse. It's said the United States government would like to do more than call him names."

"It is said!" flamed Celia. "You hear. The British government thinks. Doesn't anybody know one single thing for sure about this man?"

"I saw the *cantina* at Taos after Washakie got through his drunk there," said someone.

"He turned his bull loose in it," said another trapper. "No one man could do that much damage to a building with his bare hands."

Celia looked around the circle. "His bull?"

"He doesn't ride a horse like any ordinary man," said Little Tiswin. "He rides a coal-black buffalo bull with horns as wide as a man is tall."

"They say he deserted from Leavenworth when they wouldn't let him lead his company riding the bull," said a trapper.

"Oh, don't be fantastic!" Celia bit her lip, trying to control her anger. "Isn't there anybody who can tell me where to find this man?"

"What man?" asked Jules Veinier, coming through the outer circle of trappers.

He was the chief factor of Arnaud Furs in Santa Fe, Veinier, a tall young Frenchman in tight, broadcloth trousers and an immaculate gray tailcoat. There was a vivid, animal grace in the way he walked, striding forward with a lithe pivot to his slim hips that swung his broad, powerful shoulders from side to side with each step. His gleaming black hair was queued beneath a flat-topped hat, and his eyes reached Celia with an intense, flashing brilliance.

"I told you not to come down here," he said angrily.

"What's wrong with down here?" asked Little Tiswin.

"Yours is hardly the company a lady should seek, *m'sieu*," said the Frenchman.

Little Tiswin took a step toward him. "Listen, Veinier. . . ."

The Frenchman stiffened. "Don't come any closer, *m'sieu*."

Veinier's voice was like a rapier sliding from its velvet sheath. Little Tiswin stopped abruptly, standing there a moment with his mouth open slightly. Then he threw back his yellow head and let out a laugh that shook the few remaining leaves from the cottonwoods.

"Don't come any closer, he says, don't come any closer. Maybe you'd like me to put my hands on you, Veinier, maybe you'd like . . ."

"You won't put your hands on me," said Veinier darkly. He turned to the girl, catching her elbow. "I told you, Celia, Santa Fe is no longer safe for Americans. You had best get out of the city as quickly as possible, and out of here now."

She tried to hold back. "Jules, let me go. If you haven't nerve enough to get my furs from Armijo and run them through his blockade, I've got someone who has."

He wasn't pulling her roughly, but she could do nothing against the power in his gentle, firm hand, and was forced to follow him past the last trapper, stumbling over an *aparejo* pack. "It isn't a matter of nerve, Celia. It's a matter of being sensible. You know I'd run Armijo's blockade alone if it would gain you anything. But what would my death gain you? What would the death of anyone who tried it gain you? Your furs wouldn't be in Saint Louis. They'd be right back here where you started. If there was a way to get them through, believe me, I'd do it. But there isn't . . ." He stopped suddenly, looking at her intently. "What did you say?"

"I said I have someone who will run Armijo's blockade."

"*Oui*? You're joking, of course. No man would be that big a fool."

"Washakie Winters."

She saw the surprise pull the skin tautly across his flat high cheek bones, and then saw the slight pallor whiten the sudden drawn lines at the corner of his mouth. "Don't be a fool, Celia. Not that *homme*. You could never find him in the first place. But that doesn't signify. He's a murderer, Celia, a deserter from the United States Army, the worst cut-throat this side of Saint Louis. Three governments have a price on his head. He'd kill you before you even got to tell him what you wanted. No, Celia. . . ."

"Yes, Jules!" She tried to pull away from him, felt the harsh bark of a cottonwood against her back. "It's my last chance. If I lose Arnaud Furs, I have nothing left, no money, no home, no people."

"You have me." His body was heavy and hot against her, pressing her back against the tree.

She struggled in his grasp. "Don't, Jules. I've got to get my furs through. I don't care what Washakie Winters is. If he'll run the blockade, I'm going after him. Let me go!"

Something in her voice made him release her, step- ping back. He stood there a moment in the gloom of evening, staring at her, breathing heavily.

"You little fool," he said. "If you go out hunting Washakie Winters, you'll never get back to Santa Fe alive!"

— II —

Lieutenant Miguelito Separ stepped wearily off his dusty horse and stood there a moment, disgust plain in his thin, supercilious face as he glanced at the line of lancers behind him. This was what they gave him for soldiers. Peons, that's what they were, stupid, bucolic, gaping peons who wouldn't know a cavalry charge from a right-about-face. He had been two years at Saumur, France, studying cavalry tactics under the best commanders in the world; he had spent four glorious years in the Collegio Militar at Mexico City, riding with the most superb cavalry in the New World; the Golden Cross of Honor hung on his chest for distinguished service in the war with Texas. And here he was, stuck up in this stinking province under a drunken despot of a governor, commanding a troop of the laziest *borrachos* who ever carried their *lanzas* wrong. Contemptuously he dismissed them, pulled his bandanna around from back of his neck to wipe the sweat off his face, and moved toward the mud-walled customhouse.

Many of Governor Armijo's officers were of the *gente*, and Separ bore all the lithe, aquiline beauty of the young Mexican aristocrat, his shoulders high and square beneath the round blue lancer's coat with its red cuffs and collar, his saber scabbard popping against his blue velvet breeches, unbuttoned, as high as his knees to reveal his black cavalry *botas*.

Taos was the last official Mexican outpost between New Mexico and the States, and it was through the customhouse here that all furs going eastward had passed when the Santa Fe Trail was open. A fat customs official sat with his feet propped up on his desk in the low-roofed, adobe-walled room, talking with a woman whose back was to Separ.

"*Sí*, it was about two weeks ago. *Señor* Martino Kenna had his *burros* lined up outside for inspection. It was just dusk, and we had lit our *antorchas* to see the furs. Then the sentry up on Placita Road started yelling something about *Indios*. We thought Apaches maybe, and ran up that way loading our *escopetas*. I guess Kenna was the only one who kept his head enough to stay with the mules. All his men were running with us. We were up on Placita Road when it happened. *Señor* Kenna said they came jumping down off the roof tops over the customhouse here. He recognized Washakie Winters. *Pues*, what could Kenna do against all of them? ¡*Nada, caramba*! Nothing! They stampeded the mules before we could get back. Across the *río*, on into the hills. Sixty thousand *pesos* worth of furs, *Señor* Kenna said . . ."

"Get on your feet, you insolent *perro*," snapped Separ. "You are talking with a lady present. Where are your manners? Can't Armijo turn his back an instant without you officials letting your post degenerate to this?"

The fat man scrambled out of his chair, almost knocking it over, stumbling on his words. "*Perdóneme, teniente, perdóneme*. You are *correcto*. Where are my manners? *Caramba*."

The woman had turned. Not a woman, really. A girl. Separ could see how young she was, with a strained, pale look to her face. She wore tight-fitting buckskin leggings, covered with the dust of a long ride, and her chestnut hair fell down about the shoulders of a leather jacket, something bulging beneath it on one side. With all her apparent weariness, she still retained a beauty that quickened Separ's pulse, and he bowed low.

"*Teniente* Miguelito Separ at your service, *señorita*. Haven't I seen you somewhere before in the province?"

"How do you do," she said.

Separ gave her an intent glance, then turned to the official, flourishing a folded sheet of parchment from his breast pocket. "I come under orders direct from our illustrious Governor Armijo. A half-breed named Chefuri brought news to Santa Fe of what this *bribón* Washakie Winters had perpetrated here at Taos. Armijo has doubled the price on Winters's head. I have orders to find that head and bring it back on a lance to hang up in the plaza at Santa Fe. You are to give me all the aid possible in tracking down the man."

"*Sí, sí.*" The fat official was obsequious. "I was telling the *señorita* here how Washakie Winters stole *Señor* Martino Kenna's furs from under our very noses. . . ."

"Kenna?" said Separ. "Isn't he an *Americano*? What was he doing with pelts in Taos? The trail has been closed."

"You are from Santa Fe," said the man. "You should know more about that than I."

"I do not question my orders," said Separ haughtily.

The official shrugged gross shoulders. "*Pues*, neither do I. Kenna had an official order from the governor. A man in this office questioned an order like that last year. His widow now resides on Ojitos Lane."

Separ hardly heard him, because he had realized who the woman was, and he turned toward her. "How is it you're here, *Señorita* Arnaud? Governor Armijo issued a proclamation that all aliens in Santa Fe were confined to the limits of the city. I didn't have the pleasure of meeting you down there, but I remember seeing you on the streets not a week ago."

"I heard no proclamation," she said stiffly.

Separ made his voice suave. "Surely you must have. It was issued a month ago. I'm afraid I'll have to put you under restraint here until I send word back to the *palacio*."

Something desperate entered her voice. "No. You have no right. . . ."

"No?" Separ drew himself up. "I have every right, *señorita*. What are you doing here? Why were you interested in Washakie Winters?"

"I wasn't. . . ."

"*Pues*, she was," said the official.

"Nobody asked you to open your *boca*," snapped Separ. He called his sergeant. "*Sargento mayor*. Bring in two men. I have a person to put under guard."

"No!" Celia Arnaud started to back across the room, and the lieutenant saw what had made the bulge beneath her coat. It must have been stuck in her waistband, and it was a big Waters pistol. She had it in her hand now with her little thumb hooked around its double-necked hammer. "Don't make a move, Lieutenant. A Fifty-Four slug makes an awfully big hole in a man. You're right about my being interested in Washakie Winters. I came north to find him and nobody is going to stop me, least of all you."

"*Least* of all?" Separ laughed. "You don't seem to regard me very highly, *señorita*. Don't be a *necio*. I have a whole troop of *lanceros* outside. The alley from that back door only leads you around to the plaza again. You can't escape. Get her, *Sargento*, what are you standing there like *imbéciles* for?"

The sergeant-major and two men stood in the doorway. They shifted uncertainly into the room, then stopped again, held by the black bore of that Waters. The official made a small moaning sound. Separ looked at the troopers, feeling his thin lips curl with contempt. Peons! Then he laughed wryly, and shrugged, and began moving deliberately toward Celia Arnaud. "Lieutenant!" Her voice was strained. "Don't. Please. I told you. Not another step."

"*Señorita*"—he laughed easily, still moving forward with that lithe grace that might have come from countless hours fencing in the courtyards of the Collegio Militar—"I don't think such a beautiful woman could shoot a man down in cold blood."

Her mouth drew back against her teeth and he could see her thumb tremble on the double-necked hammer. His boots formed a soft sound against the earthen floor, taking another step, another. She made a small, strangled noise, and whirled suddenly toward the back door. Laughing, he took a long jump after her, grabbing her shoulders. She jerked back toward him, tearing out of his grasp.

"Maybe I can't shoot," he heard her gasp, "but you won't stop me." Then the gun hit the side of his neck with a dull, fleshy sound that he heard through the sudden stunning pain. He felt himself falling, and his shoulder smashed into something solid, and, when the pain had gone enough for him to comprehend things, he was crouched up against the wall. The rear doorway was empty, and legs made their dim running pattern by him as the *sargento mayor* and his two men went through the back door.

Separ's first impulse as he lurched to his feet was to follow them. Then he realized another man going that way wouldn't help. He had to block her off from the entrance of the alley onto the plaza. Stumbling through the front door past the customs official, he shouted at his corporal: "*Cabo*, take two men and cover the alley where it opens into Santa Fe. Carlos, you and Ramirez come with me. The rest of you spread out across the plaza. Stop that woman when she comes out if you have to shoot her!"

The men scattered.

The alley ran behind the customs office, one mouth opening into the plaza near La Calle de Santa Fe, the other running into La Fonda Street. Running down toward La Fonda with his two men, Separ had to keep himself from falling by putting his hand against the wall. He stumbled around the corner into the alley, head still ringing from the blow; farther down where the back door of the customhouse made its dark blot in the yellow wall, one of the troopers who had been with the sergeant was kneeling.

"That Frenchman," he gasped when Separ reached him. "Veinier? I knew him in Santa Fe. He was holding two horses in La Calle de Santa Fe. Ran in here when he saw us after the girl. Helped her onto the roof before we could reach them. Shot me. The *sargento* followed them. . . ."

This was originally an Indian pueblo, with the communal houses built three stories high, each story recessed back the length of a room on the story below, so that the building looked like three huge steps with ladders leading from one level to the next. The whole block of houses was built together, so a person could travel across the roof top of any story from one end of the plaza to the other. The wall facing the alley was three stories high, but there was a window opening above Separ's head the height of one floor.

One of Separ's men made a stirrup of his hands, and Separ mounted from there to another's shoulders, and hauled himself through the window. It must have been the way Veinier had helped the girl up because the curtain was torn off, and Separ made out the dim form of a woman cowering against the wall with a baby at her breast. He brushed aside the heavy Bayeta blanket curtaining the doorway and rushed onto the roof of the first level.

Far ahead he could make out the figures of the girl and Veinier getting down to drop off the roof where it overlooked La Fonda. He reached the edge of the roof in time to see them galloping away on two horses, driving a third riderless mount ahead of them. A man in flapping *chaparreras* was running down the street behind them, shouting, and two more *vaqueros* were standing by the empty hitch rack directly below Separ.

"Our horses!" one of them yelled at the lieutenant. "The *gringos* got our horses!"

The corporal careened around the corner from Santa Fe, followed by his two men, and Separ shouted at him. "*Cabo*, bring your *caballo* over here and dismount beneath the wall. *Pronto*, you *caracol*, *pronto*!"

The *cabo* yanked his dusty black onto its haunches, and then sidled it over against the wall and swung down. Separ sat on the edge of the roof, jumping off, twisting so he could hit, forking the horse. He struck the saddle hard, and the animal bolted, almost throwing him over backward. Then he had the reins and was spurring it into a headlong gallop up the street, shouting for the other two lancers to follow him, leaving the two *vaqueros* and the corporal there in the dust.

He crossed the Avenida Pueblo and saw the

rest of his troop streaming out of the plaza down Pueblo toward him. The red and green pennons of Mexico fluttered from their lances, held every which way, some carried horizontally along the horse, others straight up in saddle butts. The lieutenant's face twisted disgustedly. Stupid *burros*! Give him half a dozen of his cadets from Mexico City; he would show these *bribónes* how a soldier rode.

He pulled his horse around the corner and thundered past the last huddled adobes flanking the old Kiowa Trail as it led out of town. The low bunchy piñon spreading across a rise reached out and he *clattered* to the crest of a low top land, then hauled his blowing mount to a stop. The trail dropped down the other side of the rise ahead of him and hugged the purple Sangre de Cristos in a series of serpentine curves. But it was empty.

The *sargento mayor* was first to come up from behind. He was a grizzled old mercenary from Chihuahua, Sergeant Torres, and his cuirass of double-folded deerskin bore scars that he swore had been made by Colonel James Bowie's knife at the Alamo.

"It looks as if the *señorita* has disappeared like the smoke from your campfire, *teniente*," he said sardonically.

Separ turned toward him, face dark. There had always been an enmity between these two men. The sergeant's grin was mocking, and, as the rest of the troop *clattered* up with their accouterments rattling and their *lanzas* clashing, Lieutenant Separ spoke with a singular, bitter intensity that took the grin off Torres's face.

"No woman can do this to me, *Sargento*. My orders are to get Washakie Winters. But if she is after him, too, then I am after her, and my name isn't Miguelito Separ if I don't come back with two heads to hang in the plaza!"

— III —

The white mist came after the rains sometimes, like this, and it curled mordantly around the shadowy cavalcade of weary riders as they padded through the somber lanes of dripping bristle cone pine, somewhere in the Sangre de Cristos north of Taos. The leader was a square, stocky man in a heavy, black buffalo coat and a long-tailed, wolf-skin hat. He rode a big, hammerheaded mare with his *tapadero* stirrups flapped out wide, and his dark eyes burned with a driving anger deep beneath shaggy black brows.

"I told you what would happen if your damn' fool trackers missed him this time, Chefuri," he said acridly.

Chefuri rode directly behind the buffalo-coated man. Half white, half Apache, his face was an evil mahogany enigma beneath a flat black hat with a tattered brim, his lean body moving sinuously to every shift of the rawhide pinto beneath him, the tails of a long coat flapping soggily against the horse's damp, steaming hide.

"You know what happened, Kenna," said the half-breed. "He saw us coming, that's all. Nobody else in the world ever saw us coming when we didn't want them to, but he did. It's up here now."

Martin Kenna jerked his mare upslope, hunching deeper into his buffalo coat, and the others followed him. There were four of them, carrying long Jake Hawkins guns across the pommels of their saddles, tall, angry Yankees with the scars of the trapper patterning their sinewy brown hands. The horses were breathing heavily by the time they reached the little glade high on the slope. From here, Kenna could look through a cut of burned timber to the bottom of the valley where the Pecos River flowed, narrow and sluggish. He stepped down off his horse to kick viciously at the soggy ashes of a fire.

"You can see how close we missed him," said Chefuri. "They must've had camp all set up when they heard us coming."

Kenna became aware that his four men had dismounted and were standing around something beyond the fire. He moved over to see the body lying in the wet wheat grass. The woman had been scalped, and disfigured, and the back of her buckskin dress was soaked with blood, and the hilt of a big Bowie still protruded from her side. Kenna whirled on Chefuri.

"You fool!" he shouted, grabbing the man by his long black coat. "Haven't we got enough troubles without a murder on our hands, too?" He began to shake Chefuri violently, so filled with rage now that he was almost screaming. "You fool! I don't know what the hell I put up with you for . . . !"

"Kenna," gasped Chefuri, and tore free of the man's heavy hands, staggering backward with his evil face flushed dark, grabbing for the ivory-handled Remington belted around the outside of his coat. Then he stopped, and straightened, with the gun only half out of its smooth holster. Martin Kenna's move hadn't been violent or noticeably fast. He had done it almost without thought, dipping his elbows inward until their tips caught the edges of his buffalo coat. When his elbows flopped back out, they carried the two edges of the coat away from his stomach, and automatically swung his hands back in until they were directly above the two Cherington pistols stuck in his wide belt with their gold-chased butts pointing inward for a cross-arm draw.

"Go ahead," he told Chefuri, and his hands hung above the Cheringtons without actually touching their curved handles. "Go ahead. I want you to."

Chefuri stood there a long rigid moment, holding his Remington. His harsh breathing was the only sound in the clearing. Then he dropped his gun back into its holster carefully.

"Listen, Kenna," he said. "Listen. I didn't do it. I swear. Ask Tovar, ask Romero. She was like this when we came. Her and that Ute buck."

Kenna had seen the other body, a man's, farther away. "Where are Tovar and Romero?"

"I sent them out to follow the tracks," said Chefuri. "The rain's probably washed the trail away by now, though."

"If you're lying to me, Chefuri," said Kenna, "if I find out you did this, I'll kill you."

Chefuri's face was pale, and he held up his hand to say something. No words came out. He was looking past Kenna, and it made Kenna turn around.

Four riders approached.

Tovar and Romero were Chefuri's two Apache trackers, and they came in flanking two other horsebackers. Celia Arnaud was riding a buckskin that the Mexicans called a *bayo coyote*, her bare chestnut hair wet and curling from the rain. Jules Veinier was the other.

Veinier bent forward in his saddle to peer at Kenna, then swung down angrily.

"What's the meaning of this, Kenna? Your Indians come out and herd us in like cattle. You can't . . ."

"Take it easy, Frenchie, take it easy," said Kenna. "It isn't often they run across anybody up in this neck of the woods. They were out tracking a man. Maybe they thought you were him."

"What man?" asked Jules Veinier.

"Washakie Winters," said Kenna.

The girl stiffened on her horse. "What do you want with him?"

"A number of things," said Kenna. "For one, he took a passel of furs off me at Taos. Chefuri here had tracked Washakie to this camp, but when we closed in on him, Washakie got wind of us somehow and slipped out."

"I've heard it said he smells things coming as an animal does," said Veinier dryly.

Kenna looked at him, irritation making his voice harsh. "You sound skeptical."

"I'm not naïve."

"Neither am I," said Kenna. "But I know Washakie Winters."

The girl had climbed from her horse, and was staring past Kenna. Suddenly she grew white, and she turned to put her face against the saddle skirt with a small, strangled sound. Veinier took a step toward the body of the woman, revulsion plain in his face. Kenna looked at Romero, indicated the body.

"We find it that way," said Chefuri's Apache, wiping a nervous hand on his greasy blanket leggings. "Chefuri and me and Tovar. Here when we came. All chopped up an' . . ."

"Never mind, never mind," said Kenna, moving

over to squat above the corpse. He turned the bloody hand over. "Ute woman. Little Tiswin's squaw. He gave her that ring when they were married Christian down in Santa Fe."

"You say Washakie Winters was here?" said Veinier.

"Just before we came," said Kenna, nodding toward the knife sticking in the woman. "Recognize this Bowie?"

"Of course not," said Veinier. Then he seemed to sense what Kenna was driving at. "But a white man wouldn't . . . I mean this scalping . . . this disfigurement. . . ."

"Wouldn't he?" said Kenna. "You haven't been around much, Veinier. I've seen more than one white man use a scalping knife. Get them out here and it don't take long before they've caught on to most of the Indian ways. Look how this hair was taken off. An Indian would make a series of gouges all around the scalp just below the hairline and then pull straight up. This has been slashed at the brow and ripped off front to back. And what Indian would toss the hair aside like that after he'd gone to the trouble of getting it for his scalp belt?"

Veinier stood there, looking at the body for a moment, then, with a palpable effort, moved his gaze to Kenna. "Winters took the furs from you at Taos?"

Kenna rose, and their eyes met, and the corner

of Kenna's deep, chiseled mouth turned up in a mirthless smile. "Yes, Washakie took the furs from me, Veinier."

"You'll get them back, of course."

"Of course."

Veinier bent closer, his voice soft, insistent: "I'm just Jules Veinier. You knew me down in Santa Fe, that's all."

Kenna glanced at the girl, still turned against the saddle skirt of her horse, and his cold smile grew. "I see what you mean. All right. You're just Jules Veinier."

"*Bien*," said the Frenchman. "And now, what?"

Kenna toed the body of the squaw, looking at the Bowie again. "If this was Tiswin's squaw, Tiswin will be along soon. He must have left her up here when he hit for Santa Fe and meant to meet her coming back. I think maybe we'll wait for him. I think maybe he'll be able to tell us something about Washakie Winters. What do you think?"

— IV —

A woodpecker was working industriously on a juniper tree, knocking loose a steady stream of alligator bark that dropped to the ground fifty feet below where the man sat with his back against a spruce, watching the sloughings come down. Almost all the fringe running down the seams of his buckskin leggings had been hacked off to use as whangs for repairing worn moccasins or broken pack saddles or torn clothing, and his elk-hide shirt gleamed with grease from the countless times he had wiped the remains of bear steak off his fingers.

He stood up suddenly, with no apparent effort in the movement, and paced nervously toward the other side of the clearing, something wild and covert in the way he glanced swiftly into the trees. There was a taut, ferine look to his whole lean body, as if he would jump at the slightest sound, and he carried a five-foot Jake Hawkins rifle in one hand so that it swung with his stride.

"Sit down, Washakie," said Little Tiswin where he squatted over an unloaded pack. "You're getting worse every time I see you. Jump at your own shadow, I swear."

Washakie Winters shoved his gray, wolf-skin hat back on hair so black and slick it looked wet. He stooped forward to peer, narrow-eyed, down the dark lanes of timber surrounding the glade. His face matched the lean, drawn refinement of his body, almost wolf-like in its bearded gauntness, saddle-leather skin drawn tautly across his high, flat cheek bones. Little Tiswin threw a W hobble on his ornery lead mule and turned to unload another animal, looking strangely at Washakie.

"So they got my squaw," he said finally, and his voice had a guttural, dead sound.

Washakie turned toward Little Tiswin, placing his back instinctively against a tree, holding out one hand in a helpless gesture. "I was trying to bring myself to tell you, Tiswin. You know?"

Little Tiswin unhitched the Mexican breeching and breast band on a gray mule and took the double hitch off the lash rope, still watching Washakie in that odd, calculating way. "Think I wouldn't? How did you?"

"Word passes," said Washakie. "I left here every day to scout my back trail while I was waiting for you to come. Met Old Gotch stringing beaver lines down at Mora Creek. He told me."

"What happened?" said Little Tiswin.

"I thought you knew?"

"I mean with you," said Little Tiswin. "You were supposed to meet me in that camp above the Pecos last week, too."

Washakie nodded. "I hit there about half an hour before the rain. Your squaw and her brother had already arrived from Pecuris, and told me they'd had word you'd left Santa Fe, and should be in that day. I knew someone had been tailing me for about a week, and I'd just started stripping some jerky with my Bowie when Nailla's brother came back from getting water down-slope. . . ."

"With your Bowie?" said Little Tiswin.

Washakie glanced at him, puzzled. "Yes, I told you. Your squaw's brother came back and said two Apaches were coming up on my back trail. He said he knew them and there wouldn't be any trouble for him and Nailla, but I'd better shuck out and head for this camp at Mora Peak, and they'd foller me as soon as you came. After that little job of work at Taos, I didn't want to be spotted by anyone tailing me, so I left. It started to rain, and I knew that would wipe out my trail, so I headed straight for Mora Peak. I been waiting here ever since. Tiswin, how was I to know? Nailla's brother said they'd be all right. Nobody ever connected you with me. They wouldn't have done it for . . ."

"Yeah, yeah, I wasn't thinking about that. Not your fault, Washakie. No cause for you to stay with 'em. They'd been traveling alone all the way from Pecuris. Nobody to blame, is there? Just happened, that's all." Little Tiswin had been speaking absently, dully, but suddenly he looked up, eyes glittering strangely at Washakie. "Who do you think done it, Washakie? Those Apaches, maybe? Got drunk, you think?"

"We'll find out," said Washakie.

As if jerking himself from a trance, Little Tiswin turned down to the *aparejo*, unlashing the nigh pocket. "Will we? I reckon."

He looked up at the black-haired man again, and Washakie frowned nervously at him. "What's the matter, Tiswin?"

Little Tiswin opened the pocket, lowering his

curly head. "Nothing, Washakie. Just losing my woman that way. You know."

They were both silent for a long time while Little Tiswin unloaded the *aparejo*, taking out beans in a clay *olla* and strips of jerked beef from Santa Fe. Finally Washakie moved away from the tree, walking to the other side of the clearing in that wild restless way, peering here and there, his black eyes never still in his face. He turned back to study Little Tiswin, then he held out his hand again.

"Tiswin, you and I been friends a long time. . . ."

"Never mind," said Little Tiswin. "I know how you feel. And you know how I feel. That's why we don't have to talk about it. I wouldn't have mentioned it at all, but I didn't know you'd heard. You did hear?"

"Of course, I told you," said Washakie. "What's the matter?"

"Nothing," said Little Tiswin, glancing oddly at him from under hoary, golden brows. "Sit down, Washakie, you make me nervous. I swear nobody follered me here. Nobody knows I been trailing with you."

Washakie grunted, his head cocked like a listening dog. "You find out anything in Santa Fe?"

"Nothing," said Little Tiswin. "Leastwise nothing that would be any harm to you, and that's what you sent me down to find, wasn't it?

Armijo's got too much gout to worry about anything else. Most of the trappers are heading north. Celia Arnaud's trying to find you."

"Celia Arnaud?"

"One gal west of the Mizzou you ain't met, I guess," said Little Tiswin, and glanced at Washakie in that strange, enigmatic way again. "Daughter of Pierre Arnaud, Arnaud Furs. She came West when the old man died, been trying to hold the business together. Veinier's been chief factor down there for some time, you know. He tried all he could to help the gal, but it looks like she's through, what with Armijo closing the trail. I got a lot of *tiswin* left here, Washakie. How about some?"

Washakie rubbed a calloused hand across his stubble beard. "I'm about to bust open for a drink of any kind, Tiswin, but we can't afford it now. Wait'll we hole up at No Agua. What's this Arnaud girl want with me?"

"Seems to think you're the only one who can get her plews through Armijo's blockade. I tried to head her off, but it was no good." Little Tiswin took a flat wooden keg from the *aparejo* and pulled out the plug. "Come on, Washakie, just one drink. A man's got to let loose somehow when he's been up here as long as you or he'll blow up."

Washakie licked his lips and paced restlessly past Little Tiswin, cocking his narrow, black head. Little Tiswin was right. Washakie could feel his nerves tightening up inside him day by day like a slipknot on a lash rope. It seemed his whole life had been spent up in this somber, gloomy timber, running at the slightest sound, never able to sleep more than an hour or so without his animal instincts waking him to prowl nervously about camp after something that wasn't there. A man could live like that only so long without a release of some sort. Normally the trappers obtained that release at the rendezvous, where they went at the end of each season to Taos or Green River, selling their furs and spending all their money in a wild orgy of liquor and gambling and women, and then returned satisfied for another season to their lonely trade. But there had been no rendezvous this year, and Washakie had been running like a hunted animal a long time now, and he could feel his breath begin to come faster as he glanced again at the keg of *tiswin*.

"You never think about anything else except finding out if you're being tailed?" said Little Tiswin, tipping the keg back and making a deliberate gurgling sound as he drank. "What's life worth that way? Have a drink, Washakie. I knew you'd be here if you wasn't at the Pecos camp, that was our agreement. But I'm the only one in the world knows that, Washakie. You can put on the biggest drunk you want. I'm here, ain't I? You get drunk and I'll watch. Then when you're sobered up, I'll get drunk and you watch."

"I tell you we can't afford to get drunk."

"One little sip."

Washakie's voice rose. "If I take one, I'll take more. Kenna's out there. No telling who else."

Watching Winters in that strange, calculating way, Little Tiswin gurgled at the keg again. "Been a long time since you had a drink. Been a long time since you let yourself go. You been holding in and walking on eggs and sleeping with one eye open so long you're tied up in diamond hitches. One drink won't hurt you, Washakie."

Washakie took a single lithe step over and swept the keg from Little Tiswin's hand. The big, curly-headed man watched him tip the keg back, a slow grin spreading across his heavy, bearded face.

Washakie's Adam's apple bobbed up and down his lean brown neck; finally he lowered the keg, tossed it to the ground with a curse, wiping his lips. He could feel the heat of it rising up, and he choked on the fumes in his throat. It was good, though, it was good. His teeth flashed white in his mordant face for an instant, like sunlight splashing momentarily on a dark pool, then disappearing as suddenly as it had come.

"That's the stuff." Little Tiswin chuckled. "I told you. Have some more, Washakie."

Washakie grabbed the next keg, feeling all the caution and stealth and discretion of the last months slipping away from him in the fiery precipitation of the *tiswin*. He pulled long at the second keg, then lowered it to look at Little Tiswin.

"What are you watching me like that for?"

"Nothing, Washakie, nothing." Little Tiswin's grin held something Washakie couldn't read. "I'm your friend, ain't I?"

Washakie threw back his head and laughed harshly. It was like his smile, short and fleeting, the sound dying down the dark lanes of Douglas fir behind him almost before it had begun. His face was sober when he again raised the keg.

Little Tiswin sat cross-legged beside the Mexican pack saddles, watching him.

"So they killed my squaw," he said.

Washakie lowered the empty keg, blinking his narrow eyes. "Huh? Listen, Tiswin, I told you . . ."

"I know what you told me," said Little Tiswin. "Have another, Washakie."

Washakie took the third keg, frowning at Little Tiswin. Then he shrugged, raised it to his lips. Little Tiswin took a long Bowie knife from his broad black belt and began to turn it in his hand. "Who do you think did it, Washakie? A drunk Apache maybe."

Washakie blinked.

"Did what, Tiswin? Oh. We'll find out, Tiswin. I swear we will. I know how you felt about Nailla . . . where'd you get that Bowie?"

Little Tiswin looked up. "A man gave it to me, Washakie."

Washakie bent forward, trying to focus his eyes. "Looks like my old Bowie. Lost it between here and the Pecos somewhere. Where'd you find it?"

"Lost it?" said Little Tiswin. "I didn't find it myself, exactly. Take another drink, Washakie. It's doing you good. I told you a man gave it to me. He found it near the Pecos."

"Oh." Washakie had raised the keg. His Adam's apple bobbed up and down once, then stopped. He lowered the keg, staring at Little Tiswin. The big, yellow-haired trapper seemed to sway in his vision, and the grin on his face looked to Washakie like a leer. Washakie heard his own voice come out as if from someone else. "Pecos?"

"That's what I said, Washakie." Little Tiswin leered. "Have some more, Washakie. Your old friend'll watch out for you."

Washakie took another drink. The circle of timber seemed to recede, and then sweep in on him. He felt himself swaying and laughed again, that short, harsh way. He lurched to his feet, reeling backward.

"Gimme a woman, Tiswin. I want to fandango. I'm gonna roar like a bear and dance like a caterpillar in a hot frying pan. Tell Nailla she's got a ring-tailed buffalo bull on her hands. Bring your squaw out and we'll dance. . . ." He stopped suddenly, shaking his head. "Whatta you looking like that for?"

"Nailla ain't here any more, Washakie, remember?" said Little Tiswin. There was no grin on his heavy, florid, sweating face now. There was something ugly in the way his eyes had begun to glitter. He tossed the Bowie knife in the air and let it slap into his beefy palm. "What do you suppose that is on the blade, Washakie? Blood? Who do you suppose did that to her, Washakie? Scalped and chopped up like that. A drunk Apache?"

Washakie reached out for a tree to keep himself from falling, and it wasn't there, and his face struck the ground. He sat up, spitting out dirt, head spinning. Little Tiswin seemed to be leaning toward him, and the look on the big man's face chilled Washakie suddenly. "Who do you suppose did what, Tiswin?"

The giant's voice was shaking, and there was a wild, almost bestial look twisting his face. "Look at the knife, Washakie. They found it in her, Washakie. It was sticking. in her when I saw her, Washakie. Scalped and chopped up, Washakie. By this Bowie, Washakie."

"Shut up, will you!" shouted Washakie. Then he laughed crazily. "I'm drunk, Tiswin. . . ."

"Damn' right you are!" screamed the huge man suddenly, jumping erect with the knife over his head. "Just drunk enough. You killed her. You stuck her like a pig and ripped her hair off and left her lying there like that. You killed her, Washakie, and I'm going to kill you!"

Washakie heard the words through a drunken

haze, and looked up to see the huge, yellow-headed man leaping at him with the wicked Bowie knife upraised, face twisted savagely, eyes glittering with an intense hatred. Washakie tried to rise, but his legs refused his will; the best he could do was a fumbling roll to the side, throwing up his feet to tangle them in Little Tiswin's legs. It tripped the giant, and, still leaping forward, he fell face down on Washakie, driving the Bowie hilt deep into the earth beside Washakie's head.

Washakie felt as if he were swimming through viscid ooze. Each movement was a battle against the lethargy of the corn brew, and half the time he couldn't feel what he was doing. He knew dimly that he had fought out from beneath Little Tiswin, rolling away from the man. He saw Little Tiswin jerk the knife out of the ground and get to his hands and knees, still screaming wildly.

"Tiswin!" shouted Washakie. "Don't be crazy. You know I didn't . . ."

He was on his hands and knees, facing Little Tiswin when he stopped. There were other men in the clearing, shadowy forms rushing in from every point, tall men in buckskin with bearded faces, lean brown Apaches with their faces painted bizarrely. Washakie whirled from one to the other, eyes wild, and then he saw the man in the black buffalo coat, and knew.

"He's mine!" screamed Little Tiswin, and was

44

coming down on Washakie again. "I'll kill him, Kenna, I'll kill him!"

"Damn you, Tiswin!" shouted Martin Kenna hoarsely. "I told you to wait till he was dead drunk. Don't let him get away, don't let him get away. . . ."

Washakie had jumped to where his Jake Hawkins lay, landing sprawled on his belly, clawing for the gun. He had known it wasn't loaded, but it was the only thing in sight, and he jumped to his feet, meeting the first man with the rifle clubbed, knocking him rolling clear across the glade. Shouting drunkenly, Washakie swung around to club the next man. They were all around him now, Little Tiswin's yellow head looming above all the rest.

"I'll kill him, Kenna. . . ."

"You will not!" yelled Kenna. "Take him alive."

Like a wild beast in their midst, Washakie swung this way and that, clubbing with his rifle, trying to break through, yelling and snarling. He beat down an Apache and stumbled over his falling body, free for that instant with only the timber in front of him. He kicked free of the Indian's clawing hands and ran blindly for the trees. But his legs wouldn't work like they should, somehow, and he kept tripping and weaving, and then they were on him again, and someone hit his back, and he went to his knees with a hoarse scream. Gasping for air, he fought madly to get out from under them, kicking and biting and butting in a frenzy.

"He's loco!" shouted one of the men, reeling away with his hands pawed over an eye Washakie had thumbed. "He's loco. . . ."

"He's Washakie Winters!" bellowed Kenna. "I told you. Get him, you fools, get him!"

Then Kenna's voice was right in Washakie's face, and Kenna's spasmodic grunt, and Kenna's big Cherington pistol striking Washakie's head. Winters reeled back under the blow, fighting to keep his arms from being torn around behind him, then it was the sharp pain of green rawhide whipped around his wrists, and the jerk of a hitch being thrown on. He lay on his back, kicking a man in the face who tried to grab his legs. Someone threw himself across Washakie's thighs, and they had the rawhide on his ankles, and he couldn't move after that.

They spread away from him, one man bleeding from the nose, another sitting on the ground farther out holding a broken arm. It had knocked most of the *tiswin* from Washakie, and in the sudden strained silence he looked toward Little Tiswin.

"You," he said, and his voice was unbelieving, "you . . ."

"Yes." Kenna grinned without mirth. "Little Tiswin. Your best friend, Washakie. Nobody knew he was your friend, did they? Nobody knew he'd traveled your trail so long. That was slick going. You could send him into Santa Fe any time to find out what was going on, and nobody would know he came from you."

"But why, Tiswin?" said Washakie desperately. "Why?"

"Don't act smart," said Kenna in a sudden anger. "Tiswin wanted to come after you all by himself at first. When he hit that camp above the Pecos and found Nailla that way, he was just about crazy. He told us all about you and him. He was for striking right out after you alone. We had a hard time convincing him it would be plain suicide. Finally we got him to remembering how many others had tried to get you, Washakie. He agreed to come in and get you so drunk you couldn't even squeal when we all hit you. You almost messed things up, Tiswin, jumping the gun that way."

"I couldn't wait," said Little Tiswin in a strangled voice. "I couldn't hold it in any longer, Kenna. Now let me at him."

"If we hadn't been here, he would have gotten away," said Kenna. "Probably killed you in the bargain. I told you no man could do it alone. You can have him as soon as we find out where he cached those furs he took from me at Taos."

"You said I could have him if I got him drunk!" shouted Little Tiswin. "He killed Nailla and I'm going to kill him and nobody can stop me. I've waited long enough, Kenna. . . ."

"Get him!" yelled Kenna.

It took the bunch of them to subdue the giant, a writhing screaming tangle of men for a moment. When they got him down, one of Kenna's trappers had to club him with a rifle butt until he stopped fighting. Little Tiswin tried to get up and couldn't, then he began crawling on his hands and knees toward Washakie. The trapper hit Little Tiswin across the back of the neck once more. Little Tiswin fell on his belly with his face in the dirt.

"No!" shouted Washakie suddenly, jerking from side to side like a wolf in a jump trap. "Tiswin, I didn't kill her, you hear me, I didn't kill her. . . ."

Martin Kenna took one step to Washakie and hit him across the mouth with the long brass-bound barrel of a Cherington. Washakie's head slammed back against the ground and he lay there in a spinning daze, blood salty in his mouth.

"I'll kill you," moaned Little Tiswin.

"Sure you will, after we find out where he cached those furs," said Kenna. Then he looked at Washakie. "I'm turning you over to Chefuri, Washakie. There isn't a man in the world can stand up under his persuasions. You'll be screaming for us to let Tiswin have you before Chefuri's through."

— V —

The fire made a soft snapping sound in the ominous quiet of the glade. Over to one side, the pack horses shifted restively in their hobbles. Celia and Veinier had come with Kenna, and now the girl stood looking at Washakie Winters where he lay beside the fire Chefuri had built. She thought she had never seen a wilder man. Like some forest animal, his unshaven face bearing the same ferine, hunted look she had seen in the face of a trapped beast, his jet black eyes never still in his narrow, dark head, his lips peeling back off his teeth in a soundless snarl whenever someone approached him.

"You should take him back to Santa Fe for trial, Kenna," Jules Veinier was saying. "You have no authority to do anything up here."

"I have all the authority I need," said Kenna, slapping his pistols. "Ready, Chefuri?"

"I think the fire is hot enough," said Chefuri, and began to untie Washakie's ankles.

"Get started, then," Kenna ordered.

"Kenna," said Celia. "You can't do that . . . even to him."

"We're doing it," said Kenna.

"You didn't do it this way for me," said Little Tiswin, on his hands and knees now. "You had me get him drunk and let you jump him so you'd have him for this. I'll kill you, too, Kenna. You can't stop me from it. I saw her. All chopped up with his knife still in her. I'll do it with my bare hands, Kenna. . . ."

Still raging, he stumbled to his feet, lurched toward Washakie. Celia had never seen a man draw his guns in such a way before. Martin Kenna snapped his elbows together in front of him till they almost touched, and, when he snapped them back out again, it flopped his heavy buffalo coat open across his belly, and automatically slapped his hands onto the butts of his pistols, all in the same motion, and the guns came out before Little Tiswin had finished his first jump toward Washakie.

Kenna shot once.

Little Tiswin tripped on his second leaping step. Celia felt the ground shudder as the prodigious man sat down suddenly. He looked uncomprehending at the growing red blot on his great belly, then the pain crossed his face and he put his hands on the bullet hole and bent forward.

"We might as well finish this now," said Kenna.

"No!" cried Celia, jumping at him. "Kenna, no . . . !"

The second gun went off into the air as she struck it with her hand. She caught his buffalo coat and the weight of her going against him jerked Kenna off balance. Stumbling backward, he slugged at her with the pistol. The pain of it knocked all conscious thought from her mind, and the ground came up from somewhere below and struck her face.

She lay there, stunned, only dimly aware of the other sounds through the roaring in her head. Finally she managed to roll over and sit up. Whatever Veinier had done was over now, and he stood backed up against a tree, trembling with rage, held there by the guns of two trappers.

"Kenna, this isn't our bargain," he said, face bleeding from a cut on his forehead. "You can't torture a man like that. Any man. No matter what he is. You have no right."

Martin Kenna uncorked the brass powder horn at his belt and poured a measure of powder into the charge cup, then dumped it carefully into the barrel of one pistol. "I'm tired of all this foofaraw, Veinier, I'm tired of being told what I can do and what I can't do. The next one who interferes I will shoot dead, and that goes for the girl, too."

He drew a ball from his shot pouch, placing it in the bore of the gun as he moved so that his square body blocked off part of Washakie's lank frame from Celia's sight. Chefuri was squatting over Washakie now, sweat gleaming on his evil features. Celia couldn't see the lower part of Washakie's body, but she caught his face. It was set into an awful mask, eyes staring toward the sky in a grim, terrible concentration.

Chefuri was holding something in his hand. He turned toward the fire, and it snapped loudly, and then he turned back to bend over Washakie.

"You'll never walk on those feet again if you don't spit it out, Washakie," said Kenna.

"What's the difference." Chefuri laughed. "He won't have to worry about walking again when Tiswin gets him."

"You do less talking and more work," growled Kenna. "Where did you cache the pelts, Washakie?"

"Washakie is a stubborn *hombre*, Kenna," said Chefuri. "I told you. The trick is not to get impatient. It is a delicate business. *Así . . .*"

The muscles twitched at one side of Washakie's mouth, drawing the skin taut across his flat cheek bone until it gleamed like wet leather. For a moment, his eyes closed, then they opened again to stare back up at the sky in that awful concentration. Celia Arnaud turned away with a little moan.

Little Tiswin was still sitting where he had fallen from Kenna's bullet, holding both hammy hands over his stomach, a stupid, dazed pain twisting his florid face. He looked at Celia, and tried to say something, and no sound came from his lips. Chefuri held a smoking stick.

Chefuri's two Apaches were scattering Little Tiswin's *aparejos*. One of them dumped out several flat kegs of corn liquor. The other Apache had kicked open the last pack saddle, and he called to Kenna.

"*Esta polvora.*"

Kenna jerked his massive head impatiently. "Leave it alone. Get that stuff near the fire and you'll blow us clear to Colter's Hell."

The girl looked at the pack saddle. Gunpowder?

Chefuri took a heavy breath and tossed the butt end of a burned stick behind him, turning to choose another fresh one from the fire. Martin Kenna shifted restlessly, shoving his wolf-skin hat back on his head.

"*Pronto*, Chefuri, *pronto.*"

"What's the matter, Martino?" chuckled the half-breed. "Is it getting on your nerves? Washakie's the one it's hurting. I told you. These things take time. If I put his feet directly in the fire, he might faint before we got anything out of him. However, a burning brand, applied so . . ."

Washakie Winter's eyes closed momentarily again. The girl bit her lip, stifling the cry that rose in her throat. She felt her nails digging into her palms. She didn't think she could stand it much longer. But the other was still in the back of her mind. *Polvora.* Gunpowder?

She took a careful breath, and began to crawl toward the keg of *tiswin* the Apache had thrown down. The two Indians had moved over to the fire, squatting by Chefuri, and Kenna blocked

Celia off from the pair of trappers holding Veinier backed up to the tree. The burned stick Chefuri had cast behind him was still glowing at one end. If she could do this before it went out entirely. . . .

"Get this over with, Chefuri!"

Kenna's voice stiffened the girl. The strain was telling on all of them. One of the Apaches rose, moving restlessly around the fire, then squatted again with his back toward Celia. Washakie Winters had made no sound yet. Celia reached out for the keg of *tiswin*.

"He isn't human," complained Chefuri. "At least he could squeal a little. I've worked on *Indios* that broke before this."

Celia had the keg uncorked by now. The fumes of the *tiswin* rose from the open bottle, strong and gagging. She became aware of Little Tiswin's eyes on her; he had been watching intently, and suddenly he tried to get up, turning toward Kenna with a strangled sound.

Celia jumped to her feet and whirled toward the brand Chefuri had thrown down, tipping the bottle of *tiswin* over onto it. The first of the ferment to touch the glowing end of the stick blazed up with a startling puff.

With the bottle upended, Celia ran backward toward the *aparejos*, pouring a steady stream of *tiswin* out onto the ground, the flame following her from the stick of wood in a blazing red trail. Kenna had whirled from the fire, and Chefuri had jumped up. The Mexicans used straw to pad the bottom of their pack saddles, and, when Celia dumped the remains of the corn brew across the *aparejo*, the living train of fire licked after her and caught greedily at the *aparejo*'s padding.

"Stop her!" screamed Kenna. "If that fire reaches the . . . !"

His voice was drowned in the first booming explosion. Celia had caught up a horn of powder from the open pocket of the saddle, tearing off the plug and dumping the horn into the fire as she threw herself backward. She rolled across the ground with the flash blinding her. The first explosion set off the other horns and kegs of powder, and the ground shuddered and rocked beneath Celia as she fought to get on her feet.

The clearing was full of shouting, screaming men that passed back and forth like shadows in front of Celia as she ran toward the campfire. She bumped into a naked torso, and caught the gleaming eyes of an Apache as he tried to grab her. She tore loose from him, stumbling through the embers of the fire. It was only when she kicked free of the last blazing stick that she realized Washakie Winters no longer lay there.

Another explosion rocked the clearing, and smoke swept, black and thick, across the frenzied, fighting, squealing pack animals. Celia saw Kenna coming toward her with his pistols out, face stamped with a terrible, lithic rage.

Then another tall, broad-shouldered figure loomed out of the smoke, clubbing a long rifle. Kenna whirled toward the second man, but the rifle caught him on the side of his head, and he went down. It was Jules Veinier, then, running toward Celia, catching her arm.

"Why did you do that?" the Frenchman shouted, pulling her after him toward the trees.

"I couldn't stand to see them torture him any longer," she panted. "No matter what he did. I couldn't stand it. . . ."

One of the mules had broken its hobbles and came squealing through the camp. Celia and Veinier had to throw themselves violently out of its way. The man lost his hold on Celia, and she went stumbling blindly through the smoke, tripping finally over a body and going to her knees.

It was one of Kenna's mountain men, and it might have been a piece of metal powder horn, thrown out by the explosion, that had struck him down, because his head was covered with blood. She saw another man staggering through the carnage toward her; he was taller than Veinier, and lacked the Frenchman's shoulder breadth. The first thing Celia thought of was a weapon, and she clawed at the long skinning knife thrust through the belt of the man who lay beside her. But before she could rise with it, the running man had thrown himself at her, and his sweaty weight carried her backward into the trees. Together, they rolled across the popping cones and smashed to a stop finally against the ragged trunk of a pine. Her startled eyes looked up into a gaunt, wolfish face.

"Cut my hands loose," gasped Washakie Winters, "or I'll hold you down till Kenna comes!"

Jules Veinier crouched there in the timber, big chest heaving from the run. He hadn't realized he'd lost the girl. How far had he come without her? He'd thought she was right behind him when he ran out of the glade. And now he suddenly felt as if he couldn't breathe, and it wasn't because he had run so fast. Why should it make him feel this way? And even asking himself, he knew.

Back in Santa Fe, when she had first come, he had looked upon her as a haughty, foolish young girl, trying to take over a business she knew nothing about, turning everything upside down with her stupid innovations, making a fool of him by countermanding the orders he issued to the clerks and *engagés* at the Arnaud Agency. He hadn't come up here meaning to help her find Winters, or even because of any sense of responsibility for her safety; he had come, primarily, to keep her from finding Winters and trying to run Armijo's blockade. But a subtle change had been taking place inside him as he had ridden with her from Santa Fe to Taos, and then from Taos on up into the Sangre de Cristos, a change he had refused to recognize at first, a change he wouldn't name until this very minute. She was no longer a stupid young girl. He had seen the fire of her, and the courage, and the beauty, and realizing she hadn't followed him from the clearing, he suddenly felt as if he couldn't breathe.

"Celia?" he called softly, and began moving back toward the dull sound of another explosion. Someone came crashing through the pines, and Veinier jerked up the Jake Hawkins gun he had wrenched from one of Kenna's trappers. Two running figures lurched into view, one long and lean, limping as he ran, the other smaller, chestnut hair caught out behind her with the wind. "Celia!"

"Run, Jules," sobbed the girl. "Kenna's right behind us."

"Not with this *paillard*!" spat the Frenchman, looking at Washakie Winters.

"Don't be a fool," panted Celia. "We can't stop to argue now. We can't stop to do anything. If Kenna gets us this time, he'll kill us."

Washakie jerked her on after him by the hand, and she had to break into a run to keep from falling. Cursing, Veinier followed them down the slope. The girl began to stumble and falter soon, and the two men had to slow down. Jules was catching at Celia's shoulder to pull her away from Washakie when the crashing through the timber came from behind. Washakie Winters grabbed the girl around her stomach and swung her up on his shoulder, face down.

"Let me go!" cried girl, knees drumming against his chest. "Put me down, you . . . you murderer!"

"Put her down or I'll shoot you, Winters!" shouted Veinier.

"You're just as liable to hit her as me," said Washakie. "You better put your mind to running, Frenchie."

Washakie Winters broke once more into that long, loose stride of a man who had spent most of his life running the timber, only this time he wasn't hampered by having to slow down for the girl, and her weight on his shoulder had no apparent effect on his speed. Veinier lurched after him, trying to catch the man, but after his first spring the Frenchman couldn't get close enough to touch Washakie.

Then Veinier became aware of the sound. It was a small, strangled, grunting noise that seemed to come every time Washakie Winters put a foot down. In that moment, Veinier realized what it was; he wondered if the girl had heard it, too, and realized she had quit struggling. Veinier was looking at Washakie's bare feet, and he wondered how any man could bear to run when each step caused him that much agony.

Veinier didn't know how long they ran. When sounds of pursuit had faded behind, he had dropped so far back of Washakie that the other was almost out of sight. The Frenchman was running in a blind, exhausted haze, crashing into trees, tripping and falling all the time, drawing in great painful gasps.

Finally, when he thought he couldn't take another step, he saw that Washakie had stopped ahead, and had put the girl down. Jules stumbled somehow to where they were and dropped to the ground, tears streaming down his face from exhaustion. When he could look up at last, he saw Washakie standing above him, the rise and fall of his chest hardly perceptible.

"I guess we'll go again," said Washakie, bending to help the girl up. She drew away from his hand, her mouth twisting faintly. He stared at her a moment, then the understanding showed on his sweating, bearded face. "Oh," he muttered, "Nailla."

The girl seemed to force it out. "Nailla?"

"Tiswin's squaw," he said.

"Yes," she said, moving farther away from him. "How could you murder her like that? A woman. What made you do it? It's unspeakable."

"You think I did it?"

"I saw her." Celia's voice was bitter. "I didn't believe half the stories they told about you. I didn't think any man could be like that. If I'd known, I wouldn't have come. I couldn't stand to see them torture you any longer. I couldn't have stood to see them do it to a wild animal. But now that's over."

"That's right," said Veinier, rising with difficulty. "Everything's through. I think you'd better leave us, *m'sieu*."

"I don't care much what you think," said Washakie, still looking at the girl. "Little Tiswin told me you were looking for me."

"I wanted you to run my furs through Armijo's blockade," she said dully. "I couldn't get anybody to help me, and they told me you might."

"Why should I?"

"Excitement, *m'sieu*," said Veinier sarcastically. "They say you will do anything for excitement. What more exciting than bucking Armijo's whole army?"

"Did you come all this way on that idea?" said Washakie.

"Don't be a fool," said the girl. "Veinier is talking nonsense. I was going to make you a business proposition. You'd get a quarter of the profits on the furs if you got them to Saint Louis."

"How many pelts?" said Washakie.

"What does it matter now?" she said acidly. "I wouldn't let you touch one of my plews if I had them."

"How many pelts?"

She turned from side to side, but her answer came at last, sullenly. "Ten thousand."

"At six dollars a pelt . . ." Washakie hesitated.

"Is sixty thousand dollars," said the girl contemptuously. "And a fourth of sixty thousand is fifteen thousand. More than a trapper like you makes in a lifetime."

His laugh broke out, short and harsh, cutting off abruptly. "Maybe you've hired a man."

"I told you. . . ."

"When you started out to find me, you'd heard them tell of all the other scalps I'd taken, hadn't you?" he said.

"Yes, but . . ." She made a helpless gesture with her hand.

"But to be brought up face to face with it is different," he said.

"I guess so," she muttered desperately. "To see Nailla, and the knife you did it with, and Tiswin, and everything . . ."

"I'd like to make fifteen thousand dollars," he said musingly. "And I owe Armijo a few dead dragoons."

"Do you think we'll let you do it?" spat Veinier. "Do you think we'll even let you go on talking like this? A murderer. Armijo had the right idea about hanging your head in the plaza."

"Maybe you'd like to try getting it for him," drawled Washakie.

Jules Veinier stiffened, the blood draining from his dark face and leaving it a sickly putty color. For a moment his rage was so hot that he couldn't see. He had a savage impulse to get his hands on Washakie Winters, just to get his hands on the man. Then, coming up through the blind curtain of rage was thought of the girl. More than anything else, now, he wanted to get her safely back to Santa Fe; he hadn't cared about that, at first, but things had changed, inside him, and outside. He saw clearly enough what would happen if he fought with Winters. He would kill the man, or Washakie would kill him. As simple as that. It could end only that way. And if Washakie killed him, it would leave the girl alone with a murderer. Battling every instinct within him, Veinier forced himself to speak quietly, his voice shaking with his terrible effort at control. "You are getting a chance for your life only because of the girl's presence, *m'sieu*," he said. "I'm asking you to leave us."

Washakie shook his head. "I said I wanted that fifteen thousand dollars. If the furs were there to be run through the blockade before you got so finicky about who I murdered and who I didn't, then they're there now."

Jules Veinier hardly recognized his own voice. "I'm giving you one more chance to leave."

"No. I guess I'll take your furs through." Washakie glanced sideways at Celia, a sly grin splitting his stubble beard for an instant. "Besides, I never leave a pretty gal so soon. . . ."

"Jules!" screamed Celia.

It had been a blind, explosive reaction for Veinier. His body struck Washakie Winters with all its powerful young weight, carrying the gaunt mountain man backward. Washakie caught himself somehow, and kept from falling. Veinier tried to hit him while he was still off balance, but Washakie blocked the blow with a bony elbow. Jules caught the elbow while it was still up, ducking under the arm to grasp Washakie about the belly and heave him off his feet.

He might as well have grappled a wild animal. He felt the catgut muscle ripple and swell beneath his arms, and Washakie erupted in a writhing, kicking, shouting tangle of arms and legs and twisting, leaping torso. Veinier tried to shift his weight and spread his legs for leverage, but all the strength in his great shoulders couldn't hold Washakie's feral body. The mountain man tore free with a yell, and Veinier's head jerked sideways to the foot that came up from below and slammed him in the face.

The Frenchman stumbled aside, throwing up an arm to block Washakie's first punch as the man came in. But Washakie didn't punch. He threw his whole body at Veinier, using his head and feet as much as his hands. Veinier gasped sickly as Washakie butted him in the stomach, staggered backward. He jerked his head aside to dodge Washakie's kick, and found Washakie's hand spread across his face, a horny thumb seeking his eye. He tore the hand off, stumbling away.

"*Sacre bleu!*" he shouted. "You don't fight like a man, you fight like an animal. . . ."

"That's my style!" whooped Washakie, leaping

at him. Veinier shifted his weight forward and stuck one arm out. He saw his fist go into Washakie's belly, and heard the man's spasmodic gasp. It didn't stop Washakie.

Face contorted with pain, he was on Veinier, catching Veinier on the side of the head with a vicious backhand blow. Veinier reeled back, trying to catch one of Washakie's feet as the man kicked at him. But Washakie spun away and came into him from the side, putting an elbow into his face.

"Jules!" the girl was crying. "Stop it, Jules! He'll kill you!"

But there was no stopping Veinier now. With a choked sound, he set himself, spitting blood from his mouth that Washakie's elbow had smashed. He lowered his head and whirled squarely into Washakie with both fists pumping. Again he felt his blow strike that belly, and heard the gasp, and shouted with a dazed triumph. He stepped on into the mountain man, bent almost double, striking blindly. He jerked to Washakie's hands on his face, and then a bony fist hit him hard behind the neck, and he was down on his face. Dimly he was aware of Washakie swaying above him, dripping sweat and blood off his gaunt face, his lips drawn back flatly against his teeth in that wolfish snarl.

"Get up, Frenchie," gasped Washakie. "You ain't seen nothing yet."

The girl tried to catch Washakie, but the mountain man swept her off as Veinier got to his feet. Driving into the man, Jules saw Celia stagger and fall to the ground, then she was gone from his sight, and all he could see was a muddy, bloody elk-hide jacket in front of him, and now and then that set of snarling white teeth in a stubble beard, flashing in and out of his vision.

He was fighting mechanically now, in a haze of pain, head seeming to explode every time Washakie kicked him, nausea sweeping him when Washakie butted. He was past trying to box Washakie, or even block any of Washakie's blows. He staggered headlong into the mountain man, slugging desperately. One of his blows missed, and he spun around with his own momentum, and Washakie grabbed his outflung arm.

Veinier tried to throw his weight backward, but the mountain man had his arm across one shoulder. Veinier felt himself pulled upward by that leverage, and spinning through the air with Washakie behind him somewhere, and, when he struck the ground, it was as if a great roar shook his whole body.

He rolled over on his belly and tried to get up, but his arms wouldn't support his weight. He sank back, vision coming to him dimly, slowly. He could make out Washakie Winters first, standing above him. But Winters wasn't looking at him. Then he saw the girl. She must have managed to load the Jake Hawkins gun, because she was crouched over it on the ground.

"Go ahead." Washakie's harsh laugh came hazily to Veinier. "Go ahead and shoot. I don't think you've got the guts."

The girl held the long rifle aimed at Washakie Winters for another moment, her eyes big and dark behind the rear sight. Then the barrel began to waver, and she dropped the gun, and, crouching over it on the ground that way, put her face into her hands and began to sob.

— VI —

An Abert squirrel was chattering somewhere up in the spruce and a pinto mule was arguing plaintively with a little gray *burro*. There was an old Cheyenne teepee of tattered, blackened elk hide to one side of the clearing, and a huge buffalo robe thrown over something beside the teepee.

Washakie Winters was first into the open. The fight was a week behind him, but his face was still puffy and discolored from Veinier's fists. The Frenchman had hurt him more than Washakie liked to admit. Veinier himself had been too weak and beaten for much more resistance, as Washakie took him and the girl southward into the Sangre de Cristos where this camp was.

"El Andale?" called the mountain man.

The Mexican came out of the wild grape that spread down toward the creek. His greasy, black hair was shot with gray, and his scrawny shoulders were stooped consumptively beneath a dirty white cotton shirt. Behind him came another, built like a keg of Pass Brandy, five feet tall maybe and not much less broad, his fierce mustaches hanging long below the fat rolls of his chin. He held a coach whip in his hairy hand, and, when he spoke, it was like the growl of a brown bear.

"We hide in the bushes till we see who it is, eh?"

Washakie threw back his narrow head, and that strange, short laugh echoed back through the cottonwoods, and died almost before it had begun, and he turned to Celia, waving his hand at the short Mexican. "This is El Carajo, the best muleteer in all Mexico. . . ."

"No!" shouted the other one. The effort sent him into a spasm of coughing, and he bent his thin shoulders over till his face was hidden. Finally he straightened, gasping for air. "How can El Carajo be the best muleteer in all Méjico when I am? I, El Andale, the *hombre* who drove Santa Anna's whole supply train single-handedly from San Antone to Monclava when we were retreating before General Houston. I, El Andale, the man who . . ."

"Oh, *pállate la boca*, you old rat mule, close your mouth," grunted El Carajo, flicking the tip of his mustache with his leather-wrapped whip-stock. "You couldn't drive a louse out of your hair." He turned to Celia with a grin, jerking his thumb at the older Mexican. "He thinks the mules go because he pokes them with that prod pole of his, when it is really because they can't stand his proximity any longer. He hasn't taken a bath since he fell in the Río Grande three years ago, and he smells like . . ."

"*Basta, basta*," said Washakie. "Enough. The girl can't stand here and listen to you *necios* fight all day. She's walked her moccasins through and she's about ready to drop. How about some food?"

"Oh, *sí, sí*," said El Andale, bowing. "We shall eat. There is nothing better for a *señorita* than my tamales. They are so big you can wrap yourself up in them like a blanket, *señorita*, so succulent the *burros* cry for them. . . ."

"Get along, *viejo*," growled El Carajo, giving the stoop-shouldered old man an affectionate shove. "If work were talk, you'd be dead from your labors now."

Grumbling and quarreling, the two Mexicans disappeared into the skin lodge. The girl dropped listlessly onto a buffalo robe that Washakie spread for her, and Veinier squatted in sullen silence next to her.

None of them spoke until El Andale came out again, coughing a little from the smoke, carrying a clay platter of tamales and another of steaming *chili con carne*. Washakie deftly rolled his meat into a tamale, the juice dripping down his fingers as he ate. He finished the first one, wiping his fingers on his elk-hide leggings, restless black eyes settling on Celia for a moment.

He wondered what it was about her that drew him. She was beautiful enough, even grimed and weary from the long trek, but there had been other beautiful women. Her hair? Somehow, he hadn't been able to keep his eyes off it, all the way from Mora Peak. Why? There had been women with hair as black and glossy as a midnight pool in the moonlight, and women with hair as red as the Sangre de Cristos at sunset, and they had not drawn him like this. Why should it be a woman with hair the color of ripe chestnuts?

Celia caught his eyes on her suddenly, and, as she straightened, something *crackled* in her jacket. For an instant, he saw the confusion on her face, as if she were trying to read his glance. Then, frowning, she drew a piece of paper from her buckskin coat.

"I forgot about this," she said. "Veinier and I spent a lot of time hunting you before we met Kenna above the Pecos. We found several of your old camps. A Pecuris Indian guided us to that one at No Agua. It looked as if you hadn't been there in a long time, but some of your stuff was in that *aparejo* inside the cave. I found this."

70

He looked at the paper, shrugged. "Last time I pulled out of No Agua it was in a hurry. Guess I left some of my truck behind."

"Don't you want this?" she asked.

"Why should I?"

"It's your honorable discharge from the United States Army."

He nodded. "I guess so."

"They told me you were a deserter," she said.

"Did they tell you I rode a black buffalo bull with horns as long as a man is tall?"

Celia made an impatient gesture with one small hand. "I know, I know. But this is different. I should think you'd want to prove you were honorably discharged."

"Why?"

She flushed angrily. "Everybody thinks you deserted from the Army."

"All right."

She got up, breathing heavily. "Don't you care what people think of you?"

"Not particularly," he said.

She looked at the paper, apparently only then aware that she had crushed it in her hand, and she made a small, choked sound, throwing it to the ground. "I don't know why I even bothered telling you. I don't know why I talk with you at all."

She turned on her heel, walking stiffly to one side of the teepee. Frowning at them in a puzzled way, El Carajo reached for his bundle of *hojas*, the oblong pieces of corn shucks every Mexican carried in a pouch at his belt, along with a horn bottle of powdered tobacco. He began rolling himself a cigarette as Washakie rose.

Veinier got to his feet, grabbing Washakie's arm. "*M'sieu*, you will leave the girl alone."

"I thought we'd decided that I'd have the say so about what I was to do and what I wasn't," said Washakie.

"We decided nothing," Veinier answered hotly.

Washakie backed away a little. "Think you're well enough to try again?"

Veinier bent forward a little, the blood draining from his face, and for a moment they faced each other like that, and Washakie shuffled his feet a little to find a solid footing for meeting the Frenchman's rush. They were so intent that when the girl called, it jerked Veinier up a little, as if pulled from a trance.

Celia was bent over the buffalo robe she had taken off a pile of beaver bales beside the teepee.

"Where did you get these plews?" she said.

Washakie took a heavy breath, still watching Veinier. "From Martin Kenna at Taos."

"These are our furs," she said.

Veinier turned and ran to her side, helping her up-end a bale. The girl's voice grew high-pitched with excitement.

"Look, Jules, this is that shipment Jackson asked us to send with the heads on. No trapper would add weight of the heads to his bales, and no other company packs them that way. These could only be from the Arnaud Agency."

"Impossible!" cried Veinier.

"I didn't figure on that when I picked them off Kenna," said Washakie. "He and Chefuri had poached my lines up on the Green, and, when I got wind of Kenna running a big train through Taos, Andale and Carajo and me jumped it that evening. I sent Andale up past Placita Road to start shooting, and, when the soldiers and Kenna's men ran up that way, Carajo and me came down from the roof and stampeded the mules. Kenna was the only one who'd stayed there, and he couldn't do much."

The girl was looking at Washakie. "But I . . . I don't understand."

"Don't you?" said Washakie.

"You mean Armijo was sending Kenna to Saint Louis with *our* furs?"

"Armijo had confiscated your pelts, hadn't he?" said Washakie. "Kenna didn't get them from his customhouse by force, did he?"

"That's unbelievable," said Veinier. "Are you sure these are the furs you got from Kenna, Winters?"

"Don't be a fool, Jules," said the girl. "If Washakie was the one working with Armijo, do you think he'd have brought us here?"

"Armijo was a trader before he set himself

up as governor of New Mexico," said Washakie. "And he's been doing some shipping over the Santa Fe on the side while he held office. He isn't the kind to let ten thousand plews rot in his customhouse."

There was a pensive look on the girl's face. "One of our biggest problems was getting the furs out of Santa Fe. But now, if they're here . . ."

"Celia," snapped Veinier, "you're not thinking of . . . ?"

Her lips were parted slightly, and she seemed to be trying to fathom Washakie's lean, mordant face, and she spoke almost to herself. "We'd never make it alone, Veinier."

"You can't," said Veinier. "He's a murderer."

"I'd still like to have fifteen thousand dollars," said Washakie Winters.

"We'd never make it alone," she said again.

"Celia"—Veinier almost shouted—"I forbid it!"

The girl whirled on him. "You forbid it! What right have you to give me orders? That's just about all it took, Jules! I'm going to run Armijo's blockade with those furs, and, if Washakie Winters wants to help, I don't think I can stop him, can I, and I don't think you can either, seeing what happened the last time you tried."

Veinier's eyes flashed white from his darkly flushed face, and he stiffened so violently that he rose onto his toes, turning with a jerk to look at Washakie, opening his mouth, then closing it again, and turning back to the girl. His breath had a harsh, driven sound, and finally he whirled back to Washakie, biting off his words.

"*M'sieu*, if you try to come with us . . ."

El Carajo broke it off, starting to run past Veinier toward the man who had ridden into the clearing. Washakie saw who it was, and jumped after the squat, hairy Mexican.

Together, they caught Little Tiswin as the huge, yellow-haired man rolled off the gaunt gelding.

They sat him down on the ground where he bent over, clutching his belly. "He came like that . . . all the way from Mora Peak?" gasped Celia.

"Yeah," groaned Little Tiswin. "Was trying to reach Santa Fe. Kenna left me at Mora. Guess he thought I was done. Saw your fire from over yonder peak. Wouldn't have come if I'd known it was you, Washakie. Didn't think I could make Santa Fe. Looking for anybody that'd help me. Anybody but you. Don't touch me. I won't take no healing from you. Rather be dead. Your scalp'd be on my belt if I hadn't listened to Kenna. He wanted you for his own purpose, that's all. Help me get you? Like hell. He just wanted me to get you dead drunk so's he could take you alive and find out where those furs was hidden. . . ."

He groaned and bent over, and Washakie hunkered down beside him, trying to make him drink the Pass brandy El Andale had brought in

75

a flat keg. "Take this, you damned old bear. All we got here for that belly wound is lard and gunpowder. We're heading north with some plews and we'll drop you at Bent's Fort."

"Heading north with some plews . . ."—Little Tiswin laughed feebly, choked on the brandy, shoving it away—"heading north with some plews. That's funny. Riding the Santa Fe to Bent's Fort with some furs. That's the funniest thing I heard in a long time. You put one foot out of this camp with a pack train and you'll have Armijo's dragoons on your neck before you can say Black's Fork of the Green. Maybe you can run around the Sangre de Cristos alone without being spotted, but you know you couldn't hide from a blind varmint with that many mules cutting a trail. You'll be spotted before you've had your first dinner out-side this holler. It ain't only the dragoons, either. Martin Kenna's out there, Washakie. I'd rather have a dozen Armijos after me than that kyesh. I guess I don't need to worry about paying you back for what you did to Nailla. You're taking care of the whole thing yourself. I hope they send me to hell when I die, Washakie. I want to see you down there roasting in the fire you built for yourself."

— VII —

Lieutenant Miguelito Separ shivered in his short blue coat, slapping his hands against his thighs to get some of the numbness out of them. To the devil with this snow. Had he asked to go out in it? No! To the devil with Washakie Winters. Had he asked to go chasing around the province in the middle of winter after some legendary *gringo* who probably never existed anyway? No!

Separ had lost count of the days since he had left Taos. He had fumbled Celia Arnaud's trail long ago, and had spent weeks coursing the Sangre de Cristos in search of Winters without avail, following false alarms that took him farther north than he had ever been before, listening to a thousand and one stories about Washakie Winters, seeing old camps some wild-eyed Apache claimed had been used by the mountain man. All for what? All for nothing!

He straightened in his saddle as the *cabo* came toiling back up the slope on a gaunted, steaming horse. "Well, who is it?"

"No Mexicans, *teniente*," said the corporal wearily. "We are sure of that now. My two men saw Yankee trappers with the mules."

"Don't be a *pendejo*," snapped Separ. "No *gringo* would be fool enough to drive a hundred mules up the Santa Fe in the middle of winter, with Armijo's proclamation closing the trail still hanging on the walls of the *palacio* at Santa Fe."

The corporal shrugged his shoulders. "I don't know, *teniente*. It is as I said before. I was riding advance guard a mile ahead of the main column when I first sighted this mule train. They must have been traveling by night, for it was just dawn, and they were pulling into camp. I left my two men on watch and reported."

"*Sí, sí*, that is obvious," said the lieutenant impatiently. "And I sent you back to watch the train till we arrived. Where is it?"

"We cannot see anything from here," said the *cabo*. "My two men are farther down the slope, but if you try to move the whole troop down, we will be sighted. They have scattered the animals in hobbles, the Yankee, so that the timber hides them, and have secreted their camp in the river bottom so well that we might have passed right by without seeing them, if we hadn't come on them before they made their halt."

The Cordovan leather of Separ's high-cantled saddle *creaked* faintly as he turned to look at the line of lancers straggling out behind him. "Straighten your *lanzas*. Are you *soldados* or farmers?"

"The men are tired, *teniente*," said the veteran sergeant from Chihuahua.

"*¡Pállate la boca!*" fumed Separ. "Whether

these be friends or enemies ahead, we will meet them like soldiers. Button your coat, Torres. You look more like a stable boy than a sergeant major."

Sergeant Torres flushed. "*Teniente* . . ."

The shot cut him off. It came from below. Separ's horse whinnied and reared, and by the time he had fought it down, he could see the rider coming hard up the slope. It was one of the men the *cabo* had left down there to watch, and he hauled his frightened horse to a halt in front of the lieutenant.

"They have sighted us!" he shouted, wild-eyed. "One of them came up toward Carlos and me. He shot Carlos at three hundred paces, I swear it, three hundred paces. Washakie Winters . . ."

"Washakie Winters!" Separ stiffened in his saddle. "And you ran away, you deserted your post?" screamed the lieutenant in a rage, and drew his pistol and shot the man from his horse.

For a long moment after the sound of the shot had died, there was no sound. Then a horse shifted nervously in the snow, grunting. Separ jammed his pistol back and drew his sword, whirling in the saddle.

"Anybody else who doesn't know what a *soldado* was made for will get the same thing. Lower your lances for the charge!"

"*Teniente*," called the sergeant, "you aren't riding down there? It would be suicide. This is for the *escopetas*. . . ."

"*¡Silencio!*" thundered Separ. "Do you think I will sneak into battle like a dirty *Indio*? That is Washakie Winters down there, and you'll never get him with these pea-shooters the armory issues for guns. Nothing can stand up to a cavalry charge. We'll have the whole bunch of them spitted on our *lanzas* before they've loaded their rifles once."

"*Teniente*," pleaded *Sargento* Torres. "You don't know these mountain men. They are inhuman with those long guns. I fought them at the Alamo. There was a man there named Davy Crockett. I tell you, if that Washakie Winters has put himself in between us to hold us off till the other Yankees can get the mules out, we'll all be emptied from our saddles before we even get out of the trees."

"Another word from you and you'll get the same as that deserter!" yelled Separ. "*Trompetista*, blow the *degüello*!"

The trumpeter raised his brass instrument, and Santa Anna's call for no quarter rang out, and the timber was suddenly full of the crashing thunder of the charge.

This was the way a man should ride to battle. The brazen call of the *degüello* and the drumming beat of his horse beneath him and the militant *clatter* of his troop coming down behind him. Separ's blood pounded through him in rhythm with the galloping hoofs and his legs stiffened unconsciously until he was standing in the saddle.

He didn't hear the shot. He saw the trooper on his right flank jerk up in the saddle and reel backward off his horse. Then Washakie Winters appeared ahead of Separ, a long lean shadow of a man flitting from tree to tree, loading his long gun as he went. Swept with the terrible excitement of the charge, Separ hardly heard his own wild shout.

"Run, you *perro*! That's the way. Run! I've come for your head. I'll have it with my own sword. We'll spit you all on our *lanzas* like fat pigs and carry you back to Santa Fe for the people to see . . . !"

There was a puff of smoke from Washakie's gun, and someone behind Separ howled in mortal pain, and a riderless horse came into his vision, quartering away through the trees. Washakie had reached the dry riverbed, and he dropped coolly behind the cutbank.

Separ burst from the snow-laden timber into the open, turning in his saddle to wave his troop on. They surged down behind him, blue coats catching the meager sunlight as they came from the dark timber one by one, *lanzas* swaying and glittering in saddle butts. He was still turned that way when two of the men fell from the saddle at the same time, one catching a foot in the stirrup and dragging across the broken ground.

Whirling to the front, Separ saw that the other mountain men had quit loading the mules and were running across the river, firing. There was a girl with them. Separ caught a glimpse of her chestnut hair.

Then the mountain men were down behind the cutbank beside Washakie Winters, poking their long rifles out over the snow-covered sand. A last man came staggering across the river, a huge, yellow-haired giant, weaving and stumbling like a drunken *borracho*, shouting hoarsely. "Wait for me, damn you, wait for me! Think you can leave me out? I can shoot a Jake Hawkins as good as any man, hole through my belly or not. . . ." The giant tripped and fell, and tried to get up. Failing that, he pulled himself around till he was sitting cross-legged like an Indian, and, propping his elbows on his knees, raised the long gun.

The bright flashes along the embankment blinded Separ, and he could hear horses screaming behind him, and men. Only a few more yards now, you *bribónes*, only a few more yards! He turned to wave them on again, standing in his stirrups, and couldn't comprehend, at first, what he saw. Half his men had been emptied from the saddle, lying strung out behind the charge in a pitiful line of sprawled, grotesque figures. Even as Separ watched, the *trompetista* stiffened on his horse, and then reeled off backward, his *degüello* choking off in a brassy discord. Three empty horses ran directly behind the lieutenant, froth whitening their muzzles, eyes glassy with fright, and a fourth was rolling belly up where it had fallen. The sergeant from Chihuahua was off to one side, shouting something.

"Close in your ranks!" screamed Separ. "Keep your order! Charge, you peons, charge!"

But they were breaking, unable to go on into that withering, deadly fire, rearing their mounts back and wheeling them aside. Cursing bitterly, Separ pulled his black up on its haunches and jerked it around.

He galloped back through the remaining men, jumping a dead body, beating at them with the flat of his sword. The Chihuahua sergeant came to his aid, circling back to the rear and closing them up from there. Separ formed them into a ragged line again. A trooper screamed and clutched at his chest, sliding off to one side.

"Now, you *cobardes*," screamed the lieutenant, shaking with rage, "you cowards, give me a charge or I'll put my blade through every one of you! There are only four men. We still outnumber them three to one. Nothing can stand before a cavalry charge, I tell you. If you'd followed me through, they would be pigs on our *lanzas* now. Charge, you *borrachos*, charge . . . !"

Again it was the *drumming* hoofs and the *clatter* of his troop behind him and his own unintelligible screams filling his head. Sweat streamed down his dark face and soaked his blue coat beneath the armpits. Sword held high, he

83

drove his black straight for that embankment. He didn't look back again. If they weren't following him, he would do it alone.

The cutbank flamed bright and he could see their faces dimly behind the flashes of red and puffs of gray smoke. Something hit him on the shoulder and almost knocked him from his horse. Reeling, that pain blinding him, he leaped the bank. With a desperate shout, he leaned out of the saddle, Washakie Winters's face looming up out of the smoke and flame, and hacked viciously with his sword. But when he swung erect again, the blade was clean, and he knew he had missed.

He couldn't stop his horse before he was through them. Then, wheeling the animal on the hard-packed snow of the riverbed behind the line of riflemen at the embankment, he saw the yellow-haired man sitting out in the middle struggle to his feet and raise his long gun. Separ heard the shot, and felt his horse shudder beneath him.

"I told you!" shouted the giant gleefully, waving his rifle. "I told you! I can shoot a Jake Hawkins as good as any, hole in my belly or not . . . !"

Separ was already jumping from the animal as it went down, stumbling across the snow. A tall, powerful Frenchman with queued hair whirled from the bank ahead and ran toward Separ, the lithe pivot of his hips causing his heavy shoulders to sway from side to side with every long step. Separ knew that pivot; it was the same thing that had come to him from countless hours in the courtyards of the Collegio Militar, practicing with the foil. He set himself to meet the man, thrusting with his saber.

He heard the shout of pain, then the weight of the Frenchman struck him, heavy and hard, and almost took him off his feet. His sword was caught between his own body and the other, and he tried to jerk it free, but the Frenchman's hands were on his arm, and he thought he had never felt such a violent strength. Then he felt the blade jerked from his hand, and the man took a step back with Separ's own sword.

"*Riposte, m'sieu,*" said the Frenchman, and shifted his weight with a skillful piece of foot-work, "*touché!*"

The hot pain of the blade through him sent Lieutenant Separ to his knees. He crouched there, unable to move for that moment. The Frenchman had already turned away to run toward the embankment. A red haze seemed to be in front of Separ's eyes, and he had trouble seeing them up there. Dimly he could make out the Chihuahua sergeant, on his knees, grimly holding onto the knife arm of a Mexican who must have been as broad as he was tall. The Mexican jerked from side to side, long black mustaches flapping, but Sergeant Torres wouldn't let go. Then the Mexican jammed a knee into the sergeant's face, forcing him backward, breaking his grip. Torres made one last effort to rise before the Mexican put the long blade through his stomach.

Two horses lay on their backs at the lip of the embankment, lancers pinned beneath them, and standing up in the tangle of bodies was Washakie Winters, fighting with a third mounted man. Winters fought like a wild animal, teeth snarling white in his dark face, body twisting and writhing viciously. He caught the trooper's arm and, warding off a lance thrust, climbed up on the rearing horse. The soldier finally lost his balance, falling back with Winters, and they disappeared from Separ's view into the bodies on the embankment.

Separ tightened his hands across his belly, as if to hold in the life that was pulsing so hot and red and viscid through his fingers, and the last thing he saw was the remnants of his troop, fleeing in wild disorder back through the timber. *Stupid peons,* he thought, falling face down into the sand, *didn't they know nothing could stop a cavalry charge?*

— VIII —

The Sangre de Cristos were no longer red in the sunset. The snow was like a soft, white hand across their rugged slopes, bowing the pine branches with a glistening mantle and piling up in the coulées and fighting the passage of the mules with a soft, relentless intensity that never ceased. It seemed to Celia Arnaud, hunched over in the Navajo blanket El Carajo had given her, they had been winding up and down these narrow mountain trails forever. It seemed she had never known any other sound but El Carajo's incessant conversation with every mule in the line.

"¡*Carajo*!" he called from ahead now. "Get along, you execrable little result of a blind hinny and a deaf stallion. I'll whip you till your useless ears turn red. No rat mule is going to hold up my train. I'm the best muleteer in all Méjico. . . ."

"Ha ha ha, ha ha ha!" El Andale's cracked laugh floated back from somewhere in the white mist at the head of the train. "He is the best muleteer in all Méjico. Listen to the man, little *burros*. He thinks he can make you go with a coach whip."

"General Ampudía gave it to me himself!" shouted El Carajo.

"And who is General Ampudía?" El Andale laughed again.

"If the war with Texas had been in his hands, we wouldn't have lost!" yelled El Carajo. "He is ten times the general Santa Anna is."

"You are defiling our dictator!" shouted El Andale.

"To *el diablo* with your dictator," said El Carajo. "To *el diablo* with all of them. You can put Santa Anna and Manuel Armijo in the same *aparejo* and drive them to the moon and leave them there and this country would be much happier."

Washakie drifted by on a tall horse, grinned fleetingly at Celia, and, for a moment, she caught herself smiling back. Veinier followed, sidling up to the girl. "So now you're smiling at him. Do you forget what he is?"

She jerked her head impatiently. "Maybe I do forget, sometimes. He hasn't acted like . . . like . . ."

"Like a murderer?" said Veinier. "How do you know what murderers act like? Maybe he acted like this with Little Tiswin's squaw."

She stiffened. "Oh, stop it, Jules. Aren't we having trouble enough without making more? Washakie's getting the furs through, isn't he? Who stopped those Mexican soldiers? Who put himself between us and the troops so we could have time to get ready? Not you."

"I was there," said Veinier.

"Yes, and I must say you were just as savage as Washakie when you got to fighting," said Celia. "I saw your face when you put the sword through that Mexican lieutenant."

He shrugged angrily, and urged his horse on. The snow began to fall again, loose at first, touching Celia's face with feathery fingers; she pulled the Navajo blanket tighter about her neck. Soon the front of the train disappeared in the swirling storm, and then Celia could see only the mule ahead of her. El Carajo loomed up out of the whiteness, sitting, short and squat, on a little calico mule, his mustaches dripping snow.

"Looks like a real *ventisca* building," he said, "a real blizzard! Washakie says we make camp as soon as we hit a level spot . . . !" He stopped yelling above the rising wind when her horse stumbled. She felt the snow give way beneath the animal, and it slid off sideways. The mules behind her kept on coming, jamming the horse farther toward the outer edge of the trail.

"Keep its head up!" shouted El Carajo, trying to reach her. "Let that *caballo* get its head down and you'll go over for sure!"

"I'm in a drift!" she cried. "Carajo, I'm going over! It's a drift and I'm going over . . . !"

The horse squealed, and then there was no sound. It was all soft, suffocating whiteness, with the animal going out from beneath Celia, and a bottomless sensation of falling through that snow. Rocks reached out suddenly, black and clawing, ripping her blanket off, and then were gone again as she went on down.

There was no pain till long after she had hit. She lay there with her breath melting the snow about her face until there was a hollow. It felt as if she were floating in a cloud, with no sense of pressure from any direction, only the feel of the cool whiteness enveloping her body. First then pain bit into her consciousness and she realized she must have caught her back on the rocks above. A strange lethargy gripped her, and she only wanted to lie there, soothed by the snow. But it was growing hard to breathe, and snow was in her mouth, choking her, and the pain was growing worse.

She moved feebly at first, trying to find bottom. Her flailing feet struck something solid finally. It had been all right while she was still, with that hollow place formed by the heat of her breath, but now the snow gagged her with every movement and the sense of suffocation swept her, bringing panic up through the pain. She began to call for help, not really knowing what she said at first.

"Washakie," she sobbed, fighting the thick, lacteous snow. "Washakie, I'm down here, Washakie . . ."

She stopped suddenly. For a moment, it surprised her. Why him? Jules, or El Carajo, maybe, but why Washakie Winters? Then she broke out laughing hysterically, fighting the snow blindly.

She didn't know exactly when she found the rocky ledge, or how long it took her to follow it through the snow, head below the top of the drifts half the time. Finally, choking, sobbing with exhaustion, she found herself in the open, and threw herself on the rocky ground.

The hoarse, rasping sound impinged itself on her consciousness slowly. When she realized it wasn't coming from her, she raised her head dully. The abrupt constriction in her chest stopped the breath through her.

It was the biggest bear she had ever seen, standing there on its squat legs, curly golden coat frosted with snow, breathing in that hoarse, rasping way. Its little eyes glittered malevolently at Celia. She made a little sobbing sound, and tried to move, and couldn't. Paralyzed? With fear? She had heard of that happening. Somehow her body wouldn't answer her mind. She had no will to move. The bear remained motionless, not ten feet in front of her. Then she saw the cubs behind. They were squealing and growling and rolling in the snow before the mouth of a cave.

"Don't move." The voice came from above. "Don't move till I reach you. Must have started a slide that knocked snow off the front of that cave. Raised her out of hibernation. You would have to pick one with cubs. Don't move."

He kept on talking like that, soft and strangely soothing, and Celia was surprised to feel the swift pound of her heart lessen. He came climbing carefully down a ridge of black rock, tall and lanky in his blackened elk hides, the gaunt profile of his face turned toward the bear.

"What is it?" she asked in an awed voice. "I never saw one so big."

"Grizzly," said Washakie Winters. "Never saw one this far south before. You fell into a coulée.

Soon's I get between you and the bear, start back up the rock."

"But you . . ."

"Do as I say." His voice had lost its softness. "Start up now. Slow. No fast moves. Don't talk any more and start up."

She saw El Carajo and Jules Veinier coming down from above. The grizzly began shifting restlessly, her low, guttural sounds growing louder and more belligerent. Celia started climbing the rock, then stopped.

"I can't leave you here like this."

Washakie held his Jake Hawkins across his belly. "I'll be right up after you. Just don't make no fast moves and we'll both get out."

The sudden slide of snow and rock down the face of the slope cut him off; one of the men above had started it, and the bear roared in a surprised way, jumping back. Then, shaking snow from her great shaggy head, she leaped toward Washakie. Celia wouldn't have believed such a heavy beast could move so fast.

Washakie's gun deafened the girl and she saw the grizzly stiffen in the middle of her leap, then plunge on. Washakie braced himself, stepping aside at the last moment to plunge the long rifle into the stumbling bear's chest like a spear. It stopped the wounded beast, but the grizzly caught the rifle in her great paws, smashing it with one blow. Washakie leaped backward, placing himself between Celia and the bear again, jerking out his long Bowie.

"Get up the side, I tell you!" he yelled.

"I can't leave you here!" cried Celia. "You can't fight a grizzly!"

"Hugh Glass did!" shouted Washakie desperately. "Get out of here while you can! She's wounded now and there won't be any stopping her!"

He jumped toward the bear as the beast set herself to charge, plunging his long knife hilt deep into the shaggy golden breast. He had leaped part way to the side as he went forward, trying to keep free of the bear, but as he pulled the Bowie out and jumped back, the bear caught him with a sideswipe of one heavy paw.

Washakie Winters rolled through the snow, leaving a track of red blood across the white drifts. The enraged grizzly whirled around, shaking her head, then she caught sight of Celia, and squared toward her with a terrible roar. She could see blood on the bear's chest from Washakie's knife thrust.

"Celia," shouted Veinier, coming down from above, "get out of it! Celia . . . !"

She heard a choked, sobbing sound, and realized it was her own. The bear shook her head, roaring again, then Washakie Winters leaped in from the side, shouting hoarsely to attract the animal's attention, his face covered with blood from her claws.

The movement of his long body was so swift Celia couldn't follow it. Like a lobo he struck, catching the bear in the side of her furry throat before the beast could turn toward him, jumping backward with his blade streaming red. The grizzly bellowed, jerking her hulk back toward him.

Washakie darted in again, his feet making a swift, shuffling sound in the drifted snow. He lunged at the bear like some frenzied animal, shouting with the lust for battle that seemed to grip him whenever he fought like this, black hair down over his eyes, blood splotching the snow wherever his foot touched it. The grizzly ripped his leggings half off him as he sought to avoid her claws, stumbled on, shaking her head, coat matted with blood now from her wounds.

Celia saw Washakie dart in again, and the snow rose in a white cloud from the scuffle of the bear's great body, and then Washakie was writhing in her two front paws. Celia heard herself scream as the grizzly reared up, bellowing insanely, hugging the man to her chest. Washakie jerked back and forth, plunging his knife into the animal's throat time after time, feet beating a spasmodic tattoo against her great belly. Slowly, inexorably those huge paws closed on the man. Washakie bent backward, groaning in agony as he struck again with his knife. The bear bellowed thunderously, and tightened her hug, and the man's spasmodic struggles ceased abruptly.

Finally the bear dropped Washakie's body, and went down on all fours above it, shaking her head and peering about with myopic eyes. Celia was leaning back against the rock, and some small movement she must have made attracted the grizzly's glance. With an enraged bellow, the beast whirled toward her and broke into a lumbering run.

Then Jules Veinier's broad-shouldered figure dropped from above Celia, blotting out the bear from her sight, and she heard the *crack* of his pistol. He was carried violently back against her, and held there a moment by a huge weight, and then released suddenly.

The Frenchman turned, pulling the girl away from between the rocks and the bear, and for a moment the two of them stood there, dazed, beaten, looking stupidly at the huge carcass. Veinier still held the pistol he had taken off the Mexican lieutenant, and its ball had made a round hole between the bear's eyes.

With a scatter of rocks, El Carajo finally reached the bottom of the coulée, running directly to where Washakie Winters was, and squatting over him. Celia and Veinier followed, and, when the girl saw how limp and bloody the mountain man lay there, her voice sounded hollow. "Is he . . . dead?"

— IX —

Somewhere east of Bent's Fort, Jules Veinier made his way laboriously through the snow that lay among the giant cottonwoods of the Big Timbers in soft, high drifts. It was the way he felt about the girl, really. Maybe it was a fool thing to do, and maybe this was a fool way to do it, but it was the way he felt about the girl, after all.

He stopped for a moment at the edge of the small clearing. The group of horsemen sat their steaming animals not five paces beyond. Kenna was the only one who had dismounted, standing by his great hammerheaded mare, his square, thick shoulders hunched into his black buffalo coat.

"Hello, Jules," he said.

"I thought you'd be somewhere east of the fort," said Veinier. "We didn't meet you on the way up from Taos. I knew you hadn't quit."

"I hear Washakie Winters tried to run Armijo's blockade," said Kenna.

"Washakie Winters *did* run Armijo's blockade," said Veinier. "It wasn't any Mexican that stopped him. It was a bear."

Kenna laughed, and it was a grating, mirthless sound. "Leave it to Washakie Winters to find a fight like that. I'll bet it wasn't any little brown

96

bear. I'll bet it was the biggest, wildest grizzly this side of Colter's Hell." He stopped laughing suddenly. "What about the furs?"

"That's what I came ahead to see you about," said Veinier, and could feel his muscles begin to tighten up across his belly. "I want you to leave the furs alone, Kenna."

The flicker that lit Kenna's dark eyes momentarily might have been surprise. "You what? Do you think I've come all this way for nothing? Do you think I'm letting Washakie get away with poaching those furs from under my very nose at Taos? You and I had an agreement, Veinier, and we're keeping it."

"That agreement didn't include the girl," said Veinier. "I don't want Celia hurt."

Kenna made a disgusted motion with his hand. "I don't care what happens to the girl, Veinier. You can do what you like about her. I'm going to get those furs, that's all. I'm going to get them and take them to Saint Louis like you and me and Armijo planned, and you'll get your third and Armijo'll get his."

"No," said Veinier, feeling his first anger heat him. "Do you think Celia will let her pelts go without a fight, now that she's gotten them this far? I know you, Kenna. If you take those furs here in Big Timbers, you won't leave anybody alive to tell how you took them. You can't leave anybody alive to tell how you took them if you hope to do any business in Saint Louis. We'll do it another way."

"Will we now?" said Kenna. His eyes burned intensely from beneath shaggy brows, and he was leaning forward till his face almost touched Veinier's. "What way, Veinier? Your way? What can you do that I can't? You're not in the most favorable position of all, exactly. Don't you think Celia's begun to wonder how I got those furs to Taos, and what I'd planned to do with them?"

"It's obvious you and Armijo were working together, but that doesn't implicate me," said Veinier.

"Doesn't it?" Kenna said. "Celia isn't thick. She'd know I couldn't just walk into Saint Louis with sixty thousand dollars worth of pelts and say I got them on a trap line. I'd be the only one in from Santa Fe this year, Veinier, and that would put the light on me. Whatever I did would have to be pretty legitimate. Don't you think she's figured that out? What's left then? I couldn't sell under another company's name, because it would be known none of them had any shipments in. All that's left is official sanction from the Arnaud Agency that would let me sell to the buyers who had already contracted. Celia'd know she didn't give that sanction. Who else, Veinier? Don't you think she's figured that out? Who else at the Arnaud Agency is big enough to send official sanction with me?"

"Will you stop saying that?" snapped Veinier. "I tell you she doesn't know. You're not taking the furs when we pass here, that's all. I don't want the girl hurt."

"You'll rob her blind," said Kenna contemptuously, "but you don't want her hurt. Is that what a gentleman does, Veinier?"

Veinier grew rigid. "You wouldn't know what a gentleman does, Kenna."

"I know what you're doing," said Kenna, closing his hands slowly as if holding his anger in them. "You made the deal with me because you couldn't have gotten the furs through any other way. You couldn't have taken them through Taos yourself because you didn't want the girl to know they were gone, and you had to ring Armijo in on the profits to get them out of his custom-house. But now Washakie Winters has run Armijo's blockade for you, and you think the rest will be easy sledding to Saint Louis, and you don't want to split with Armijo and me. You ain't worried about the girl. You'll have to get rid of her anyway if you want to profit from those furs." His hands worked again.

Veinier could hardly get his words past the anger clogging his throat. "You're letting Celia pass unmolested, understand. I'll get rid of the furs in Saint Louis without having to hurt her, and you'll get your third."

That wasn't so. It was in Veinier's mind; it had

been in Veinier's mind a long time now. Kenna wouldn't get anything. Armijo wouldn't. He himself would not. Only the girl. It was strange how she had become the paramount thing. It had been the money, in the beginning, even after Celia had arrived in Santa Fe. The $20,000 that Veinier would get as his third of the furs. It had meant a lot to the hundred-a-month factor in the Arnaud Agency at Santa Fe. Now it meant nothing. Only the girl.

"I got to admire your nerve, coming here alone and telling me this," said Kenna. "What did you think I'd do? Agree and let you walk away with the whole sixty thousand in pelts?"

Nerve? Veinier smiled thinly to himself. He hadn't thought of it that way, exactly; in fact, he hadn't thought much of it at all. He had only known this was the way it had to be done, and he had come to do it. It amused him, somehow, because he had never seen a thing so simply and clearly before. He heard his own voice come out, and it sounded strangely calm. "You aren't taking those furs, Kenna."

Kenna's lip curled. "The hell with you!"

Veinier grabbed Kenna's buffalo coat, the jerk of his powerful shoulders throwing the smaller man off balance. "I want your word on it, Kenna. You'll get your share of the pelts, but not this way. I want your word you won't harm the girl."

Kenna's yell made the big mare shy away. "Let go of me, Veinier!"

"No!" The calmness was gone now, and Veinier felt his blood pounding against his temples, and he shook Kenna. "Your word . . . !"

Kenna shoved his arm up between Veinier's elbows, levering it against the taller man's big chest and heaving hard with all his weight. It broke Veinier's grip, and the Frenchman stumbled back. He saw Kenna's elbows dip inward, and knew what that meant. He tore aside his blanket coat, going after the big Spanish pistol he had taken from the lieutenant. He had his hand on the butt, and felt it coming up out of his belt, and then Kenna had cross-armed his Cheringtons out, and their flame blinded Veinier, and their thunder deafened him. He felt a great shock. He felt himself falling into a vortex of pain that spun black and bottomless beneath him, and that one last thought passed dimly through him, almost as if he had spoken. It was the way he felt about the girl.

— X —

Big Timbers extended thirty miles south of Bent's Fort along the mountain route of the Santa Fe Trail, and the mule train had taken two days to reach this point from the fort, making heavy going of the desolate country. There was no doctor at

Bent's, and they had been advised to take Little Tiswin on to St. Louis. They had obtained a light wagon to carry him in, and Celia was driving it behind the mules.

Sitting the high box seat, she could see Washakie Winters humped over on his big gray gelding far ahead. He had gotten out of a sickbed to come with them from the fort, when Bent had advised them to start as early as possible if they wanted to be out of the mountains before the worst of winter settled down.

"I'm worried about Washakie," Celia told Little Tiswin. "He should be in the wagon with you. He still had a fever when we left Bent's, and those scars on him aren't healing right."

Sitting propped up inside the white tilt, face pale and haggard, Little Tiswin spat disgustedly. "Don't you mention his name to me. Put him inside this wagon and I'd finish what the bear started. You're getting mighty teched up about a murderer, it seems."

She flushed.

"He saved my life there with the bear, didn't he?"

Little Tiswin scowled blackly. "And you saw my squaw, didn't you?"

"Oh, Tiswin," she said angrily, snapping her reins on the nigh horse. She wished she weren't so mixed up about Washakie Winters. It wasn't right, the way she felt. Or what did she feel? He had killed a woman and, whenever Celia thought of that, even to look at the man filled her with revulsion. Yet, at times, when she wasn't remembering Nailla, and she felt Washakie's eyes on her.

The gigantic cottonwoods spread in a deep grove across the bank of the Arkansas, brooding over the drifted snow like gnarled spirits, filling Celia with a sudden uneasiness. She looked to the right of the wagon where the trees climbed the slope, bare and leafless; on the other side was the river, ice gleaming, slick and white, across to the midstream islands, where more huge cottonwoods spread their bare winter branches.

"Celia!" called Little Tiswin. The tone of his voice made her turn around, and she saw him staring at a clump of barberry bushes in the grove. "Did you see something move there?"

She studied the thicket for a long moment. "No."

"Give me a gun," said the curly-haired giant. "This is Pawnee country and I don't want to ride through it like a fool hen sitting on a limb waiting for some buck to come along and knock me off."

She shook her head. "You know you'd only be after Washakie if we left a gun with you," she said. "Besides, the Indians don't raid so much during the winter. Veinier told me . . ."

She stopped at the name. Yes, Veinier. What had become of him? Acting so strangely those days after the battle with the bear, so quiet and moody, watching her all the time with that dark, almost puzzled look in his eyes, and then disappearing as soon as they reached Bent's Fort.

"Celia!"

It was Little Tiswin's voice, and it stiffened her on the wagon seat. Then it was the thunder of the first gun, and her nigh horse leaping into the air with a scream. The wagon tilted to one side as the wounded animal fought to get out of the traces, kicking and whinnying in terror. Celia had a dim sense of men charging from the cotton-woods where they grew down to the river.

"¡Carajo!" shouted the muleteer from some-where ahead. "Carajo, you calico sons of *el diablo*, *carajo*!"

The charging men were close. A tall mountain man in tattered buckskins swept by Celia, shooting his Jake Hawkins at Washakie Winters. The girl had all she could do to fight the plunging team and keep her wagon from going off the embankment into the ice. Panting, she tried to rein the frenzied animals to the right; they responded blindly, and crashed into a pair of Apaches who burst from the trees on pied mustangs.

One of the Indians leaped from his horse, crashing belly down over the off animal of Celia's team. He threw his legs over onto the tree and whirled toward the girl, leaping up for the seat. She felt the sweaty weight of his body strike her, and then both of them went off.

Her back struck the wheel, and she cried out with pain, and then the ground shuddered against her body. Dimly, above her, she could see the twisted face of the man, his eyes glittering. The tails of his long black coat flapped against his bare calves as he caught her by the hair, jerking her head upward. She saw the flash of a long skinning knife.

"Chefuri," she gasped. "No . . . !"

Martin Kenna had chosen the spot because of the way the cottonwoods grew down to the river. It left only a narrow space between trees and bank, perfect for ambush. And now his men were spread out along the line of mules, stampeding them. Two of the trappers came down the line of running animals, howling like banshees, throwing their horses into the pack train. Knocked out of their line, the mules in that section broke wildly for the trees. El Carajo suddenly appeared on the other side with his *peso*-tipped coach whip.

"¡*Carajo*!" he yelled, the sharpened *peso* biting into the stampeding mules. "Back into line, you four-footed *brujas*. I am the best muleteer in all Méjico, and nobody stampedes my mules."

"What are you saying, you big *caracol*?" shouted El Andale, galloping up from the rear to help him herd the mules back into line. "*I* am the best muleteer in all Méjico. If it wasn't for me, you'd be chasing these mules all over the Sangre de Cristos now. You and your coach whip!"

One of the trappers drew a bead on El Carajo and fired. The squat Mexican's straw sombrero flew off his head, and he screamed some Spanish obscenity at Kenna's man, driving the mules on back into line. Kenna swept aside his buffalo coat to get one of his Cheringtons, booting his horse madly to try to bring up with those ahead. Then, far ahead, he caught sight of Washakie Winters. The mountain man was deliberately turning the head of the train onto the ice of the river, and his voice came back, warped and faint.

"Carajo, turn the mules toward those islands in mid-river. Get them in that timber and we can scatter them so they won't stampede."

"You heard him!" shouted El Carajo. "Turn those mules, you *cabrón*. Are you afraid you can't run them across the ice?"

El Carajo's lash turned the first mule off the bank suddenly, and it went slipping and sliding across the ice, followed by the next one Andale drove. Kenna had his pistol out now, and he threw down on Andale. But the man disappeared beneath the steep cutbank before Kenna could get a shot, and then appeared again, far out on the ice, out of range.

Cursing, Kenna jammed his gun back into his belt, and slid his own mare down the bank, holding her head up with both hands on the reins, sending up a shower of white ice as he struck the river. His horse skidded across the slick, and, for a moment, Kenna was set to jump. Then the animal righted itself.

El Carajo had rounded up the mules and was running them into a line after the others that Washakie had already driven onto the ice. Kenna's two trappers came up on the other side of the line, as before, trying to break through and scatter the pack animals. One of them was loading his rifle as he rode.

"Will you get that gray *simplón* back in line?" El Carajo bellowed at Andale. "What's the matter with you? You couldn't drive a mouse across the kitchen floor."

"A mouse?" shouted the old man. "You couldn't drive a flea across your arm! I'll show you how a muleteer . . . !"

His shout turned into a broken, strangled sound, and he dropped his prod pole, and slid off his horse, bouncing as he struck the ice. Across the backs of the running mules, the trapper lowered his rifle, grinning in his dirty beard.

El Carajo took one look at the sprawled body of Andale back there on the ice, then jerked his calico mule over into the running line of pack animals, leaping from his saddle into the other mules. For a moment, Kenna thought he had gone down amidst them. Then El Carajo appeared on top of one, clawing at the *aparejo*, and threw himself bodily from that across onto the trapper.

"You stinking *borracho*!" screamed El Carajo. "He was the best muleteer in all Méjico!" The two of them went off the trapper's horse and disappeared from Kenna's view beneath the mules.

Kenna tried to catch the mules and scatter them before they reached the islands, but Andale and El Carajo had started them on the headlong run that carried them after Washakie's section of the line into the timber, and by the time Kenna had caught up with the last of the pack animals he was almost to the trees. It was then that his horse went down. The way it stumbled, he knew it had struck a snag in the ice, and his feet were already kicking free of the *tapaderos* as the animal fell. Kenna struck running, and then let himself go over, rolling because he knew he couldn't keep his feet at that speed.

The first snowbank beneath the trees stopped him, and he rose, spitting out the acrid white stuff, bleeding from a cut on his face. The mules were plunging shadows in the gnarled skeleton timber ahead of him, and he broke into a run after them, face turned to a pale, lithic anger by the thought that Washakie Winters had thwarted him again. He caught up with the first three mules to find them alone, standing there, blowing and snorting. Kenna could get these three going again, all right, but it wouldn't cause the rest to stampede, scattered through the trees as they were.

Well, maybe he didn't care so much about the mules any more, now, anyway. Maybe his anger had carried him beyond that. He began to walk forward in a heavy, deliberate way, shoulders hunched down in his black buffalo coat, eyes burning like the coals of a banked fire. Yes, maybe his anger had carried him beyond that.

He heard the shots ahead, and the sound of running animals, and another last shot, and then it was still again except for the steady, *slushing* sound of his heavy boots through the snow. He came across the body in a moment, lying by a plum bush. One of Chefuri's Apaches, clutching an empty *escopeta*, a neat round hole in his head just above the eyes. Washakie Winters? Washakie Winters.

Martin Kenna's smile was cold and mirthless as he stepped across the body and went on ahead. The anger in him was subordinate to his purpose now, a calm, deliberate purpose that had been there, he supposed, even before he had heard of the Arnaud furs. There had been other things between him and Washakie before these furs. This would be the last. From ahead, he heard a small, scuffling sound, then silence. His heavy head raised a little as he called.

"Washakie?"

"Kenna?"

"I'm coming."

Washakie Winters stepped around the black bole

of a huge cottonwood with his Jake Hawkins held across his belly and that wolf snarl drawing his flat lips back against his teeth, and Martin Kenna flapped his elbows inward, and the butts of his Cheringtons slapped his hands, and he cross-armed them out, and the thunder of guns filled the Big Timbers.

Celia Arnaud felt the cold steel of Chefuri's blade against her forehead, and her cries died in her throat, and her lithe young body stiffened for the searing pain. Then Chefuri was torn bodily off her, and the knife dropped into the snow. Dazedly she got to her knees.

Little Tiswin must have jumped Chefuri from the high box seat, and he was straddling the half-breed, huge hands around Chefuri's neck, shaking him like a dog would shake a pack rat.

"You was going to take her hair front to back!" screamed the yellow-haired giant in a fury. "That ain't the way the Indians do it. They gouge the flesh in a circle clear around the hair and yank it off. Front to back. That was the way Nailla had hers taken. My squaw, Chefuri. Was it you? Tell me, by Colter's Hell, tell me . . . !"

Chefuri writhed in Little Tiswin's grip, screaming with pain, choking, gasping, his face contorted. Finally he could stand it no longer. "All right," he sobbed hoarsely, jerking from side to side. "All right. Your squaw and her brother

110

was there above the Pecos when we came up on Washakie's trail. I tried to make Nailla tell where Washakie had gone. Her brother got mad and started to fight. My trackers took care of him. Washakie must have left his Bowie behind. Nailla got hold of it and tried to use it on me. I got the knife away from her. I was so mad I didn't know what I was doing, Tiswin. . . ."

"I know what I'm doing," said Little Tiswin. Celia turned away, hearing Chefuri's last scream, and then nothing but Little Tiswin's hoarse, heavy breathing. Dimly, then, she saw Washakie Winters stumbling across the ice toward them from the mid-river islands. She ran to help him up the bank.

"Kenna . . . ?"

"Over on the island," Washakie told her. "He told me what they were doing, before he died. Veinier had given Kenna letters of introduction and recommendation from your Arnaud Agency in Santa Fe. As chief factor, he had enough power to do that. With the official sanction of the agency, Kenna could have sold the furs legitimately, under the Arnaud stamp, to the buyers who had already contracted for the pelts. Veinier and Kenna and Armijo were to split it three ways. But Veinier met Kenna in the Big Timbers yesterday and tried to stop Kenna from taking the furs off you. Kenna couldn't figure that out. It had been Veinier who started the whole business."

The girl felt her breath stop in her. It wasn't the

shock of finding out Veinier had been behind it, although that in itself was surprise enough. It was more the sudden realization of why Veinier had gone to stop Kenna. Kenna couldn't figure it out? She could. She could, and she felt a sudden, poignant sadness for the young Frenchman, and, somehow, she couldn't blame him for what he had done with the furs. She remembered how strange and quiet Veinier had grown these last weeks, watching her with that puzzled softness in his eyes, and then, as if he had suddenly solved a great problem, that last day before he had left them at Bent's Fort, the puzzled look had been gone. That was why he had gone to Kenna. Because of her. Was it that strong an emotion, love, that it could change a person so? Then she looked at Washakie Winters, and knew it was.

"Chefuri told us he killed Tiswin's squaw," she said, looking up at Winters's lean, mordant face. "And you didn't even bother to deny it. You didn't care enough what I thought of you even to deny that you killed Nailla. . . ."

"I used to deny things," he said. "It didn't make any difference. They went on telling stories about me. Like that poaching in the British Territories. I never got near the British Territories. I don't think the British Crown even knows I exist. Some drunk Chippewa up at Fort Union just thought he saw me near there, and, when a bunch of Cree bucks came down and burned the fort and poached the furs, trappers down here started saying it was me. Same way about my desertion from the Army. You saw my discharge papers. I guess I had to be a little wild even to give a basis for those stories, but what man wouldn't get wild if he runs the woods long enough, without friends . . . or a woman? And I care what you think of me. What do you think of me?"

"I think you're the man who's going to get my furs on to Saint Louis," she said. "And after that . . ."

"After that?"

"I'll be coming back to Santa Fe," she said. "Will you?"

"I'll be coming back."

"And if you had something interesting enough in Santa Fe, would you come down out of the mountains once in a while . . . to see it?" Her voice was growing softer.

"Come down out of the mountains?" roared Little Tiswin. "If he has something that interesting in Santa Fe, he won't even go into the mountains to begin with. I sort of hankered for you to hitch up with a squaw, like me, Washakie, but I think you got something just as good here."

"What do you think?" she asked Washakie.

"What does he think?" guffawed Little Tiswin. "Never ask a man . . ."

"Tiswin," said Washakie Winters, "now that you know I didn't kill your squaw, I hope we're friends again. And as a friend, can I ask you if all this ruckus didn't give you an ache where Kenna shot you? And if it did, why don't you climb back into the wagon where you'll rest easier, and let me do my own talking?" He looked down at Celia. "It's going to be a long time before I'm really finished. Years, maybe. A lifetime, maybe."

Traitor Town

Santa Fe was one of Savage's favorite settings, and in 1951 for this story he turned to the background of events in the province of New Mexico during the time of the Mexican War. It was this period that would also serve as the background for his novels, *The Cavan Breed* (Five Star Westerns, 2001) and *Doniphan's Thousand* (Five Star Westerns, 2005). *Zane Grey's Western Magazine*, a digest-sized publication issued monthly by Dell Publishing, was edited by Don Ward, and any fiction Savage wrote for it commanded 4¢ a word, twice as much as he received from Fiction House or any other pulp magazine publisher at the time. Beginning in late 1950 virtually all of Savage's magazine fiction was intended for submission to Don Ward. "Traitor Town," the eighth story by Savage to appear in this magazine, was published in *Zane Grey's Western Magazine* (11/51).

— 1 —

Uncle Hondo found Tony Ferrar playing solitaire at one of the short card tables in the rear of La Fonda. The old man came across the crowded bar-room at a hobbling walk, apprehension deepening the furry seams of his face.

"George Manatte is in Number Five, asking for you," he told Ferrar. "Don't go in, Tony. Cimarrón Garrett is with him."

Ferrar grinned, getting up. "Would you have me hide from that blowhard?"

The old man shook his white head. "Short men and fools, they are recognized from afar."

Chuckling, Ferrar moved through the crowd of peons and trappers that filled the inn this summer evening of 1846. He was a tall man, with curly black hair and startling blue eyes that came from the Irish trapper who had fathered him, and a darkness to his long face, a sharp height to his cheek bones that were the heritage of his Mexican mother. The exotic mixture seemed to extend to his whole personality. While his solid-muscled upper body was clothed in padded waistcoat and tailored fustian, he wore elk-hide leggings that were black and greasy from years on the trail.

Reaching the door of Number Five, he knocked, and was told to enter. George Manatte and his daughter Julia sat at the small deal table, while Cimarrón Garrett stood against the wall, arms folded across his massive chest. Ferrar took a chair, tilted it back against the wall, and relaxed immediately into his indolent sprawl. He smiled at Julia, but she did not answer it. Her wide blue eyes were solemn as a child's in her softly rounded face, gazing at him with disturbing fixity. Her cloak was pushed back, revealing deep breasts swelling at a prim calico dress, and her hair spilled like a cascade of honey onto her shoulders.

"You take your daughter into strange places, George," Ferrar said.

"I want her to know what's going on," Manatte said. He put his elbows on the table, a tall man, well in his fifties, with a face scored by the weather and eyes faded by the sun. One of the biggest fur traders in this town of Santa Fe, he still wore a simple broadcloth suit and beaver hat.

"As you probably know, Ferrar, the war with Mexico is going against the Mexicans," he said. "General Kearny has taken Las Vegas. He's going to march on this town in a couple of days. We have one chance to stop the bloodshed, to convince Governor Armijo how useless it is to stand against the American Army."

Ferrar's heavy brows raised. "Captain Cordenza is coming from Chihuahua with four companies of cavalry. Add that to Governor Armijo's dragoons and they can cut Kearny to pieces in Apache Cañon."

Manatte shook his head. "Captain Cordenza and his four Chihuahua companies were captured by an American force last week."

Ferrar came forward, chair legs slapping the floor. "How do you know?"

"Cordenza accepted the surrender terms by note. Kearny now has the note. I heard that from my last contact with him. But no more of my men can get through. Governor Armijo was close to Cordenza. He'll know Cordenza's signature and hand-writing. Armijo won't be able to stand against Kearny without Cordenza's cavalry. If Armijo knew Cordenza had been captured, he'd capitulate immediately. General Kearny could walk into Santa Fe without a shot. We want you to go to Las Vegas, Tony, get Cordenza's note of surrender from Kearny, and bring it to Armijo."

Ferrar settled back, frowning deeply. Cimarrón Garrett stirred against the wall, speaking disgustedly.

"I told you Ferrar was more greaser than Yankee, George. He wanted Cordenza to get through and help Armijo."

Ferrar's eyes flashed with anger, swinging up to Cimarrón. The man was one of Manatte's muleskinners, six feet tall and almost as wide, with a mane of yellow hair and a yellow beard that curled against his keg chest like foamy hoar frost.

119

His greasy rawhide jacket was fringed with the black hair of a dozen Indian scalps, and his leggings were held up by a belt of gold *pesos*.

Manatte leaned farther toward Ferrar. "You know how the Americans in this town have been clamped down on. Any white man who tried to leave town would be shot. Even if he did get out, he'd never make it through that strip between here and Las Vegas. Only a Mexican could get through, but we don't know any Mexicans we can trust. You're the only one, Tony. The Mexicans trust you. You could get through."

Ferrar shook his head. "I'd betray every friend I have if I helped Kearny take this town."

"You don't number the Americans among your friends, then?" Manatte said thinly.

"That proves he's a greaser," Cimarrón said.

Ferrar stood up, nostrils pinched with anger. "Don't use that word again, Cimarrón."

The man grinned evilly. "Why not? Any grea—"

"Never mind, Cimarrón." Manatte got up angrily, almost upsetting his chair. "I can see there's no use talking any more. But you've made an unwise choice, Ferrar. It will be hard for those who fought Kearny, when he takes the town."

He turned and stamped to the outer door, swinging it open and stepping out into the alley. With an enigmatic grin, Cimarrón followed him. It left only Julia in the room. She had risen, and she came slowly around the table to face Ferrar.

"Why did you refuse, Tony? You're more Yankee than Mexican. You've got to help your own people."

He waved his hand toward the noise of the main room. "These are my people as much as the Yankees. I was born here. My life is here. I speak Spanish as easily as English."

"But you'd *help* them by bringing Kearny in! You know what the government has been here."

He shook his dark head. "I admit there's a lot of graft under Armijo's rule. . . ."

"Not Armijo's rule," Julia said. "He's nothing more than a figurehead. Morina Garcia is the power behind the throne, and you know it. She doesn't represent Mexican rule any more than a cat represents a dog. Graft is the smallest part of it, Tony. The kind of life you've led has blinded you to it. Drinking, gambling, living high, off on your trap lines half the time, you have no real picture of what's going on. The people are suffering under that woman's domination. She's gotten Armijo to bleed them dry. . . ."

"Stop it!"

He checked himself, surprised that it had come out so hotly. They stood there, staring at each other a moment, white-faced. Then Julia took a deep breath.

"I've thought for a long time that Morina Garcia had come between us, Tony. Now I know it's true."

He tried to catch her arm, protesting. "Julia . . ."

She stepped back, her voice shaking a little. "Never mind, Tony. If it's over, it's over. You can't force something like that."

She looked at him for a last instant, with an intense hurt shadowing her eyes, then turned and went out. He stared after her with a sense of deep loss. Then, shaking his head helplessly, he turned back into the outer room.

The bar was filling with peons and Taos Indians and young *vaqueros*. Tomás was throwing three-card monte for Uncle Hondo and Ferrar made his way through the crowd toward Tomás's table.

"What did they want, Antonito?" the old man asked.

"Just some fur deal," Ferrar said.

Tomás went on shuffling the cards. He was Morina Garcia's Navajo servant, an enigmatic statue of a man with a face that might have been carved from some dark wood, so little did it change expression. A bright red band held his long black hair, and his pants and shirt were of doeskin, white as milk and always immaculately clean.

Ferrar poured himself some *pulque*, trying to relax, trying to take the pleasure he should in being here with his friends. Life should be like the taste of good wine in the mouth. He should savor the reek of the place as he always had—the piquant scent of chile peppers drying out front and the stable stench drifting in from the rear and the smell of grape wine and rot-gut whiskey and sweat and leather and sawdust. He should drink in the soft sound of Spanish and the slap of cards. It was the life he loved.

But somehow he was disturbed. "Uncle Hondo," he said. "You are a peon. Are your people happy?"

"They sing all day. They drink all night. I would live no place else in the world."

"How about Armijo?"

The old man looked around him. "Is that wise?"

"You are among friends."

Uncle Hondo leaned forward, wagging his shaggy head from side to side. "The governor, he is at times hard. But we are certainly better off than we were under Spanish rule."

"And you don't want the Americans?"

"If all *gringos* are like that Cimarrón Garrett, I would do to them that." Uncle Hondo spat on the floor. Then he turned his wise old eyes up to Ferrar, the wind wrinkles deepening at their corners. "Something, she is troubling you, Antonito. I have been your man since a baby you were, and I know that look."

Ferrar shook his head. "Nothing."

Uncle Hondo put a gnarled hand on his arm. "It is sometimes hard to be a child of two races."

Ferrar glanced sharply at him, surprised at his insight, then chuckled softly. "I can't hide anything from you, old one."

Uncle Hondo grinned at him, then glanced over his head, the expression changing on his face.

Ferrar turned to see Captain Seguro Ugardes coming through the door. He pushed through the knots of peons and *vaqueros*, answering their greetings with a jaunty grin. He made an elegant figure in the round blue jacket of the Mexican dragoons, with its red cuffs and collar. His blue velvet breeches were unbuttoned at the knees to show white stockings above the deerskin boots, and the Golden Cross of Honor glittered brazenly over his heart. He came right to where Ferrar was sitting, clapping him on the shoulder.

"It is good to see someone who can relax, *amigo*. I have had a trying day."

"Governor Armijo been keeping you busy?" Ferrar asked.

Captain Ugardes took a chair and dropped wearily into it. "The palace is in an uproar. All kinds of rumors. Some say Kearny has ten thousand men. Some say only a handful. Armijo is in one of his rages. Nothing is right. I wish Cordenza and those four Chihuahua companies would get here. It would make us all feel safer."

"Cordenza's coming, then?"

"*Pues*, of course . . ." Ugardes broke off, studying Ferrar. "You make a point of that. Do you have any information?"

Ferrar frowned, realizing for the first time what a position Manatte had put him in. Ugardes's reaction convinced him that Governor Armijo did not yet know Cordenza had been captured. Thus

Manatte had put Ferrar under an obligation of secrecy by telling him the news. But why had Manatte been so sure he would keep their secret? Captain Ugardes was Ferrar's oldest friend in Santa Fe; they had grown up together. Didn't his loyalty to that kind of friend place a deeper obligation upon him than the mere fact his father was white? Wouldn't Manatte know that?

He looked up, on the point of telling Ugardes. Yet something checked him. Perhaps Ugardes saw the struggle going on within him. He leaned forward and put a hand on Ferrar's arm.

"I have always known it would be hard for you, if something like this ever came up, Antonito. I will not press you. Just remember this. No matter what happens, no matter which side you choose, we will always be *compadres*."

They stared into each other's eyes a moment. Then the embarrassment of a man who has touched deep emotion flushed Ugardes's face, and he leaned back with a laugh.

"Enough of this. I came here to forget the war. Like the old days, no? Wine and monte and maybe a pretty *doncellita* to amuse us."

They had their drink and wandered to Ferrar's monte table and for a short while the laughter and pleasure that only this country could afford filled the two men. Then Ferrar noticed a change in the sound about him. First it was the rough laughter dying out. Then the *clink* of glasses seemed to

125

diminish. Ferrar turned to see Cimarrón Garrett shouldering his way through the knots of men. With him was Pitch, his swamper. The man was shorter than Garrett, but just as broad. The muscles of his chest and shoulders bulged like sides of beef beneath a hickory jacket. A barrel of hot pitch had been dumped over his face while he was doping a hot box on the trail, many years before. It had burned most of his hair off and left one eye blinded, and the left side of his face was badly scarred. Behind Garrett and Pitch were three of the buckskinned trappers who worked for Manatte. They were tall, raw-boned men from Tennessee and Kentucky, their elk hides black with bear grease and stinking of beaver medicine.

"That fool," Ugardes said under his breath. "Doesn't he know better than to come in here? With the feeling against the Yankees he's liable to be torn apart."

"He's drunk," Ferrar said.

Garrett pushed his way heedlessly through the crowd, ignoring the curses and hateful looks that followed him. He halted before Ferrar's table, hooking thumbs in his waistband and swaggering drunkenly.

"I thought I'd better check on you. Manatte was a fool to trust you. Ran right to your greaser friends with the news."

Ferrar felt his fingers close around the edge of the table. "I haven't said anything you wouldn't,

Garrett, and you'd better not stay in here. You're taking too big a chance."

"But you aren't, are you?" Garrett asked, swaying toward Ferrar. "Put you in a bunch of chiles and nobody could tell the difference."

Ugardes's voice was a drawn blade. "*Señor*, you are insulting my friend."

"I expect," Garrett said. "Too yellow to dodge for himself. Has to hide behind the Mexican army."

"Are you blind as well as a pig?" snapped Ugardes. His face was dead white. "If Ferrar hit you and a fight started in here, you'd be torn to pieces. The feeling is so bad against you the slightest thing will set it off. Ferrar is giving you this chance. Take it and get out."

"Git out, hell," Garrett said. He grabbed Ferrar's shoulder, twisting him around in his chair. "Did you think I wouldn't follow you in here just because this place was filled with Mexicans?"

Ferrar was trembling, unable to contain himself much longer. "I notice you didn't come while you were alone," he said thinly.

Already there was an ominous muttering from the crowd, and Ugardes grabbed Garrett's arm. "They'll kill you if anything starts, *señor*. Will you get out?"

Garrett jerked his arm free. "There ain't enough greasers in all Santa Fe to cause us trouble. You're the one who'd better get out, Ugardes. In a couple of days there won't be any chile army left."

"You make a bad mistake," said Ugardes in a voice so low it was barely audible. "I am not so noble as Ferrar. Do not insult my service."

"Service?" snorted Garrett. "A bunch of donkeys in rags with a sheepherder for a general. . . ."

"¡*Pordiosero*!" It escaped Ugardes in a hissing curse, as he slapped Garrett across the face. For one instant, the immense muleskinner stared at Ugardes, disbelief in his gaping mouth. Then he made a snarling sound and lunged for the captain. Savage vindication in his face, Ugardes jumped backward, unsheathing his saber. But it caught on the underside of the table, and Garrett reached him before he could bring it into play. Garrett's blow made a sharp, meaty *crack* in the room. It bent Ugardes back across the monte table like a bow.

Ferrar lunged up out of his chair at Garrett, but Pitch caught his arm, spinning him halfway around. Ferrar saw Garrett snatch the saber from Ugardes's limp hand and swing it high. With only that moment left, Ferrar sank his fist into Pitch's belly with all his weight behind it. Pitch doubled over with a gasp. Ferrar tore free and threw himself bodily at Garrett as the saber swung down.

He smashed heavily into the man, knocking him aside. The sword bit into the edge of the monte table an inch from Ugardes's hip. Ferrar carried Garrett on down the table and the man had to let go of the saber to catch hold of the edge and stop himself. Before Ferrar could recover, he felt the man's arm snake around his neck. The great bicep bulged. There was the *pop* of tendons. A shooting pain in Ferrar's head. Holding Ferrar in the crook of his elbow, Garrett brought his other fist into Ferrar's belly. The wind left Ferrar in a gasp. He hung there in a moment of limp helplessness, sensing the shift of Garrett's weight as the man brought that fist back for another blow. With the last of his will, Ferrar doubled up and jackknifed a knee to block the fist.

He heard Garrett grunt in pain as his fist cracked against Ferrar's knee. That arm around Ferrar's neck tightened spasmodically. The congestion in Ferrar's head was so great now he thought it would burst. Sound and sense spun. He felt Garrett shifting for another blow. With a gasp, Ferrar brought his right arm around behind Garrett, into the kidneys. Garrett's grunt was full of pain. Ferrar hit him there again, a vicious hooking blow. This time he felt it slacken Garrett's death lock on his head. He tore free. Garrett tried to follow up and grapple again, but Ferrar hit him in the belly. It stopped the giant for a moment, pain twisting his face.

Ferrar knew he would be finished if Garrett could get in close and grapple again. As the big man recovered and took a step toward Ferrar, arms outthrust, Ferrar weaved off to one side, brushing aside the right arm, smashing at his belly again. Garrett grunted sickly and doubled forward. It left his face exposed. Ferrar put all his weight behind the blow. Garrett's head jerked up and his whole body spun. The nearby *chusa* table caught him waist high and bent him over. It left the back of his neck open. Ferrar made a hammer of his fist and hit the man there.

Garrett stiffened, then went limp, rolling off the *chusa* table and onto the floor. Ferrar caught at the table to keep from going down himself, surprised at how drained he was. Garrett lay unmoving at his feet. The room was filled with wild shouting and cursing, the sound of cracking furniture and vicious blows.

Ferrar turned to see the *chusa* dealer and the bartender struggling with Pitch against the bar. Ugardes was on his knees astraddle one of the trappers on the floor, slamming his head into the hard adobe. The other two trappers were struggling in the midst of half a dozen Mexicans, and more peons were streaming in the door, drawn by the fight. The bartender broke a bottle over Pitch's head, and the man went to his knees. Ferrar staggered over to Ugardes, pawing at him.

"Stop it, Seguro! We've got to get them out of here before a mob gathers, get off him . . . !"

Ugardes spun over onto one knee, eyes blank with rage. Then his eyes cleared, and he saw who it was. Shaking his head, he got to his feet. His black hair was torn from its queue and hanging down over his eyes.

"Get that one out!" he shouted to the bartender. "Get him out before he's killed."

The *chusa* dealer and the barman got the stunned Pitch between them and half dragged him to the rear door. The trapper on the floor rolled over with a groan. The other two broke and ran suddenly before the growing crowd jamming in the front door. Ferrar staggered back to Garrett, rolling him beneath the *chusa* table and standing in front of him.

"That way!" he shouted, pointing toward the rear door. The first wave of peons streamed past him after the trappers, and there was a momentary break. He caught Garrett by the collar and dragged him over to one of the side doors, rolling him into a small room. There was an outer door here leading onto a back alley. Garrett was coming around as Ferrar dumped him against a wall.

"You'd better get out fast," Ferrar told him. "If they catch you, they'll cut you to pieces."

Garrett got to his feet, sagging heavily against the wall. His eyes were bloodshot and vindictive.

"This isn't the end, Ferrar," he said thickly. "You'd better not stay in this town when Kearny comes."

Ferrar slammed the door on him and went back into the bar. More peons were coming in from the front now and milling around Ugardes, who stood at the bar with a big drink. He hailed Ferrar with a grin.

"Are they all safe?" Ferrar asked in a low voice.

"A bunch of *vaqueros* are still chasing the trappers." Ugardes laughed. "But those mountain men have long legs. What a fight, Antonio! We haven't had so much fun since the bull got loose in the palace. I owe you a drink. Garrett would have cut me in two with that sword." He poured Ferrar a drink, and then jumped up onto the bar with his own, raising the glass high.

"A toast, *compadres*, a toast to Antonio, the *gringo* killer. He saved my life. He defended the honor of Santa Fe. Truly he is a *hidalgo* and one of us."

A knot of the men who knew Ferrar gathered around, slapping him on the back and making obscene jokes at the expense of the *gringos*. Their hands were callused and the reek of them was strong and it was the kind of a thing that struck deeply at the roots of a man. Ferrar took a drink, smiling around at their sweating, grinning faces. It was as if the old life had returned, with all the strange tensions and conflicts swept away.

— II —

San Francisco Street was full of black shadows and thick silences when Ferrar and Ugardes and Uncle Hondo left La Fonda near midnight. They crossed the plaza with a hot little wind rustling tawny dust against them, passed the deserted market place, lonely and ghostly now in the moonlight. Ahead of them lay the Palace of the Governors, the center of Mexican rule for all New Mexico. It was a long building of adobe with towers at either end. The arcade running the length of its front was supported by a row of peeled *puntales*.

"What do you keep looking around for?" Ferrar asked Uncle Hondo.

"Is somebody following us." muttered the old Mexican.

"You're an old *burro*." Captain Ugardes chuckled.

"Even a hair casts a shadow," moaned Uncle Hondo. "We had better be careful going home, Antonito. That Cimarrón Garrett does not give up so soon. . . ."

He broke off with a sharp intake of breath as a figure suddenly stepped from the black shadows beneath the palace arcade. Ferrar wheeled sharply. But he saw that it was Tomás. His immaculately white doeskins turned him to a pale wraith in the darkness. He stopped before them, staring with enigmatic eyes at Ferrar.

"*Señorita* Garcia," he murmured. Ugardes looked with envy at Ferrar. "She wishes to see you, Ferrar. I wish I were so honored."

Ferrar grinned, gripping his hand. "See you tomorrow, Seguro. Uncle Hondo, it'll be safe for you to go home. It isn't you Garrett wants."

Ferrar left them before the palace and followed the Navajo down past Burro Alley, where a single *burro* still stood, loaded down with faggots, his master rolled up in a blanket against the wall, fast asleep. The massive oak door of Morina Garcia's gambling *sala* was half a block beyond the alley. It opened into a hall that led to the large gambling rooms at the rear. Ferrar could hear the *click* of the roulette wheels and the metallic voices of *chusa* dealers. Before reaching the gambling rooms, however, Tomás turned through a door halfway down the hall that opened into the woman's private chambers.

Morina Garcia's parlor was probably the most sumptuous room in Santa Fe. The floor was of red Spanish tile; a polychrome frieze ran around the wall. Hangings of velvet and silk draped corners of pier glass mirrors that reflected the pendants of the cut-glass chandelier in a hundred glittering shards. Diagonally across one corner was a Turkish divan upholstered in jade silk. Upon this sat Morina Garcia.

Light from the candles in their silver sconces caught up a soft blue-black glow in her hair. Bare shoulders gleamed like alabaster against the contrast of a taffeta dress red as blood. A single cabochon emerald rode the deep upper swell of her breast. Until this woman had come to Santa Fe, two years before, Ferrar had thought Julia

Manatte was the woman he wanted, had been on the point of asking her to marry him. Then Morina Garcia had come north from Mexico City, filling the whole province with the legends of her fabulous rise from a ragged peon to one of the most famous gamblers of the period. Within a few short days after the establishment of her gambling salon in Santa Fe, every man in town was vying for her affections. A general had fought a duel with a judge, and had gotten but a rose from her hair for his trouble. Captain Ugardes had sworn he would die for her, and all she had asked of him was an introduction to Tony Ferrar.

"Antonito."

Just the single, husky word from her. But it sent an excitement through him he had never felt with Julia. Her magnetism seemed to permeate the room.

"*Chica*," he murmured.

Her eyes became veiled. "You are the only man in Santa Fe who has the right to use that name. Perhaps I should take away the privilege. You have not been to see me for so long."

"Business," he said.

"Like smuggling your furs into the hills pelt by pelt so you can make up a fur train that will run through Armijo's blockade to Saint Louis?" she asked.

His eyes widened in surprise. "Do you know everything in this town?"

"Everything." Her ripe lips spread in an indulgent smile, and she rose from the divan. "If I help you get those furs through, will you help me in something?"

He could not help chuckling. "It's a long time since we made a deal."

"Your greatest threat is Armijo's fur patrol, no?"

"If they catch me, I don't have enough men to fight them."

She moved toward him, voice growing husky. "What route were you planning to take?"

"Glorieta Pass, Apache Cañon."

"Don't do it. That is where the patrol will be tonight."

He caught her by the arms, and the satiny feel of them went through him like fire. "*Chica*, you're wonderful. What do you want from Saint Louis?"

"Not from Saint Louis," she said, looking down at her fine strong hands. "I have helped you, Antonito. Now you will help me. Have you heard of the Cordenza note?"

The humor left him in a rush; his hands slid off her arms. Face tight with wariness, he played it close to the vest. "No. What is it?"

"As you know, Captain Cordenza was bringing four companies of cavalry from Chihuahua to help Governor Armijo here. The Americans now claim Cordenza has been captured, and they have his note of surrender as proof. But it is not his note. It is a forgery."

"How can you be sure?"

"My agents inform me that Cordenza was not captured. He is but a day's march from Santa Fe. Have I ever been mistaken before, Antonito?"

"If anybody has the truth, you have."

"I am glad you have so much faith in me," she said. "Governor Armijo is not so easy to convince. You know him under pressure. He is ready to run at the drop of a pin. If that forged note reaches him, he will be convinced Cordenza is captured. He will think he can't stand against Kearny with the dragoons he has here. We are afraid he will capitulate and give Santa Fe to the Americans."

"I thought Armijo knew Cordenza's handwriting."

"The Americans must have taken that into consideration," she said. "Maybe they actually got some of Cordenza's handwriting and copied it. I don't know the details of their plot. All I know is it will lose the war for us if the note reaches Armijo. All the talking we can do in the world won't convince him once he gets it into his head that Cordenza has been captured." She looked up. "I know Manatte sent word to Kearny that he was trying to get you to take the note through to Armijo for them."

"Your spies have been working overtime," he said wryly.

Her chin lifted. "I also know that you refused Manatte. I am proud of you, Antonito. Now you will get the note for us. We will see that it does not fall into Armijo's hands."

Ferrar moved restlessly to a heavily shuttered window. "There must be somebody else who could do as much."

"Nobody!" There was a sensuous *hiss* of taffeta across a full hip as she moved. "You are the one Kearny is expecting. He will not trust another without proper credentials from Manatte, which we can't get. You can't ride the surface any longer, Antonito. It's fine to gamble and drink and sing and be everybody's friend in normal times. But there's a war going on. You are on one side or the other. Think of your people."

"My people?"

She came toward him. "You are more Mexican than Yankee. Perhaps your father was Yankee, but it is where you live that counts, who are your friends. Men like Uncle Hondo and Ugardes would die for you. Will you let them down now? If Kearny takes over, we will be nothing but dogs in the dust. You know the Yankee attitude toward us. Greasers . . ." Her lips writhed on the word. "You know what will happen the minute Santa Fe is in American hands."

He frowned with the picture of Cimarrón Garrett before him. Somehow it symbolized what had been brought to his attention so often these last years, the contempt so many Americans seemed to hold for the Mexicans here. And yet something else was trying to resolve itself in his mind.

"It's funny," he said. "I was given the same kind of talk earlier this evening. Only the Mexican rule was represented as despotic then."

"Despotic?" She laughed softly. "Your mother must have told you what went on under the Spanish regime here, before the Mexicans revolted. Haven't we advanced a thousand years from that? You've been listening to the wrong people, Antonito. You know where your heart is. Say you'll do it. Say you'll start tonight, and meet me at the old Pecos pueblo tomorrow night after dark with that note."

He shook his head, realizing how right both Morina and Manatte had been. He had ridden the surface too long. And now, when he wanted to look beneath and see the hidden issues at stake, he couldn't. His indecision must have shown in his face. The woman came closer. Her voice dropped to a husky whisper.

"If you will not do it for your people, Antonito, will you do it for me?"

He felt the blood thickening in his throat. "You . . . *Chica*?"

"You told me once you'd do anything for me."

"But this . . ."

"Yes . . . this."

The kiss started as something rich and ripe; suddenly it was savage. Her lips flared beneath his, the curves of her body flattened to him; he

139

was swept by the passion of it. Finally she pulled her head back, staring, heavy-lidded, into his eyes.

"If you start tonight, you can reach Kearny at Las Vegas by dawn."

He shook his head, trying to pull away. "I don't know. I can't think with you this close."

"Do you have to think?"

"Yes."

She tried to kiss him again. He pulled free. The pupils of her eyes distended.

"*Tu borracho*," she hissed. "I was right. You are nothing but a drunken fool meant to spend his nights in some *cantina*, swilling and gambling. ¡*Chica*! You shall never use that name again. How could I have ever thought you worthy of my confidence?"

All the primitive, savage force of her Indian blood darkened her face and blazed in her eyes. He could not help the sardonic smile that crossed his face.

"You should have done this in the first place," he said. "I always thought you much more fascinating in your barbaric state."

"¡*Bribón*!" she panted.

With a husky curse, she wheeled for a tankard of brandy that sat on one of the marquetry tables. He had already reached the door and swung it open by the time she wheeled and threw the tankard. The silver pitcher made a clanging crash against the door as he pulled it shut behind him.

— III —

Tony's father had been an Irish trapper for Hudson's Bay who had drifted down to Taos and Santa Fe in the early part of the century, establishing a fur business there. Prospering, he had married the daughter of one of the most aristocratic houses in the province. With her had come the dowry of a sprawling *hacienda* on the hills overlooking Santa Fe. The walls were adobe, thick and high, built in the days when Indian attacks necessitated that the home be a fortress. On the death of his parents, Tony had taken over the fur business, using much of the house on the hill as a storage place for the pelts his trappers brought in every spring.

He knocked three times on the immense door of the *zaguán*, and it was opened for him by Uncle Hondo. He rode through this wagon entrance into the patio.

"Troops have been up in the hills half a dozen times today, watching the house," Uncle Hondo said. "They know you make a run for it soon now, Antonito."

"Do you think they suspect when?"

"No. The last load of pelts went out in a *carreta*, covered by a load of onions. We unloaded it at the old woodcutter's house. If troops were watching, they will think we were merely giving him his winter's supply of onions, as we always do."

Ferrar nodded in satisfaction. They had been sneaking furs out like that for days now, under loads of vegetables, beneath the cover of faggots on a woodcutter's *burro*, even under the shirts and *tilmas* of laborers and peasants whose comings and goings around the Ferrar house were so usual they would not arouse suspicion. Each load had been picked up in a safe spot along the road or in the hills and transferred to the train of mules Ferrar's men held back in the mountains.

"And now we are ready, old one," Ferrar said. "Get your horse and we will ride."

North of Santa Fe the cedars filled the hills with their stunted ghosts, and the yucca stood like lonely candles in the pale moonlight. They picked up the Pecuris Trail and followed it for an hour, and then turned off for the meeting place in the mountains. Deep in timber, at a deserted and crumbling hacienda, they found the mules. Twenty-five of them, their straw-matted *aparejos* bulging with the swart beaver pelts that had piled up in Tony Ferrar's warehouse since Governor Armijo had closed the Santa Fe Trail to any trade with the United States.

Little Joe was standing by the lead mule, a short, squat, bowlegged man in white cotton shirt and buckskin leggings. He looked like a Gypsy with the brass ring in his ear and the spotted bandanna drawn over his greasy black hair. But he claimed pure Castilian descent, and would cheerfully knife anybody who doubted it.

"Were you followed?" he asked.

"We circled back three times to make sure we weren't," Ferrar said. "I think we can start safely. Morina gave me a tip that the fur patrol would be in Apache Cañon tonight. The only thing we'll have to worry about is the customs troops at Taos."

"I don't know," Uncle Hondo said darkly. "In Santa Cruz it is said that the toll of the bell is not for the dead, but to remind us we, too, may die tomorrow."

"And the time I will really start worrying is when you quit grumbling, you old *bribón*." Little Joe leered.

"*Vámonos*, you lazy *burros*. Let's go!" He swung onto his ratty little pony and the four other drivers stepped into their saddles, prodding the mules with their pointed poles. There was a great groaning and grumbling and twitching of ears, and the train was under way.

They found the Pecuris Trail again, and turned north. It led through dry washes where *chamiza* turned the sand to gold and primrose lay like patches of blood so red it was almost black in the feeble moonlight. They passed Cuyamangue while it was still dark, a huddle of adobe huts surrounded by fields of alfalfa sighing like a lonely woman in the wind. And beyond that was Pojoaque, with the Indians sleeping in their mud hovels and a dog howling at the cavalcade passing above the town through the hills. And all the time they were rising toward the mountains around Taos. The hour before dawn was the blackest, with the stars blinking out. Then light began to come, milky at first, finally flushed by a rising sun. They were south of the Pecuris pueblo now, climbing a shelving trail that looked across a vast expanse of timbered ridges and sheltered valleys. It was a country Ferrar loved, but somehow the familiar exhilaration, the sense of freedom did not come. His mind was still on the Cordenza letter.

He had tried to tell himself that he had done right, that he would be gone a month, and it would all be resolved before his return. But that did not satisfy him. Yet, even if he returned now, what could he do? Was Morina right, was his allegiance to the people of Santa Fe? Or was his white heritage too strong? It seemed that he could not turn either way without betraying someone with whom he had ties. It would do no good to go back, with the decision unresolved.

"What are you always looking behind for, old one?" Little Joe asked.

"Didn't something move up there on the hill?" Uncle Hondo said.

"Yes, and we were followed all the way from

Santa Fe. By our shadows. You live in dreams, you old *bribón*."

With the full light of the sun came the cry of a great blue fool hen perched beside the trail in one of the spruces. Ferrar's buckskin shied at the sound and he fought it with numbed hands. The shadows swallowed the cañons and gorges beneath him with hungry mouths.

They reached the top of the cut and began descending. The trail shelved down through a deep cañon, with the silvery flash of a river far below. Ferrar's attention was still turned down when the sound came. It was like a great clap of thunder. The buckskin reared, bugling shrilly. The mules brayed behind Ferrar and began to bolt, banking up behind the buckskin in wild ranks. One of them was shoved off the edge and crashed down the cliff side like a broken rag doll.

"Let the mules go, Antonito!" shouted Little Joe. "They'll all go off the side."

Another shot crashed, its echoes rolling across the gorge. Ferrar put the spurs to his buckskin. The frenzied beast squealed and plunged forward down the rocky trail, with the *burros* streaming out behind.

All Ferrar could do was let his frantic horse have its head on the narrow shelf. He risked one glance up but could see nothing on the timbered slope above. The trail was getting steeper, dropping swiftly toward the level of the cañon floor. His horse stumbled and almost went down. He knew it was only a matter of time before it spilled, or was shot from beneath him. He heard another mule slide off the treacherous shoulder behind him and plummet down the steep escarpment with a lost bray.

He saw a point ahead where the cliff became a talus slope and knew it was his only chance. If he were thrown beyond it, where the wall became sheer again, he would be broken to bits before reaching bottom. Another volley of shots put his buckskin into a new frenzy. He tried to pull it down before the slope. It fought the bit, stumbled. He realized it was going down and kicked free, diving right over the horse's head. Its impetus threw him far enough to strike a shoulder of the slope. He sprawled flat, stunned, and slipped and flopped through the shale. It seemed as if he slid a thousand feet before he rolled off onto a sandy beach.

He lay there a moment, dazed, bleeding. His shirt had been ripped completely off his back, his body was a mass of bloody bruises and wounds from the rocks, his leggings hung in shreds. As from far off, he heard the shots begin again. Sand kicked up a foot from him.

Groaning, he rolled over and crawled into the water. It cleansed his wounds and revived him. He threw himself deeply into the current and let it carry him down till he reached a rocky shallow where he could cross into the timber on the other bank.

Crouched here, sobbing with exhaustion, he could see the mules just streaming out onto the floor of the cañon from the end of the trail. Some plunged into the river, and their pack saddles immediately overturned them and they were swept downstream until the packs were torn off by the rocks and they could start swimming for the opposite side. Others charged on down the other side of the cañon, braying wildly. Little Joe plunged off the trail and into the river. A shot chipped rock off in the face of his horse and the man had a wild time forcing him into the current.

Ferrar came to his feet and ran toward the point Little Joe would reach. The horse lunged onto the bank, dripping wet. Little Joe saw Ferrar in the timber and reined the squealing animal toward him. He dropped off, holding the reins, and they both hunkered down behind a screen of brush, looking out at the carnage. Then they realized how silent it had become.

"The shots, they have stopped," Little Joe said.

"Sure they have," Ferrar said bleakly. "They've done their job. Half the pelts have been ripped to pieces on the rocks and the other half will be swept all the way down to Santa Fe in this river."

"Is right," Little Joe said mournfully. "A dozen of them mules must have gone over the side. Saint Looey will get no fur this year."

Ferrar shook his head. "What are we thinking of? The hell with the furs. What about the men?"

"I saw Ramirez go over the side with the mules. The others were ahead of me. They were chasing what few mules got into timber, the last I saw."

The *clatter* of hoofs on the rocky trail brought both their heads up. Uncle Hondo had been at the rear of the column. His frightened horse had settled down to a spooky, skittish trot. The old man was bent over the big saddle horn, hanging on grimly, his wizened body jerked from side to side. Ferrar's face went white. Both he and Little Joe left the trees at a run, plunging into the creek, fighting its turbulent spring current across to the other side. Ferrar came out a hundred yards farther down than where he had gone in, crouched on the white sand, sobbing for air. The old man's horse *clattered* from the trail onto the beach. Gasping, Ferrar rose to his feet and stumbled to catch it before the animal went by. He blocked it up against the cañon wall, got its bit. Little Joe was there to help him lift Uncle Hondo off. They lowered the old man to the ground. His eyes fluttered open; he tried to grin.

"They are right about the bell in Santa Cruz, no?"

Ferrar clutched his shoulders. "Uncle Hondo, who did it, who was it?"

"I get a look at one of them . . ." The old man broke off, to cough feebly. Blood bubbled from his mouth. He settled back, fighting for breath. Finally the words left him, on a dying whisper: "A man with long yellow hair, and a beard, all yellow . . . all yellow . . ."

Ferrar stared down at him with bleak eyes. His voice, when he finally spoke, was barely audible. "Cimarrón Garrett."

— IV —

They got back to Rancho Ferrar near dusk, with Uncle Hondo's body wrapped in his poncho and hung across his horse. Little Joe went to the cathedral in town and came back with the priest and after a simple service they buried Uncle Hondo by torchlight in the cemetery where Sean Ferrar and his wife lay, and a dozen of the retainers and faithful peons who had died in their service.

Before the services were over, Ferrar saw a wagon coming up the road from town, and, when he led the procession back to the house, it was waiting before the front door. Julia Manatte had just gotten down from the front seat, with one of George Manatte's teamsters still up in the wagon, holding the reins.

"I heard Little Joe was in town for the priest," she said. "What happened, Tony? The caretaker at the church said something about Uncle Hondo."

Bitterness and deep fatigue turned his face gaunt, forming shadowy hollows beneath the cheek bones, lending his eyes a sunken, feverish look. He stared down at her without answering, unable to believe she did not know. Her face was thrown into deep shadow by the hood of a cloak that covered her to the knees, but he could see her eyes, guileless and deeply worried.

"I guess your father doesn't tell you the dirtier side of his business," he said. His voice was ugly. "That was Uncle Hondo we buried up on the hill. My fur train was attacked. They couldn't be satisfied with merely making sure the furs were ruined or lost. They had to kill a harmless old man."

"Who had to? Tony, please, who had to . . . ?"

"Cimarrón Garrett."

Her lips parted; the blood left her face till it had a parchment hue. There was a restless murmur from the people around them. A torch spat softly. Then she began shaking her head.

"Tony, you can't believe that, you can't! Dad had nothing to do with it. If Cimarrón did it, Dad didn't know about it."

"What did your father want to do? Make me think Morina attacked me, make me turn on her? Then maybe send you up to convince me when I came back, is that it? So I'd take the letter through for you? Only Cimarrón made the mistake of getting seen. Maybe that's why he killed Uncle Hondo. He knew Uncle Hondo had seen him."

"No, no, Tony. . . ." She was almost crying. "Dad wouldn't do anything like that, he wouldn't." She came up against him, seeming to forget the rest of the people, her thrown-back head tossing off the hood to let the torchlight shine like wet gold in her hair.

"Did I ever lie to you, Tony? Even after that Garcia woman came between us, did I lie to you? Maybe you're right, maybe it was Cimarrón Garrett. But he doesn't represent all the Americans here, any more than Morina Garcia represents the Mexicans. . . ."

"Cimarrón works for your father, doesn't he?"

"Yes, but . . ."

"Just how bad does your father want the Americans in Santa Fe?" he asked her.

She pulled away, staring blankly up at him.

"That's what I thought, you're afraid to answer it," he said. "And just how far would he go to bring them in?" He paused, and her lips parted slowly, as if she would speak, but she did not. He said bitterly: "Your father wanted me to get the Cordenza letter of surrender. You tell him I've gone to get it."

She pulled away from him, forcing the words out. "Who . . . who will you bring it to?"

"Who do you think?"

She grabbed his arm as he tried to wheel away. "You can't do it, you can't betray your own people."

"I guess I didn't really know who my people were, up till now," he said. "You decided for me, by killing one of them."

He tore loose and went inside with long, savage paces. She tried to follow, but the servants blocked her off, coming after him. He told one of them to saddle up his best horse. The powder in his Dragoon cap-and-ball was wet from his swim in the river, and he reloaded the cylinder, primers and all, before buckling the five-shot on again. Then he hooked the powder horn onto the other side of his belt and put the buckskin bullet pouch in a coat pocket and went out into the patio, where the horse was saddled.

Little Joe wanted to go with him, but he knew he could travel with more secrecy alone. Julia's wagon was gone when he rode through the gate in the *zaguán*, and turned down toward the Santa Fe Trail.

Through his bleak fury, his grief at Uncle Hondo's death, one thought drove him. George Manatte had always been highly representative, to Ferrar, of the Americans in Santa Fe. And now what had happened became just as representative of how it would be if the Americans took over. If they were capable of killing one innocent man to gain their ends, they were capable of killing a thousand.

In this bitter mood he reached Glorieta Pass, with the cedars standing like stunted ghosts on the slopes. He passed through Apache Cañon and went by the cut-off to Pecos, the deserted pueblo at which Morina had promised to meet him if he got the letter for her. He knew she would hear of what had happened, would know he was going after the note, and would be waiting at the pueblo for him on his return.

He pushed his horse to the small farm of a peon he knew and had something to eat and got another horse. He reached the cañon in the mesa south of Las Vegas about noon of the next day, where a Yankee patrol picked him up and took him to Las Vegas, a hundred squalid adobes huddled along the west bank of the Gallinas. Kearny and half a dozen officers were gathered in one of the larger buildings in a feeble attempt to escape the heat.

Ferrar had dealt with Kearny several times before in his business along the trail, and Manatte had already sent word that he was trying to get Ferrar to carry the note, so Kearny accepted him without much question. Cordenza's letter of surrender was a short missive, written in poor Spanish, stipulating two terms beside those offered by the Americans. All the American officers seemed sure that Armijo would either capitulate or surrender once he saw the note and realized his main hope of support was cut off.

They fed Ferrar and replaced his beaten-down animal with an Army horse and a patrol escorted him out as far as the mesa. In the late afternoon he passed Starvation Peak, with its *penitente* cross stamped forebodingly against the sky, and San José, where the dogs set up a howl at the drumming of his horse's hoofs. He was stupefied with fatigue, now, and rocking heavily in the saddle. He lost count of the times he fell asleep and jerked up barely in time to keep from pitching from the horse.

It was already evening when he sighted the turn-off to Pecos ahead. It was here the first shot smashed out. The bullet struck the road directly in front of him, and the excited horse veered and pirouetted and reared high, pitching him off its rump.

He hit heavily on the bank of an arroyo and rolled to its bottom and lay there, stunned. Dimly he could hear the tattoo of the horse's hoofs, racing away into the night. He rolled over, shaking his head, and pulled out his Dragoon.

He could not be sure, but he thought the shot had come from the other side of the road. The arroyo he was in pinched off right against the cut-off into Pecos. He lay there a moment, thinking back. He had told Julia where he was going, and he knew who this was. For a moment he had the savage impulse to stop and fight and get Cimarrón Garrett for Uncle Hondo. But the Cordenza letter was more important. He had to get it to Morina first.

He crawled to the end of the arroyo, and then

snaked up into the cover of scrub timber. It was what they had been waiting for. From across the road came the *boom* of a shot. Lead *crackled* through piñons a few feet from him. He fired four times at the gun flash, and then turned and ran as hard as he could into timber.

His volley had made them seek cover, for the return shot did not come till he was deep in the trees. He reloaded his gun as he ran, measuring powder roughly into each chamber, spilling a little each time, seating the gray lead balls with the ramrod. With the cylinder reloaded, he fumbled for caps in his pocket, thumbing them home on the nipples at the rear of each chamber. He was in broken country by the time he finished, looking down into Pecos.

An early moon had risen, its light making a hazy mystery of the ancient Indian town. Pestilence and war had wiped out its people long ago, and it stood, ancient and deserted. He sought vainly in its courtyards for sight of Morina's coach.

He knew he would be foolish to remain in the open, if he had to wait for her, and dropped down a crumbling shale bank to the buildings, stepping into the first door that had not fallen in. The darkness was musty with the odor of ancient things. Broken pottery crumbled beneath his feet.

Then the waiting began. The ghosts of this lost city whispered through its countless chambers. He remembered stories of a sacred fire that never died and of human sacrifices that still went on in hidden *kivas*. Then he realized it was not his imagination causing the whispers in the crumbling buildings. While he had been watching the approach, his ambushers could have moved around and come in from behind. He heard the distinct *crunch* of pottery underfoot, from far within the city. He turned to stare achingly into the blackness. No telling how many passages led into this chamber.

Then a new rattling broke into his tension. The coach came up on the crest and *clattered* down the age-old trail. There were half a dozen outriders in blue jackets and red helmets, their lance tips silvery flickers of light. Captain Seguro Ugardes led them, a proud figure in his high-cantled saddle.

The coach pulled up with a flourish, its matched team stamping, and Tomás jumped from beside the driver to open the door. The troop of lancers formed ranks of their prancing horses, and faced the coach at attention as Morina Garcia stepped out.

"Seguro!" Ferrar called. "¡*Chico*! Get out of the open! Manatte's got his men here!"

His voice echoed into the crumbling chambers and died. Out in the courtyard, Morina turned toward the sound of his voice. She had on a hooded cloak that dropped her face into black shadow; diamonds glittered on her fingers. Finally she laughed huskily.

"Antonito, how would Manatte know we were here?"

"Move her out of here, Ugardes!" Ferrar called desperately. "They hit me on the road, I tell you!"

He saw the sharp toss of her head, the motion of anger he knew so well. There was a pause, then she laughed again. "It is all right, Antonito. We are safe. There has been a mistake. You can come out."

"A mistake?"

"I assure you, you are safe. Come out."

Slowly he moved into the open, gun held tightly, peering at the doorways of the buildings that circled the great courtyard. But no shots came. Finally he reached Morina, gazing at her wonderingly. At that instant, there was a faint movement from the first-story roof of a building that formed the balcony of the second story.

"¡*Señor*!" Morina called sharply, as if to halt something.

But the man had already come into view, sliding over the edge of the balcony, to hang and drop to the earth below. It was Cimarrón Garrett, carrying a long Yerger rifle with the moon making a golden mane of his yellow hair. Then there was a faint *crunch* of pottery behind Ferrar, and he wheeled to see Pitch emerge from the doorway next to the one he had stood in.

"You are both fools!" Morina said disgustedly.

"How the hell did we know he was coming

here?" Cimarrón said. "He was seen talking to Julia Manatte last. You told us he'd already refused to get the letter for you."

The whole thing struck Ferrar with a sick shock, as he wheeled back to Morina. "I thought Cimarrón and Pitch were Manatte's boys."

"Everybody else in Santa Fe thinks they are, too," she said. "It suits me to have it so."

"Then *you* killed Uncle Hondo." It left Ferrar in a thin whisper.

The toss of her head slid the hood off, and moonlight made a blue-black flash in her dark hair. She stepped forward, reaching for his hand.

"Antonito, they didn't mean to. It was an accident. I had to do that, don't you see? I couldn't let you leave with your furs. You were the only one who could get the letter through. But Uncle Hondo was an accident. Cimarrón told me. He was shooting at the mules. . . ."

"The hell he was!" Ferrar pulled away from her, face white. "You knew I thought Cimarrón was Manatte's man. You knew I'd get that letter for you if I was convinced Manatte killed Uncle Hondo."

"Antonito . . ."

"No!" He pulled away again, staring at her. His breathing made a thin sound in the moment of silence. "I brought the letter to you because I realized the people who had killed Uncle Hondo would be capable of doing the same thing again

158

to attain their ends. Capable of doing it on any scale, one man or a thousand. But I brought it to the wrong one, didn't I? How many more people do you think you'll kill?" He wheeled to Ugardes. "Seguro, you aren't going to let her get away with it! Can't you see how she operates now?"

There was a hurt confusion in Ugardes's face as he looked at Morina. She turned swiftly to him, putting more intensity into her voice than Ferrar had ever heard before.

"Seguro, you can see what I had to do. It was only to save our people. Uncle Hondo was an accident, I swear it. But if it had to be, isn't it better to have one suffer that many may be saved?"

Ugardes turned to Ferrar, shaking his head. "She's right, Tony. It was tragic that it had to be Uncle Hondo. But now we must finish it."

Morina faced Ferrar, holding out her hand. "Let us have it now. Don't try to destroy it in this last moment. You wouldn't have a chance."

Ferrar realized how right she was. Cimarrón held that Yerger on him now and Pitch had a big Cherington pistol pointed at his back. Sick with his own helplessness, he took the letter from his pocket, handed it to her. She opened it, read it, smiled triumphantly.

"Hadn't we better destroy it at once?" Ugardes said.

"I want to know whether it is a forgery," she

159

said. "There is a man in Santa Fe who knows Cordenza's handwriting. We will have to leave Ferrar here. You can understand how dangerous it would be to let him go. When it is over, he will go free. Does that suit you, Segurito?"

Ferrar saw the captain's young eyes widen. "Segurito?"

"Yes," she murmured. "Why not? And there will still be but one man in Santa Fe who calls me *Chica*. That will be you, Segurito."

Ferrar saw a wild flame of adoration light Ugardes's eyes. He wondered if his own eyes had looked that way when Morina told him the same thing, so long ago. The woman had turned to Cimarrón, her brows raised in a faint inquisition.

"We'll hold him here till we hear from you," the yellow-haired man said. "We'll do that."

She wheeled and stepped into the coach. The Navajo climbed back onto the seat beside the driver. Ugardes stepped into his saddle, turned to look down at Ferrar. That shine had left his eyes. They were beginning to look puzzled again.

"I'm sorry, *amigo*. I hope we meet again when it is over."

He raised his arm, dropped it; the troop wheeled and broke into a gallop after the coach, as it *clattered* up the rise. Then Cimarrón told Pitch to get Ferrar's gun. The man stepped in behind Ferrar, pulled the cap-and-ball from Ferrar's hand.

"Now we'll wait a while, so they won't hear the

shots," Cimarrón said. "Captain Ugardes didn't look too convinced."

Ferrar's sick defeat deepened as he realized what they meant. He knew it was only a few seconds now. But he couldn't just let them shoot him. Not just bow his head and submit. He felt the sweat start out on his forehead, felt all the muscles of his body contract. A surprised look crossed Cimarrón's face. He jerked his rifle up, till it covered Ferrar's chest.

The shot made a great smashing sound. But it did not come from Cimarrón's gun. His mouth dropped open; he staggered backward with shock making a grotesque mask of his face, and a red hole staining his chest.

At the same time, Pitch swung away from Ferrar, firing his Cherington at the rise of land. He realized his mistake an instant after his shot, and tried to wheel back and jerk Ferrar's Dragoon up in his other hand. But Ferrar had already spun around and was lunging into him. He knocked the gun back down as it went off, crashing into Pitch so hard the man fell.

Ferrar went down with him, catching the Dragoon and twisting it from his hand as they fell. He struck the ground on his knees, astraddle Pitch, and raised up, with the heavy cap-and-ball in his hand, and smashed it into the man's face. Pitch made a broken sound and went utterly slack.

Panting, Ferrar got up. Cimarrón lay on his

back, dead eyes staring emptily at the sky. There was nothing in sight on the rise of land. Ferrar ran heavily up the trail, gun ready. Finally he came into sight of Captain Ugardes, lying on the ground just beyond the crest.

"That Pitch, he's a better shot than I thought." Ugardes chuckled. Then he choked, and blood bubbled from his mouth.

Ferrar dropped to his knees beside the man, trying to ease him. "Why did you come back, Seguro?"

"I got to thinking," the man muttered feebly. "It came to me how quickly Morina had changed from you to me. I had wanted it so long that I couldn't think straight when it happened. But riding back, it came through. She wouldn't have switched so easily if she really cared for you. And if she didn't care, she had only been using you. And if she could use you, she could use me. I had to make sure, Tony, I had to come back."

"Seguro . . ."

The man's eyes were getting glassy, his voice fading. "You were right, Tony. What happened to Uncle Hondo had been going on a long time, in many different ways. We didn't see it. We only saw the peons at the *cantinas*, drinking, gambling . . . we thought that represented their life as much as ours. But they were suffering under the rule. And it was her rule. Not Armijo's. She was pulling all the strings. Just like the

Cordenza letter. She knew it was real all along. But she wanted Armijo to fight Kearny, so what she had here wouldn't be overthrown by the Americans. She doesn't represent our people . . . any more than Cimarrón and Pitch represent the Yankees. Stop her, Tony. Get the letter . . . to Armijo. . . . Too much needless bloodshed . . . already. . . ."

He sagged back. Ferrar called his name. The young captain's eyes were closed. He did not answer.

Ferrar got up, a pale look to his face, a lost feeling inside him. Then he turned and stumbled through the greasewood to where Ugardes had left his horse. He mounted the nervous beast, turning it down the trail. But Ugardes had left his troop where the cut-off ran into the Santa Fe Trail, and they must have heard the gunshots, for the earth began to tremble with their galloping.

Ferrar pulled his horse off into the piñons and watched them sweep by in the darkness, lances down. He thought bitterly that it was a fitting tribute to Ugardes. Then he turned the horse and rode.

It was a wild ride, over barrancas, into arroyos, seeking short cuts across the loops and switch-backs of the trail. He had cut off the last wide turn in by the road by crossing the ridge between it and was forcing the lathered horse down through scrub oak when the coach rolled around the point, coming hard. It passed him before he reached the road, and he burst out a few feet behind it, blocked off from the view of Tomás and the driver.

He spurred the stumbling horse into its last run. It gained the rear of the coach, began to veer and weave, unable to keep the pace. Knowing it was his last chance, he rose to a crouch in the saddle and leaped for the coach. His left foot came down on the boot, his right foot caught in the rear window. His hands caught the luggage rail on top.

Tomás must have felt the coach tilt. He turned sharply on the front seat, then rose and climbed back across the top, pulling his knife. Ferrar fought desperately to get on top and meet the man. He had to use both hands, and had no time to draw his gun. He managed to sprawl out on top, belly down, when Tomás reached him. The Navajo lunged up and drove down with the knife.

All Ferrar could do was flop over. The knife drove hilt-deep into the wood of the top. Before Tomás could pull back, Ferrar caught the man around the neck, pulling him down and doubling up at the same time to smash a knee in his downcoming face. It stunned Tomás, knocking him over Ferrar's body. Wildly he tried to catch the rail, but his impetus carried him over it, and he rolled off the racing coach with a scream.

Ferrar pulled the knife from the top and crawled up behind the driver, who was still fighting to stop the horses. He put the point of the blade against the man's back, disarmed him, waited until the coach was halted, and then ordered him to jump down and walk away from the coach.

As the man reached the ground, Morina shoved open the door and started to step out, calling angrily to the driver: "Juan, what's going on, why did Tomás fall off . . . ?"

She stopped, mouth open in surprise, as Ferrar dropped off to confront her. Then she ripped the Cordenza note from the bosom of her dress. He reached her before she could tear it, putting the point of the knife against her throat.

"Don't destroy it, *Chica*. . . ." He made the word thin and ugly.

Her eyes widened. "You wouldn't."

He pressed the knife harder against her neck. "I'm thinking of Uncle Hondo, *Chica*."

Her eyes narrowed; her cheeks grew pale. Slowly the defeat came into her face, making it indefinably gaunt and old. He took the letter from her slack fingers. Then he turned and climbed back into the seat, picking up the reins.

He took one last look at Morina. It was like stirring the ashes of a burned-out fire. The passion he had felt for her, the intense attraction, seemed to have belonged to another life, another man. It had been real enough, in its way. But again he had only been looking at the surface. Now he knew what lay underneath. He lifted the reins and started the horses down the road.

Manatte, Julia, and a dozen Yankee trappers met Ferrar a mile down the road, halting the coach. "What happened?" Manatte asked him. "We heard the Garcia woman had left town and figured it was to get the letter. Julia wouldn't stay behind. She still couldn't believe you'd take it to Morina."

Ferrar handed down the letter. "She was almost wrong. I'll tell you sometime. Just get this note to Armijo. It will straighten out a lot of things."

Julia was dressed in a man's coat and blue jeans, a flat-topped hat tilted over one eye. Smiling, she climbed off her horse onto the coach seat.

"Take my horse back with you," she told her father. Then she turned to Ferrar, face radiant. "You must have finally found out who your people really are."

"I belong to both," he said. "Your people are my people, and so are the Mexicans. And soon they can all be one people, if men like Cimarrón or women like Morina don't get the power in their hands and twist it all into lies for their own sake."

She put a hand on his arm. "I have the feeling you've come back to me, Tony."

He smiled down at her. "Yes," he said. "I've come back to you."

Blood Star over Santa Fe

Les Savage, Jr., became a client of the August Lenniger Literary Agency in the summer of 1943. Prior to that, the author represented himself and sent in stories to magazines on his own. This story was the second one he wrote, appearing in *Frontier Stories* in the Summer, 1943 issue.

— I —

Paul Trent allowed the brass-studded door to close softly behind him and stood there for a long moment, one hard hand hitched into his sagging gun belt, the other holding a dusty sombrero against his buckskinned leg. His first awareness was of a tension; the whole noise and movement of the smoky gambling *sala* seemed to hold it. A *señorita* wagered her earnings against the table, laughing too shrilly. A man's nervous cursing cut the bubbling talk. Paul Trent realized that the boiling undercurrents in Santa Fe had penetrated this place.

He had not entered unnoticed, and he turned with the feeling of someone's gaze upon him. In a high, carved chair across the room sat *Doña* Barcello, regarding him expectantly. Standing beside her was a tall, dark man whose thickness of shoulders and upper torso gave him a top-heavy appearance. It was Fornier, the French-Canadian. He had come down from the Columbia River country long ago with the marks of logging on his scarred face and quick, grasping hands. Manuel Armijo had then been governor of New Mexico, and it hadn't taken Jan Baptist Fornier many months to become one of Armijo's right-hand men; he had a talent for the kind of politics the despotic governor played. But Armijo had recently been overthrown, and with him had toppled his understrappers, including Fornier. Paul questioned his presence here tonight, and felt the hand in his gun belt tighten with apprehension.

A *criado*, one of *Doña* Barcello's numberless Navajo slaves, padded by Trent, carrying a live coal to light the *cigarrillos* held in tiny golden tongs by the *señoritas*. Paul started to follow the slave toward *Doña* Barcello in her massive chair. He didn't see Colonel Price until the officer spoke.

"Paul Trent, b' God. Didn't know you were a gambler."

Trent stopped reluctantly, turning. "Nor I you, Colonel."

The tall, spare soldier Kearny had left at Santa Fe smiled slightly. "I'm only here to see *Doña* Barcello about closing her gambling *salas* to my officers. Bad for morale, y'know." A speculative look had entered his gaunt face and Paul knew what was coming. "But, say, Trent. For a long time now, I've been trying to place your . . ."

"I hope you'll excuse me, Colonel," said Paul deliberately, "but my business is rather urgent."

And he turned, telling himself he had been an ass to stop. The same thing always happened, sooner or later. And Price was from Fort Leavenworth—Paul felt surprise and an old choking bitterness that the officer hadn't already placed him. But the thing was swept from his mind as he broke through the shifting edge of the crowd and faced the woman who had risen from ragged peonage in Mexico to become the most famous woman gambler of her time. At thirty, *Doña* Gertrudes de Barcello still retained that vivid flashing beauty that had been her road to influence and fame and gold. The white *mantilla* was quite effective against her rich, dark skin; her wine dress drank in the light from the chandeliers softly. But looking into her eyes, Paul sensed something more than beauty. Power and riches had left their mark.

Fornier had been in Santa Fe long enough for his quick, slurring voice to lose its French flavor; his fluency with Spanish was almost native. "You seem on good terms weeth the *gringo* colonel, *Señor* Trent. Perhaps you knew him before Santa Fe, no?"

"Oh, quiet, Jan," said the woman. But she was looking at Trent with a strange smile; her glance lingered for more than a moment on his mouth, a mouth that might have once been generous, but that was now thin-lipped and a trifle drawn at the edges. Quickly she noted his patched linsey hunting shirt, his worn buckskin breeches, stuffed indifferently into battered boots. Her smile grew.

"Sometimes I want to laugh at you, Paul Trent. And sometimes I think you should have been governor instead of Armijo."

Trent shifted his feet, regarding her silently, not yet sure of his ground. Fornier's laugh held a taunting note. "You always act as if you were given only so many words to use during your lifetime, and did not wish to waste them," he said.

Paul looked at him without smiling. Fornier's sardonic face carried a scar-pattern of "loggers' smallpox" down the right side, the mark of some white-water man's heavy, calked boots. The Frenchman flushed uneasily under Paul's gaze, and the pox showed white. *Doña* Barcello said easily: "Come in here. We can talk with more privacy."

Three Navajo servants appeared suddenly, without a sound, preceding the woman to a heavy curtain on one side of the room. Fornier allowed Trent to go next, then followed, last. And Paul had an impulse to feel the reassurance of his cedar gun butt. The curtain swept behind them with a dull *clang* of its silver embroidery; they went through a short hall, then into a room. The Navajos in their white doeskin shirts and breeches had already disappeared by the time Paul entered the room. Through an open door, he could see a *placita*, the inner patio these buildings usually held. Were the three Indians out there? Yes, three of them, thought Paul, when one had usually sufficed. The thought made him move until he commanded both doors, and faced the woman and Fornier.

Doña Barcello was calmly turning up the oil lamp on a small, round pine table. "I hear you 'ave sold your horse herds to Beaubien and are leaving Santa Fe, Paul Trent."

He nodded, aware that Fornier had casually hitched his thumbs into the Navajo belt supporting his two, ivory-handled Colts.

Doña Barcello continued: "That is why I asked you to come tonight . . . to find out why you are leaving. New Mexico is more your country than ever, now that it is a United States military territory. And you were doing so well with your horses. Beaubien even insists they are a straight descent from Cortez's original sixteen. You had so many friends among the *pobres*, too. Why should you leave all this?"

He remained silent, sensing something intangibly wrong. Fornier was leaning forward with an almost predatory grin; the woman's intense look ill fitted her easy talk. She said with deceptive softness: "Are you running from the blue coats, Paul Trent?"

It didn't catch him off guard. His face remained impassive, but something recoiled within him—it was a question few here in Santa Fe would have asked. His mind flashed back to Colonel Price's query. Was it only a shot in the dark? The blue coats, the American Army of the West under General Steve Kearny—they had come in August of 1846, four months after Mexico declared war

173

on the United States. Manuel Armijo had been for ten years the governor of New Mexico, Mexico's northern province, but he fled without firing a shot. Kearny entered the ancient capital of Santa Fe on the 12th. He built Fort Marcy on the mesa above the old Spanish prison of La Garita; he left Price in command of the military, and appointed one of the Bent brothers governor to dispense civil authority from the Palace of the Governors in the city. Then Kearny pushed on with his main column to join Frémont in California and to annex another of Mexico's provinces for the United States.

Almost before the general had left the plaza, revolt was sweeping the city. There were factions who would not profit by the American rule, and these factions fed *mula blanca* and Taos lightning to the ignorant *pobres*, whipping them into insurrection. One plot was thwarted in December, but others leaped into its place. By January the American Army officers had relinquished their quarters in the Realito behind the palace and had withdrawn to the safety of Fort Marcy. Governor Bent had gone to Taos for his family. And with drunken *pobres* in every *cantina*, *gringos* walked the streets with hands on their guns.

Paul did not answer the question. He said: "Why should you care whether I go or stay, *Doña Barcello*?"

Her sidewise glance to Fornier was almost

imperceptible. "*Por supuesto*, Paul, we have been friends, you and I. And you have been with us for many years. The *pobres* have come to know you well, to be your friends, to trust you as they would no other *Americano*. They will tell you what they won't even tell me. You must know the things that are stirring, Paul, things that could make you more than a horse-breeder if you used them well."

"Perhaps you overestimate me, *Señora*," he said gravely. "Politics were never my line. And, there comes a time to leave. . . ."

Yes, there had always come that time, inevitably, sending him on when he would have given blood to stay. He didn't say that, though. And for a moment he seemed to detect a plea in the woman's lustrous eyes. It disappeared almost without having been there as she saw the thin line to his mouth. She spoke angrily with her inability to move this *Yanqui*; she had moved so many other men. "You were always a slow, stubborn man, Paul Trent. You did not have Armijo's swift grasp of things. You could not laugh as easily as Jan. But I did not think you were stupid."

Fornier moved forward then, hitching up his belt, heavy with gun weight. "*Sí*, Trent, she ees correct. You are stupid. We thought you would be quick enough to get what we were driving at . . . we thought perhaps some sort of an agreement could be reached. . . ."

Paul sensed that the man was keying himself up to something with the words; as he spoke, his voice took on a tight slur, his face flushed.

"*Pues*," went on Fornier, "you do not seem to see how you would profit by staying here . . . and how you would lose by leaving."

And Paul had it now; perhaps a quicker man *would* have seen the thing behind their talk sooner. Yes, Fornier was keying himself up to something, and, when he reached his pitch, Paul Trent would have no earthly chance against the swift skill of his hands. The shots would be nothing new here; those outside would ignore them, if they heard them at all. Paul set himself bitterly, knowing he would probably die without even getting his gun clear.

Jan was unhooking his thumbs from his belt now, was settling his weight forward in the manner of a man who had done this thing many times before. "*Por supuesto*, Trent, the time for talking is over."

The Frenchman's eyes flickered. Paul felt the sudden dull tingle of nerve message leaping down his gun arm. But the whole thing was suspended there by the swift pad of moccasins in the outer hall. Fornier's head snapped around to the Navajo who burst into the room. The Indian panted something in his own language. *Doña* Barcello's voice was hissing echo to the words: "Governor Bent has been assassinated in Taos!"

It was then that Fornier realized his error. He turned back to Trent with one hand twitching a little above an ivory gun butt. Paul hadn't needed a dead-man draw to get his weapon free in that moment of diversion. And now he commanded the room quietly, completely. "I guess Bent's murder will sort of start things going," he said, moving without haste until he stood a pace from the door leading into the *placita*, his back against the wall. "And I guess I won't be staying here any longer. Call your three *criados* in, *Señora*."

She spoke with a sharp intake of breath, and the trio of Navajos paced in from the patio with hardly a glance at Trent. *Doña* Barcello was watching Paul narrowly and there was something in her eyes, almost relief. Wondering at that, he stepped backward into the patio.

"It is a long trail out of Santa Fe for a man riding alone!" called Fornier.

Trent said: "Don't follow me too close, Jan."

His boots made hollow sounds on the crude tiling; a door across the way gave to his shove. He had shut it behind him and stepped to one side before the Frenchman opened up. The shots formed a wild volley; lead smashed through pine and *thudded* harmlessly into earthen floor. Then Paul moved across the *sala* and into a hallway. The ballroom was beyond that, empty, darkened. He crossed it and let himself out into Burro Alley. The night felt safe, somehow, closing around him softly; it was more his element than glittering gambling houses.

His boot heels *crunched* softly in the earth, moving toward the alley mouth. And he felt a rising resentment at the whole set-up, a rueful anger that he had been trapped by the woman. Why the hell didn't they want him to leave Santa Fe? He had been attracted by the *Doña's* vivid beauty, but he had stayed clear, not relishing her endless intrigues. Yet, somehow, he had become involved in something big enough for death.

— II —

Paul stopped at the end of the alley, holding his hat behind him to hide its revealing white, searching the darkened plaza. And he saw them, two shifting blobs of shadow over by the customhouse, two men, half hidden behind bales of beaver pelts. Perhaps he had moved back instinctively at sight of them because shots blasted the silence; piñon splintered into his face off the corral poles.

Trent was on his belly then, gun hand propped on an elbow. The thick poles made a good barricade. Paul lay there, realizing how thorough had been Fornier's trap. The men out there had him cut off neatly; they covered all exits from their position.

There were probably more of them, too, staked out in San Francisco Street perhaps, or down Palace Avenue. Paul knew the kind they would be—wild, arrogant young men who had long ridden for the Frenchmen, sons of the politicos who had become rich under Armijo. Trent had seen them too many times, swaggering behind Fornier, dressed in tight leather breeches and glazed sombreros, heavy with silver embroidery; the Frenchmen even supplied their guns—new, single-action Colts from Texas.

He stiffened at the *creak* of a door. Then someone was in the alley, someone was filling the narrow place with flashing gun thunder, throwing a hail of lead. A man standing up would have died swiftly. Lying in the dust, Paul fought to keep from turning his head; Fornier would catch the movement. And it was Fornier. No one else would have come out that way, fast and shiny and loud. Trent could understand the insolent *caballeros* following a man like that.

But he would have to move now or never. The quick, nervous advance of boots down the alley told him this. And the sound of empties being jacked out gave him that moment of time when Jan was reloading. With the thought still working, Paul was rising, throwing himself violently across the open space toward the comparative safety under the arcade. Sound was continuous—first Fornier's surprised grunt, then the steady slam of a six-shooter being triggered empty from in front of the customhouse. Bullets were whining down the alley, *thudding* into adobe. But Paul was already stomach down on the earthen walk under the arcade of *portales*. He could have fired at the gun flashes, but his own flashes would give his position away. And it was a good position, deep in the shadows against an adobe wall. The knowledge that he was there would keep Fornier around the corner. So he lay silently, drawing a shuddering breath. It had been close, with all that lead howling after his hide.

Thick silence had fallen; gun play was not an infrequent thing in this city, and people waited till it was all over before they investigated. Price had doubtlessly returned to the fort—and, anyway, these days, the blue coats weren't too eager to fool with local affairs. It left Paul alone against he didn't know how many men. Fornier's voice boomed, calling to his gunnies.

"Carlos, Vasquez, work aroun' by La Fonda. The *gringo* ees somewhere over on thees side, near the *palacio*, under the *portales*. Be careful. You know Paul Trent."

As the shadows began to shift in front of the customhouse, Fornier was calling other names, directing his riders to close in from San Francisco Street, from Palace Avenue, from the Church of San Francisco. The place became a moving pattern of ghostly shapes, flitting from cover to cover, moving inexorably in on the *gringo* who lay alone on his belly, still not wanting to reveal himself by his gun flashes.

Paul began moving, too, cautiously, along the wall toward the Palace of the Governors. He came to the first of the narrow glazed windows that lined the fortress-like building. It would be practically empty now inside. Governor Bent had left for Taos to be murdered there; the officials had taken to the safety of the fort. It would serve as well as any of the other buildings.

He raised to his knees and shattered the glass with his gun butt, cleaning the bottom part of the window out with sharp, hard blows. The *caballeros* opened fire at the sound. To the *thud* of slugs in adobe, Paul rose and sat on the sill, facing the street. He kicked violently with his feet and fell over backward into the darkness of the room. A slug plucked at his boot heel. And the flat echoes of gunfire died again outside.

He took off his boots and moved without sound across the pitch-black room. Even moonlight could not reach here. The gunmen would take it slow with the threat of his gun still holding them. It would give him a few moments.

That was all he needed, passing through door after door, working his way through the great building toward the *placitas* and Casas Reales at the rear. Paul fumbled open one door and stepped into something that brushed harshly in his face.

He leaped back, gun up. But it was only a closet, filled with some sort of uniforms. His eyes had grown somewhat accustomed to the gloom, and he saw that they were red coats, white trousers, cocked hats. Armijo's dragoons had once worn these uniforms, but they had parted with them when the Americans disbanded the governor's army. There were rumors, however, that several squadrons of dragoons had escaped with Armijo when he had fled.

He tried another door and found himself in a room larger than the rest, its walls strung with lines of small, round objects. It was a jolt to realize that this was Armijo's executive office and that these were the festoons of Apaches' ears the infamous governor had taken in reprisal for scalpings. The despot had left his marks.

Paul stumbled out of the grisly chamber and went on toward the rear, stopping now and then to listen for sounds of pursuit. Evidently the *caballeros* in the plaza still had a healthy respect for his .44, however, for the building was silent. Finally he gained a *placita* with its high walls bordering a street, and its wrought iron gate unlocked. Paul slipped his boots back on and was soon walking unhurriedly toward the poorer section of Santa Fe. The whole trap had been so thorough that he knew Fornier hadn't missed confiscating the horses he had left at the stables.

Paul had sold all but those three. He could

have left the city now, but he told himself he was staying to get the horses back. And telling himself that, he knew it was a lie. There was another reason, the real one. Something had been working in the back of his mind ever since the Navajo had burst into the *sala* with news of Bent's murder. Things were beginning to tie together, and something was holding him here when he knew it might mean his death, something he himself could hardly name. His destination was the hovel of Melquades Segura, who had spent many roundups with Paul on the mesas.

The door opened to his soft tapping and Segura muttered sleepily: "Ah, *Señor* Paul, *esta tu*. Have you come in from the pastures, have you eaten?"

"*Sí, sí, compadre*," said Trent. "I only want to sleep."

"*Es un* buffalo robe in the corner, Paulito, some blankets, too. My *casa* is yours."

"*Gracias, hermano, gracias*," murmured Trent. He pulled off boots and pants and slid under the rough blankets. His tired mind refused to consider the danger of remaining here, and sleep came almost immediately.

— III —

The *dons* of Santa Fe were descended from Spanish conquerors who had come up from the south hundreds of years before, but the *pobres* like Melquades Segura were Indians—perhaps his ancestor had been a Tlascán or an Aztec, brought along by the proud Spaniards, or perhaps he was merely from Pueblo stock, the village Indians the first *Conquistadores* had found here in the Santa Fe valley. He was typical of the *pobre*: a small, patient man whose resigned eyes asked nothing more than enough tortillas to fill his comfortable paunch and enough sun to warm him against the wall of his adobe hut. His wife might have been twenty-five or -six; she was already old with toil and the bearing of many *niños*. Her eyes were not so resigned, her face a little stronger. It was evident who ruled the hovel of Melquades Segura.

Paul sat watching her warm over some tortillas for breakfast, feeling that her flow of talk was hiding something. The man stood to one side, forcing a smile whenever Paul glanced his way. And Trent remembered the tension he had felt before.

"*¿Que hay, hermano?*" he asked Melquades.

Segura's laugh was forced. "*Nada, Señor* Trent.

184

Nothing ees wrong. Only you will go after breakfas', no? You will leave?"

"You are afraid of something, *amigo*. I can feel it," said Paul, and he eyed the peon narrowly as he said the next: "Is it Jan Fornier, is it what he is stirring up?"

The man took a step backward and his face paled a little. "Oh, no, not Fornier, not the Frenchman. He is stirring nothing."

Paul knew it was a lie. The woman had dropped a *torta* into the fire; it was burning, but she ignored it. She was standing, watching Trent with a strange expression of anger and fear.

"What is he doing, Segura?" said Paul. "You can tell me. You have always told me everything. We have shared enough *mula blanca* to fill the Río Grande. And how many nights have we spent together on the mesa. I am your *hermano*, Segura. The *pobres* know what is happening here in Santa Fe. Tell me, brother, tell me."

They were all standing now, and the *pobre* was actually shaking: his mouth worked with the effort of speaking. "*Nada, nada, Señor* Trent. I know nothing. Please don't ask. Please go. . . ."

"Segura . . . ," began Paul, but the woman cut him off.

"I think you had better go, *Señor* Trent. There is nothing here for you now."

And he realized she was right. The fear they had, denied even his friendship. Slowly he picked

185

his gun belt and holster from the blankets, buckling it on. And then he walked from the hovel into the blinding sunlight of the street. His defeat was full and complete. It had been bad enough to leave the valley, but he had been going thinking he at least left friends behind. Now, even that was denied him.

When he had first ridden in through the towering Sangre de Cristos and had seen the sleepy green valley, his thought had been, surely the remoteness and obscurity of this place will last my lifetime. And he took to breeding horses, because they had been so much a part of him before. He had gained some small fame for his *caballos* by the time the tall, fair men with the long rifles began to filter in from the outside. One of them said he came from Boone's Lick country in Missouri and his name was Kit Carson. Another was an Irishman, known to the Indians as Broken Hand because of an old gunshot wound. And although Paul knew what would inevitably come behind such men, he continued to round up his stallions in the spring, calling on his friends, the *pobres*, to help him. He sold them to such as Beaubien and Maxwell and Chisum, who boasted the finest remudas in the province. It was Beaubien who set their quality by insisting that they were directly descended from Cortez's original Arabian barbs.

But after the mountain men from Missouri and

Ireland and Kentucky came traders from Texas and farther east, long lines of wagons with their double thicknesses of Osnaberg sheeting and their payload of three thousand pounds. With that familiar sense of defeat, Paul prepared himself for a final roundup. The thing that would follow these traders was as inevitable as the sun rising on the Río Grande y Bravo. War was declared on the United States, April 24th, and, when Kearny marched into Santa Fe in August, Paul Trent had sold his herds and was resigned to leave what he had left so many times before.

Standing in the sun-bright street, looking up at Fort Marcy, Paul knew he couldn't leave now. Fornier was mixed in a revolt big enough to terrorize the *pobres*, and, if it was that big, it surely formed a threat to the troops on the mesa above La Garita. Trent thought the thing within him had been long dead. But it was what had kept him here last night when he might have left, and it was even more so keeping him here now. He had other friends among the peons; surely one of them would have enough courage to tell him.

Paul ducked suddenly into the space between two hovels. A pair of Fornier's *caballeros* were coming down the street, faces turned featureless in the deep shadows cast by their glazed sombreros. They rode side-by-side, turning nervously in the saddle, questing. Paul stood behind a *burro* piled high with *sabinas* faggots, listening to the steady *clop-clop* of the hoofs fade away. Fornier was still hunting.

The mud-walled house of Fernando Semora lay across the river from San Francisco Street. It had been a long roundabout way for Trent, dodging between houses, watching the Frenchman's riders comb the streets for him. Once he had taken refuge in the chapel of San Miguel, wondering if the insolent gunmen would hunt him even in a church. But they had cantered by, and he had scuttled from the cool darkness inside like a rat when the cats are gone.

He stood for a long moment across Agua Fría road from Semora's house, watching, waiting. But nothing stirred in the shade of the cotton-woods, no one moved down by the bubbling *acequia*. So he walked over the baked clay and entered the low door, standing just inside to focus his eyes.

Semora's voice was shaky, slurred. "*Señor* Trent, you should not have come. All the *pobres* know by now that Fornier wants your life, that he has men hunting for you everywhere."

Paul could see him now; he was a young man, dressed in the peon's flapping white pantaloons and cotton shirt. And the fear had turned his dark face pale.

"Yes, Semora," grated Paul, "he is hunting me. Why? What is going on that Fornier should want to kill me? What is he doing? You know . . . all the *pobres* know."

Fernando stepped forward, pushed his hands on Paul's chest, forced him backward through the door. "No, no. I cannot tell you, I cannot tell anyone. You must go."

"But, *amigo*, you cannot be afraid. You were always *muy valiante*. Remember the wild horse in the Jemez two years ago. You were not afraid then. . . ." Paul stopped, realizing that the boy had pushed him into the street, realizing they were talking entirely too loudly. Men were coming from down by the river, their legs hidden in reddish-brown dust as they hit the street.

Across the river by the footbridge, he could see their two stallions, silver-mounted Spanish saddles glinting with sunlight. Paul jerked himself free from the young peon as shots *cracked* dully, as lead puffed up blobs of red dust in the street. But one of the bullets didn't hit the street, and Semora clutched spasmodically at his chest with work-calloused hands; blood leaked thickly through his clawed fingers.

Paul had his big .44 out now, no split-second draw, but good enough to be ready for them as they entered effective range. There was a stubborn air in his square figure, spread-legged in the middle of the street—a look to him that made the running men slow suddenly, realizing what Fornier had meant last night in the plaza when he had called: *Be careful. You know Paul Trent.*

He didn't shoot from the hip. That was for gun artists like Jan Fornier. He held the Remington cap-and-ball out in front of him and squeezed out the first thundering shot. One of the men stumbled, fell on his face, slid a little bit with his momentum.

The other *caballero* had stopped completely and was beginning to move sidewise, indecisively, shooting as he went. Paul gritted his teeth against that deadly bee hum of .45 lead around him and deliberately cocked his gun. The second shot jarred him from hand to shoulder. It gave him a certain satisfaction to see the man go down, eyes and mouth opened wide as if in surprise. Trent lowered his weapon slowly, only then aware of the wetness on his left forearm. It wasn't a bad wound, not as bad as Semora's. Kneeling beside his friend, Paul found that there would be no more fear for the *pobre*. He was dead.

There was muted sound from San Francisco Street; a group of riders galloped around the sharp turn it made before entering the plaza. Fornier led them—Paul couldn't miss his figure, dashing, arrogant. Well, why not, he had everything in his favor.

They didn't make the mistake their dead associates had of dismounting; they forded the river in a surge. Fornier was first into Agua Fría road, his leggy roan mare glossy wet. He shouted hotly:

"You mad dog, Trent! Do you theenk you can go running aroun' town like it was San Juan's *fiesta*. I 'ave two dozen men hunting for you, Trent, two dozen. You will never leave Santa Fe alive!"

Paul moved unhurriedly, partly to gall the Frenchman, partly because that was his way. He disappeared behind a wall of adobe brick as they opened a futile fire. And as he flitted up the river, then doubled back until he was opposite the *entrada*, as he ran like a fox before the hounds, his thought was that the quest had now been marked with blood.

— IV —

It was the end of the second day of search, of questions, of seeing fear estrange him from men he had known for years. He had slept a few hours under a moldy haystack in the *vegas* outside of town; he had had piñon nuts for breakfast and two raw eggs, stolen from an outraged hen on De Vargas Street, for lunch. And he grew more bitter as each friend turned him away. His patience was wearing thin, and by that afternoon his mouth was only a slash in a face gray with dust and weariness. His arm had swollen a little and was sore to the touch; his tired eyes held a hunted look, for still the riders of the pocked, white-water man coursed the city, ready for murder.

He had told himself a hundred times that it was hopeless, that he had no reason for risking his life like this. But the thing inside him that had never been dead was keeping him going, and he knew he would either find out what was up or die trying.

At 4:00 Paul stopped above the entrance into the town from the Santa Fe Trail. Below him, he could see the road, winding in between clusters of houses. He hunkered down in the shade of some green-branched cottonwoods, watching for signs of Fornier's riders as had become his habit. A few chickens scratched and *clucked* in the dust; a *burro* cropped at sun-dried grass; a Mexican parrot chattered in its amole cage. That was all. The *pobres* seemed even too fearful to come out of their houses, and what few did venture forth were in the town, drinking to insurrection in every *cantina* and saloon.

Paul made his way to an outlying hovel, small, dirty, forlorn. The roof hadn't been repaired after the last rain and sagged dangerously; the door leaned its last days on rotten cowhide hinges. Paul wondered if Lucio Montoya had died since their last meeting. The gentleman had been very old. And if he were alive, what could a *viejo* do for Paul Trent? His fear would probably be even greater than that of the younger peons.

Paul had to lift the door before opening it. He stood for a moment in the gloom, unable to see.

How many times had he done this in the past two days?

The old man's voice sounded like wind through dry leaves. "I knew you would be here, *muchacho*. I heard you were seeking something from your friends, an' I knew you would be here."

Paul made out the old man, lying on a sheepskin in the corner. "*Buenos días*, Lucio. Are you sick?"

"No." The old man sighed. "Just old, just old. I cannot even find the strength to see the sun these days."

Paul squatted beside him. "Can I get you *agua*, or food?"

"No. I am not thirsty or hungry. And I am not afraid, either. You must not blame your *compadres*, Paulito, they are only simple *pobres*. You must not be hard on them for their fear of this thing the Frenchman is doing."

Paul's voice was tight. "You will tell me, then?"

"*Sí, sí.* I am *viejo*. What matter if they kill me for telling." He raised on an elbow, gathering himself with labored breaths. "Governor Bent's murder in Taos touched off a revolt up there. The Taos Indians, the Apaches, the Tesques, they are killing every *Americano* in the town. Price will take his *gringo* soldiers up the Taos trail to stamp out the insurrection, and will leave Santa Fe stripped of troops. And Fornier will strike down here. He will strike with a drunken mob of *pobres*. He will kill all the *gringos* in Santa Fe, then take Fort

Marcy, and finally march up the trail and trap Price between his forces and those from Taos."

"I had guessed that much," said Paul. "But what makes the *pobres* so afraid? There have been a hundred such revolts smoldering in every *cantina*. Why should this particular one give them so much fear?"

"They do not fear the revolt itself, or even Fornier. They fear Armijo!"

Paul almost whispered it. "Armijo?"

"*Sí*. Fornier is bringing him back. He will put him in the Palace of the Governors again and give him the ears of five hundred *Americanos* to hang in his office."

"*Por supuesto*," muttered Trent. "But that is impossible. The old murderer is in Durango. He ran there five months ago."

Lucio snorted, feebly. "Durango, *bah!* They said he fled to Doña Ana, too, and Socorro, and Taos. Rumors, all rumors. We *pobres* know. He is at his *rancho* at Lemitar, waiting with two squadrons of dragoons who escaped with him, waiting for word from Fornier that Santa Fe has been taken so he can ride in like the conquering Oñate did . . . the Pueblos playing their flutes, the *penitentes* chanting their dirges, the *pelados* waving their bloody machetes."

Paul didn't answer; he squatted there, trying to believe it.

"Now," said Montoya, "now you see why your

amigos are so afraid. Armijo holds them in terror. Not one of them would reveal this coming madness, though many of them are not in sympathy with it. Do you remember how many *pobres* disappeared mysteriously during the days of the *Tejanos?* They speak one wrong word and Armijo takes them to one of these dungeons in La Garita and they are never heard from again. Do you recall how he stole Esquipilca Baca's wife and exiled Baca when he protested, and how he murdered his old *compañero*, Gonzales? That is Armijo, Paul, and the *pobres* have good cause to cower in their hovels, waiting for him to come back on that huge mule with his dragoons."

Paul rose slowly. "I can understand a few things now. But not all. If the *pobres* know of Armijo, they must know why Fornier doesn't want me to leave Santa Fe alive."

"No, Paulito, they do not know," said Montoya. "That you must find out from Fornier himself."

Trent took a deep breath. "*Sí,* I almost knew it. *Muchas gracias* for what you have done, Lucio. And as you ask, I will not be hard on my *amigos* for their fear. I must do something now that is difficult for me. *Adiós.*"

The old man lay back on his sheepskin. "*Vaya con Dios.*"

— V —

La Garita, the old, diamond-shaped Spanish prison, thrust up like a stolid guardian on the winding road to Fort Marcy. In the dust, Paul was only a shadow against the thick mud walls, walking with that deliberate stride of his, bent forward a little on the slight grade. The steady pace of the sentry at the gate of Fort Marcy was like a knife thrust from the past. At Trent's insistence, the trooper called the captain of the guard. As the officer approached, Paul remembered seeing him several times in the city, once at *Doña* Barcello's.

"Trent?" he said. "Let me see, Trent . . . Trent . . . shouldn't I know you from somewhere? I mean somewhere before Santa Fe."

"Possibly," said Paul, trying to ignore the old speculation in the man's young eyes. "But look, Captain, this is extremely urgent. I've got to see Colonel Price."

"Trent, Paul Trent," mused the captain. Then he shrugged his shoulders and led Paul across the new parade ground, past the stables with their mingled odors. Trent could see a battery of the fourteen cannon that Kearny had left, thrusting their black barrels out toward the city. They would be useless in a revolt; Price couldn't fire into Santa Fe for fear of hitting the American civilians down there.

The colonel was a sick man; his tall frame was wasted beneath the blue uniform; gold braid hung slackly from his gaunt chest. The march from Leavenworth had left most of them that way. But he no longer eyed Trent with that question in his gaze, and Paul felt a sudden dread. He stood almost in the middle of the colonel's bare quarters and forced himself to speak slowly. He tried to get across to Price how deadly Armijo's part in the revolt was, tried to show with the inadequacy of mere words what the ex-governor's return would do to the *pobres*. They feared him dreadfully, but they would follow him once he got the upper hand. He represented the old ways, and the stamp of his former rule had not yet left the country. But as Trent finished, he had the sinking feeling that he had made little impression on this disease-wracked officer from Missouri.

"I have but one thing to say, Trent," grated Price, pulling himself erect. "Since I've been in Santa Fe, I've been trying to recall where I had heard your name before. I remembered, the night before last, after seeing you at *Doña* Barcello's. In Eighteen Thirty-Five it was Lieutenant Paul Trent of the Missouri Cavalry, Fort Leavenworth, wasn't it? Quite a smell in the service, your court martial! None of us knew the exact details . . .

but it leaked out that you protected that black-guard trader who was convicted the same week of selling guns to the Pawnees. Do you think I could believe anything from a man who had been cashiered from the regulars under those circumstances?"

The shock of his words was but a dull one, for Paul had come half expecting it. He stood without meeting the colonel's accusing eyes, knowing how utterly futile further words would be in the face of this.

"Shall I call the captain of the guard, Trent? Or will you leave now?"

Paul shook his head. "I'm . . . going."

He didn't see the captain of the guard as he walked past him, didn't hear the pacing sentry when the gates closed. Yes, Price had finally remembered. Inevitably it was that way—first the speculation in their faces, then the contempt. Walking down the road toward Santa Fe, Paul thought of the way he had tried at first to face men like Price who didn't know the exact details. It had taken him a month, sticking around the big fort on the Missouri after his court martial, to find out how deep his stigma was; he had only stayed that long in the hope of clearing his name. The country had been too full of soldiers, young officers from West Point to meet on the reservation, old line officers to see in the towns. So he went westward, to Council Grove—buffalo hunting, two skinners and a killer and a wagon, the stench of death in their clothes and on their leather. And he had seen a parade that would soon be familiar to him. First the Long Rifles with their fair hair, then the traders with their huge wagons, and finally the soldiers. *Trent, Trent? Oh, yes, you were at Leavenworth. . . .*

It had taken him three months to find out how many times the squadrons of cavalry escorted the traders to Chouteau's Island. And that was as long as he had stayed there. So it was, moving before the steady westward advance of civilization and knowing what it meant when he saw the trappers begin to filter in, saw the wagons follow them. Well, he could move again, out of this valley. He had done what was in him to do and he could go now. Fornier's *caballeros* would be infinitely easier to face than the officers at the fort. A shadow suddenly materialized from the blackness beneath the walls of La Garita.

Paul stopped abruptly in the center of the moon-whitened road, waiting for the thunder of a gun without too much emotion. Then the man came into the pale yellow light; he was dressed in white doeskin and it reminded Trent that he had other enemies besides Fornier.

"*Doña* Barcello sent me for you."

That was all the Navajo said. After speaking, he turned and swung on down the road, moving like a big white cat. Paul stood where he was. Did she expect him simply to follow the Indian into another trap? Did she think him that stupid—or was it a trap? He could hardly believe her that obvious; her style was intrigue and subtlety. He remembered, too, the strange look of relief in her eyes the other night, when he had escaped the first trap. Perhaps he wanted to find how she fitted in this crazy thing, or perhaps he was just weary enough and beaten enough to follow the line of least resistance. He started after the Navajo.

They went around behind the Realito and through the Casas Reales where Spanish officers and their families had once been lodged when New Mexico was a part of Spain. Once the *criado* stopped, pointing to where a pair of men sat their restless *caballos* on Palace Avenue, men with glazed sombreros. That the Navajo should shield him from the Frenchman's riders gave Paul faint hope. Finally they gained *Doña* Barcello's building and moved across the same silent ballroom, the same series of connected rooms, the same *placita*. The Indian was suddenly gone, disappearing through one of the doors in each of the patio's four walls. Paul took it that she would be in the same room as before; he stepped in with his big Remington .44 very evident in his fist.

She was the only one, sitting with her hands folded calmly in her lap, her mouth open a little, and the soft lamplight glistening on her rich under lip. There was a *rebozo* over her shoulders, its fine weave marking her wealth and station as did the serape of a man. Her smile seemed glad, somehow.

"Where's Jan Fornier?" he asked.

"Jan?"

"What trap would be complete without him?"

She rose with a rustle of satin. "Oh, Paul Trent, you are such a child in these things. If I had wanted to trap you, do you think I would have been simple enough to send a man after you? I have known exactly where you were ever since you left the house of Melquades Segura. Two of my Navajos have followed you every hour of the day and night. And if you thought it was another trap, why did you come at all?"

His mouth held a hint of a smile. "I guess I trusted you despite myself . . . though you and Fornier looked like hand-in-glove the other night."

She moved closer and he knew that feeling of awkwardness again. "You were perfectly safe then," she murmured. "I had three Indians in the *placita*. Remember how swiftly they entered when I called, how close by they must have been? A word from me, and Jan wouldn't have been able to draw a gun in our game."

"And just what is that game?" he asked grimly.

Her smile was indulgent. "I will try to explain. Jan Fornier came down from the north a long time ago. He was an opportunist and he saw his opportunity in Manuel Armijo. He was soon high in the governor's favor, and, as Armijo prospered, so did Jan Fornier prosper."

Paul nodded gravely. He remembered Governor Armijo's practice of making *diligencia*, that incredible system of graft—$750 levied on each trader's wagon coming into Santa Fe, bribes from trappers who wished to poach on what was then Mexican territory, government funds from Mexico City to be diverted. All of which had made Fornier a rich and powerful man.

Doña Barcello continued. "The Frenchman stood to lose everything under *Americano* rule. There would be no more making *diligencia*, no more living like emperors. It was natural that he should be mixed up in the insurrections. He had never offered tangible oppositions to the *gringos*, so they let him go, satisfied that the army of Armijo was disbanded, and that Armijo himself had fled."

"And you?" asked Paul.

"Me, I am an opportunist, also, but I saw that the *gringos* were here to stay. Outwardly Jan and I were still thick as *ladrónes*, just like the old days when I was rumored to have been Armijo's *inamorata*. But Jan Fornier must have suspected that my favor had shifted, for he wouldn't tell me what he was doing. I couldn't find out anywhere what he was up to, not from the *ricos* because they didn't know, and not from the *pobres* because I had never been their friend. Can't you see me, *Doña* Gertrudes de Barcello, who had put her finger into every pie in Santa Fe during the last eight years . . . I could not find out this one thing that might mean so much to all of us. When Jan suggested that you be invited to my *sala* that night, I could not risk an open breach with him, and, although I suspected his intentions, I invited you. He only told me he did not want you to leave Santa Fe. And when you refused to see the threat behind our talk, *pues* . . ."

"Sort of playing both ends against the middle, isn't it?"

"That is intrigue, Paul. It is much more fascinating than *chusa* or monte. It is my eating, my drinking, I have been doing it so long that it is a part of me."

Her hand was smoothing his linsey shirt over his chest now, and she seemed to have lost her conscious sense of power, seemed to be only a woman who was very beautiful. Paul could understand how she had ruled so many men. He swallowed against the hint of perfume in her blue-black hair.

"What ees Jan Fornier up to, Paul?" she asked. "I know you have found out. You were the only one who could have found out."

He needed someone so desperately to trust. And he was convinced of her sincerity, although he knew she had used her beauty to convince him.

Her flashing eyes had swayed stronger men than Trent. So he told her about the plot, about Armijo, and even about Colonel Price. For a moment she was silent, a half-amazed smile on her face. It was an imperceptible shift that changed her from the woman back into *Doña* Barcello; some of it may have been the narrowing of her eyes, the hardening of her mouth.

"*Dios*," she hissed. "I might have guessed it. Armijo. What a thing Fornier has there. None of your little *cantina* plots. This one has every chance of succeeding, especially with that blind Colonel Price stripping Santa Fe of all the *gringo* troops."

Paul was resigned. "You can't blame him. Bent's murder started a massacre up at Taos. The Pueblos and the Apaches under Tomásito have killed all the Americans in the town. Price has got to stamp the thing out. And why should he take the word of a cashiered Army officer on anything?"

She looked up sharply at his weary tone. "You are through trying, Paul? Is it so terrible a thing you have been running from, this . . . cashierment?"

He looked at the floor. "You have no idea. It's a thing you can't stand up to and knock down. It's a deadly thing, a subtle thing. And I was never good at fighting subtle things."

"Does Price know the real story?" she asked.

His suddenly narrowing eyes met hers. "Do you?"

"Perhaps I couldn't find out what our precious Frenchman was doing, but I told you I knew everything else here. Scouts, traders, hunters, trappers . . . they all come to my *salas* sooner or later. Maybe the Army didn't know any more about that court martial than what was on the surface, but those frontiersmen knew what really happened."

He swallowed. "It doesn't matter. It's too long past, and you can't call on ghosts to testify. The trader who was selling guns to the Pawnees is dead, and the major who connived with him and saved his own neck by pinning the charge on me left his scalp on a Kaw's belt two years ago."

Her voice held a mocking note. "A clever man like Fornier wouldn't have butted his head against a thing like that. You are soft. You let them handle you like a *burro*! It must have been like spanking a baby to fix the whole dirty business on you."

A *criado* slipped unobtrusively in from the hallway, hissing something to *Doña* Barcello. An excited flush glowed through her face and she turned to him with a growing smile. "You aren't quitting, Paul, you aren't going. You could have gone the other day when you escaped Jan through the *palacio*, but you didn't. You stayed to find out what he was up to, because you began to realize that it threatened the *gringos* at Marcy. My servant has just told me that Fornier left for

205

Lemitar an hour ago. He must be worried about your being free, must be getting nervous. He is the kind that would get nervous, too. Armijo is the crux of thees whole affair. Weeth him out of the way, the *pelados*, the peons would crumble from beneath Jan. I think maybe you could get to Lemitar before Jan, Paul."

His laugh was bitter. "What could I do? And why should I go? I owe Price and his cavalry nothing. I owed them nothing before, and I tried to help. You saw what happened."

"*Sí*, you owe them nothing. They owe you everything . . . for the pain they have given you, the bitterness, the endless running. But you were a lieutenant in their army once. That is what kept you here all along. It will keep you here now, until you have smashed the threat to them. You know it."

His boots made a muted sound on the floor, shifting. He did know it. The thing had never been dead in him. "I could beat Jan on one of my own horses," he said.

"You forget, I have a dozen of your *caballos*. They are still behind the *palacio*, in Armijo's old stables. The saddle stock are in the smaller building."

She was standing close, her chin raised triumphantly with having finally moved the slow, quiet *Yanqui*. It had taken Paul some minutes to make up his mind; he had been considering it while they had talked in the last moment, and, when he finally decided it should be done, he didn't feel awkward or thickheaded at all. It seemed natural to take her in his arms and kiss her.

He turned at the doorway. "Anybody wants me, I'll be at Lemitar."

Perhaps she was still surprised; she didn't answer.

It was good to have the magnificent beast surging between his knees. He lay along the pulsing neck, looking back now and then at the pursuit. They had been at every corner, their Colt thunder filling Santa Fe. But they hadn't expected him to come blasting out of the night on a great, raking stallion. He had hit one of them, too, had seen the man throw up his arms and pitch from his high Spanish saddle with one of Trent's slugs in him. And the others would soon be but a memory. They were mounted splendidly, but not equal to the killing pace of Paul's superb horse. The road slid beneath him, echoing dully to racing hoofs, stretching before and behind like a flowing white ribbon.

His one hope was that he could pass Fornier, could sight him on the road ahead, circle around, and reach Lemitar before the Frenchman. He didn't underestimate Fornier's courage, or his deadly skill with those Colts. He knew it was bad enough with two squadrons of dragoons at

Lemitar, but at least they would not be inside the house with Armijo. If Fornier were to beat Paul, he would be inside, and his twin guns would be more danger to Trent than the rifles of all the dragoons. So Trent talked to his horse and urged him even faster. The gallant stallion responded, perhaps remembering this *Yanqui*'s soft, patient voice from days on the mesa. His flanks grew glossy, then lathered; they heaved with the breath passing through him. And Paul knew that when they reached the end of the run, the horse would be hip-shot, wind-broken, ruined. It made him feel like a criminal.

He thought of *Doña* Barcello sometimes during the ride—standing there in the room, too surprised by his kiss for speech. She was beautiful, strong, ruthless, but a woman . . .

— VI —

The sun was high with morning when Trent neared Lemitar. And still he had not caught Fornier; it gave him an impending sense of fresh failure. He had thought his mount capable of passing the Frenchman, had thought to get to Armijo before Fornier would be able to add his guns to the opposition. Now even that hope was dying. Paul broke from the winding road and climbed to higher country, descending finally down a sloped covered with juniper and scrub pine. Below him spread Armijo's sprawling *hacienda*. It was like a physical blow over his heart for Paul to see the *caballeros* in front of the porch, three of them on lathered mounts, holding four riderless horses.

Trent swung stiffly from his shaking beast. A tributary of the Río Grande ran past the *hacienda*, lined with groves of young cottonwoods and willows. In the shade of these trees waited the dragoons, standing beside their horses, their red coats oddly dappled with shade and sunlight coming through the leaves. The *tinkle* of accouterments and desultory talk were small sound to Trent up on the hillside.

Out in the fields, he could see the *pobres*, plowing with a crude forked tree and a patient mule. They would run at the first sign of gunfire— he suspected they had no love for their master, Armijo. That would leave only a hundred soldiers, six *caballeros*, Fornier, and the ex-governor for Paul's gun.

His smile was a trifle bitter as he unsaddled the ruined stallion and slipped the Spanish bridle from its foam-flecked head. It could do no more than stand on quivering legs, looking at him with big, bloodshot eyes. There was no reproach in those eyes, and Paul was glad.

"*Querido*," he murmured, "you are free. I don't think I'll be coming back up this hill for you.

There are too many of them down there. Go up above Taos, in the high pastures, remember? The grass will be green now, none of that dry hay from the stables. Forgive me, *valiante*, for what I did to you . . . it was necessary."

It took him a few minutes to work down the slope, crossing the road and taking to the cover of sloping ground, passing by the dragoons unseen, finally legging up the rise when the mud walls of the *hacienda* cut him off from them. He entered by one of the back doors and came into the great kitchen. Something was cooking in a pair of huge caldrons; perhaps the hissing steam covered his footsteps. He was able to strike the cook on the head and catch his body before it fell to the earthen floor.

Then he was standing in the doorway that led to the huge, cool living room. It had a Moorish look, as did most of the *ricos'* homes. There were heavy, carved chests, covered with red and black Navajo blankets. Spanish saddles hung from pegs in the adobe wall. The walls themselves were hung with colored cloths up to a five-foot height so that the white gypsum wouldn't be rubbed off. And in the center, by a large table, stood Manuel Armijo, a huge man, well over six feet, carrying some two hundred and eighty pounds. Fornier was there, too; a trio of his riders standing uneasily behind him. On the table were hammered silver mugs and a jug of grape brandy; they were all flushed a little with drink.

The Frenchman was finding it difficult to control his anger. "You've got to come now, Manuel. Paul Trent is still loose . . . there is no telling what he is up to."

The mountainous ex-governor pursed thick lips and turned from one side to the other, admiring his dark blue military cloak in one of the many mirrors lining the wall. His eyes grew crafty in their pouches of fat. "*Por supuesto*, you said you would have Santa Fe like this"—he cupped one plump hand—"when I rode in. You said I would enter like Oñate, like Cortez. I cannot sneak back like a dog and hide in some stinking hovel until the *gringo* troops leave for Taos. No!"

Jan leaned forward a little, his lips curling: "You great, hulking *bacero* . . ."

But his eyes had drawn to Paul's figure in the doorway and he realized suddenly that it wasn't the cook, that it wasn't one of the peons from the fields. His mouth opened, his face turned pale with surprise, then red with a rising, impotent anger. The loggers' pox made a white scar-pattern against the flush.

"Move very carefully to the door," Paul told him. "And order those dragoons to mount and ride toward Santa Fe. Tell them you will follow with Armijo. Tell your *caballeros* the same thing. And, Jan, don't try anything foolish."

The man turned like a marionette twitched on

211

strings. No, he wouldn't try anything foolish, not with Paul's Remington dead bead on his back. He stood in the doorway, leaning forward a little; his voice was a trifle high as he repeated Trent's orders. Those outside seemed to suspect nothing. There was the *rattle* of accouterments, the collective *creak* of a hundred men swinging into leather, then the light drum of cantering horses that grew into thunder as the dragoons broke into a gallop and swept past the door in a rising cloud of dust, shouting excitedly: "¡*Viva libertad*! ¡*Viva* Armijo!"

Armijo was a murderer, a scoundrel, almost all bad. His one saving grace was a sardonic sense of humor that was almost as large as himself. "*Gracias, muchachos*," he laughed dryly. "*Sí, viva* Armijo."

Then Fornier turned back, long fingers curled tensely above his ivory-handled Colts.

Paul knew the only way he could hold them here was to shoot them, yet he couldn't do it in cold blood. So he waited until the drumming squadrons were gone and then he thought: *Frenchman, make your play*. And the Frenchman was quite willing to make that play; he began settling forward a little, began talking.

"So, you came alone, you didn't bring the *gringo* cavalry. Why not? Did you think you could buck us all with one Forty-Four?" And Paul realized that Fornier was keying himself up with the words as he had done in *Doña* Barcello's *sala*

212

that other night. The man had something—he had his own way of cracking things open. But when he had worked himself to that pitch of nervous tension, he would apparently slap leather in the face of all hell. Under the cover of his words, however, the *caballeros* were beginning to shift, spreading Paul's target. Trent took a breath, slowly, and was ready.

"An' *Doña* Barcello," continued Fornier, his hands curling. "Why didn' you bring her along? She helped you before. . . ." A *caballero* suddenly threw himself behind the mountainous Armijo, dragging his gun clear, blasting at Paul. Trent took a step to one side with the bullet jarring into him, somewhere high in his chest. He triggered a shot out that knocked the *caballero* halfway around, then sent him down with a sick cry.

Armijo threw himself forward with a great, rumbling roar, smashing the heavy table beneath his weight, then rolling off it onto the floor.

At the same time, Jan drew—Paul couldn't have sworn that his hands moved, but they were suddenly full of twin, bucking Colts. The first bullet slammed Trent back against the wall. He had his gun cocked then, and taking another deliberate step to the side, he squeezed out his second shot. Fornier grunted and dropped one of his Colts. He lurched behind the smashed table. Paul tried to take yet a third step aside, but he slid downward, dragging the cloth on the wall with him. He threw down on the two remaining *caballeros* as he slid; his gun jerked up with the roaring lead, but he knew he had missed. They were already outside the front door, hiding behind a three-foot-thick adobe wall.

The wrecked table made a solid barricade for the Frenchman. But Paul could hear the harsh slide of his body, moving into position. Armijo had gathered himself off the floor and was squatting like a huge gargoyle beside the fireplace, laughing shakily.

"Don't shoot thees way, *amigos*," he said. "You know what I always say. It is better to have the reputation for being a brave man than to be one."

Trent would almost have laughed but for his pain. He couldn't see very well, what with that and the sifting gunsmoke. It was slow work, jacking out the three empties, filling the chambers from his belt. Fornier's voice boomed suddenly, calling to his henchmen.

"Charge heem, *muchachos*! Come through the door shooting. He ees only one man, only one. I will give a thousan' *pesos* to the man who keels Paul Trent."

It was the opportunist speaking, the clever man. Fornier wasn't afraid; he had proved that by facing Paul's gun and drawing. But the flash was all over now; his dead-man draw hadn't finished things. This was a different kind of game, the game of the slow, stubborn man who sagged against the wall across the room, patiently waiting with a gun as slow as himself, and as deadly. Why should the opportunist face that when there were still his men to die?

Paul had his gun up when they came through the door after those *pesos*. Their shots *thudded* wildly into the adobe behind him, flaking it into his eyes. His gun boomed once, then again, and once again. They stumbled over one another, going down in a heap.

He didn't try to reload; he didn't think he had that much strength. He dragged himself grimly across the floor, rumpling a Navajo rug beneath his body, moving toward the table that formed a barricade for Jan. He guessed he'd been hit in the leg, too, because he could only move one. Well, he'd known it would be this way—all he asked now was one more shot at Fornier.

The thing worked both ways. Without Fornier, Armijo could never swing the insurrection—he lacked the pure guts, lacked the ability to lead men like those wild young *caballeros*. And without Armijo, Fornier was no good. The *pobres* wouldn't follow him. Paul only had to nail one of them and he wanted it to be the pockmarked man. He hauled himself up and over the broken table, his boot making a dull *clink* against one of the hammered silver mugs on the floor. Then he was looking at Jan Fornier's flushed face.

Their guns thundered simultaneously, Fornier's

fire a wild slanging volley, Paul's bucking out as deliberately as before. With the agony of more lead burning into him, Trent cocked his gun for a third shot. But the Frenchman was done. His body twitched spasmodically, rolled part way over. Then Paul realized his Remington was empty anyway.

He half slid down the other side of the table and pulled himself to where the other lay. He grabbed the man's tooled leather vest, jerking him upward, gasping: "You can't die yet, damn you, not yet, not until you tell me why you didn't want me to leave Santa Fe alive!"

Fornier's dark eyes were glazed; blood bubbled from his mouth when he spoke. "What are you talkin' 'bout? You know why I didn' want you to leave Santa Fe. You knew about the insurrection and you were riding to bring Kearny's main column back to stop it. No one could reach Kearny as fast as you . . . you had the best horses, were the best rider. An' you used to belong to the *gringo* army. I saw you talkin' weeth Price there at *Doña* Barcello's. Do you theenk I wanted the whole Army on my neck?"

Paul let him sag back, slowly, laughing a little hysterically.

"You poor fool! That's almost funny. I was cashiered from the United States Army. I wasn't riding to Kearny . . . I was riding *from* him, and from Price and all the others. I was running."

But Jan Fornier didn't appreciate the irony of that. He was dead.

They reached Lemitar that afternoon—Colonel Price and a squadron of Missouri cavalry and *Doña* Barcello in her gaudy coach, drawn by four of Paul's best blacks. Price swung down from his big mare and picked his way over the two heaped bodies in the doorway, then stood looking at the carnage for a moment, unable to speak.

Paul had tied himself into a chair with strips of his bloodstained shirt. One of the *caballeros'* Colts was in his lap, fully loaded. His eyes reflected hell; his body was caked with dried blood. But by some stubborn force of will he had kept himself conscious.

Armijo hoisted himself from a rawhide-seated chair on the other side of the smashed table. "Colonel Price, I am glad you have come. I was growing weary of sitting here with this *diablo* who doesn't know when to quit."

Then *Doña* Barcello was inside, supporting Paul, tenderly untying the strips of linsey that held him up. "*Pobrecito, pobrecito*, I should have known such a thickhead would overdo the thing. Did you have to try to get everybody connected weeth it? I'm surprised you missed those two squadrons of dragoons. But look at all thees blood. . . ."

The Army doctor drew her away unceremoniously and bent over Paul. "Though I've never worked on a man with so much daylight showing through him, I fear you will live." He sighed.

Price gave a relieved grunt. "We met the dragoons a few miles up the road . . . they scattered at first sign of our cavalry. And, on the way in, *Doña* Barcello told me a few things, Trent. She told me the real story behind that court martial, she said there are a dozen buffalo hunters who were working around Leavenworth at the time who knew how the trader who was selling guns to the Pawnees was covered up by a certain major, knew exactly why you were cashiered. They would be only too glad to help clear your name, and I'll do all I can to have your case reopened, in view of what you have done here. . . . You have no idea how badly I felt when *Doña* Barcello practically dragged me down to the plaza and showed me all those drunken dragoons. That convinced me of Armijo's part in it, convinced me that you had been right."

"Dragoons, dragoons?" muttered Trent. "There weren't any dragoons in town. Fornier wasn't fool enough to show them until you left for Taos. They were all here at Lemitar."

Colonel Price turned his head until he could look at *Doña* Barcello. There was a singularly pitiful manner in which his mouth sagged. She smiled, half mockingly. "Armijo left some uniforms in the *palacio*. My Navajos made good

218

dragoons, no? And they looked so drunk. *Pues*, Colonel, how else could I have convinced you? We must take them out of your guardhouse as soon as we get back . . . they are good Indians."

Paul had some trouble focusing his eyes, but when he did, he could see her quite clearly, standing there with one hand on her hip. Beautiful, strong, ruthless—but a woman.

Death Song
of the
Santa Fe Rebels

Les Savage, Jr.'s original title for this story was "Trigger Troubadour". It was submitted to Mike Tilden, editor of *Dime Western* at Popular Publications, by the August Lenniger Literary Agency and purchased by Tilden on May 27, 1944. The author was paid $250. For publication, the title was changed to "Death-Song of the Santa Fe Rebels," appearing in *Dime Western* (2/45). For its first book appearance, except for the hyphen, the magazine title has been retained.

— 1 —

It was 1848 and the United States had just terminated hostilities with Mexico. American troops had occupied Santa Fe for but a few months, and the enigmatic walls of the old adobe town had seen many strange things and heard many, as any town will during a war or directly after it. The strangest thing they heard, however, was undoubtedly the music played by the *trovador*, who came in the spring.

It was the children who were first drawn out by his songs, and they gathered around the weird figure in a sort of childish awe. And then it was the troopers, and, when they came, the children scuttled away into alleys or disappeared through spindled doorways in the high mud walls flanking the *entrada*, which was the entrance of the Santa Fe Trail into the town proper. Corday Vidal might have wanted to follow the children, but it was too late now, because the officer leading the squadron was already hauling his big bay mare to a halt in front of the *trovador.*

"What the devil are you doing out here this time of night, playing that fiddle?" asked the cavalry-man in his parade ground bellow. "Don't you know Colonel Price established a nine o'clock curfew?"

Their acquaintance at Monterey had been brief, and Corday Vidal saw no recognition in the soldier's grizzled face now.

"Not fiddle, Captain Dunn." Vidal bowed. "Violin. A Stradivarius. You see the inlaid purling? Me, I am Corday Vidal, a *trovador*, a minstrel. Songs, games, laughter."

He drew the first sprightly strains of a local *canción* from his battered violin, and jumped into the air, kicking his heels together. The soldiers began to laugh.

"Stop it!" roared Captain Dunn, his stocky Irish figure stiffening in his blue greatcoat. New Mexico was an isolated province where many customs of the old country still prevailed, and it was not uncommon for minstrels to wander from town to town, singing and playing for a few *pesos* and a night's lodging. But never one such as this. Vidal was tall and gaunt-looking in an outlandish coat that might have been worn by some court fool in Charlemagne's time; it was completely covered with patches of a dozen different hues, long enough to hang about the tops of his knee-high Apache *botas*, which had shaggy red tassels on the ends of their curled-up toes. The soldiers were still grinning at the queer sight.

But Captain Dunn was closer, and he was looking at Vidal's long pale face with its strange, melancholy eyes that might haunt a man if he looked too deeply into them—and Captain Dunn was not grinning. He jerked his gloved hand to the pair of troopers directly behind him.

"Conners, Glover . . . take this fool to the Palace of the Governors. Out after curfew will do. Colonel Price'll tend to him in the morning. I haven't time now. You can catch up with us."

The man he had addressed as Conners saluted and swung down. Corday Vidal took a step backward, holding up a long slim hand. "You are heading north, Captain?"

Dunn's saddle *creaked* sharply as he jerked forward, the surprise plain in his weathered face. Then he seemed to catch himself, and straightened, voice suddenly wary. "I'm riding under sealed orders, mister. How would you know where?"

"What happened to the other squadrons that went north, Captain?" said Vidal, and saw Dunn's face pale. "Lieutenant Wells and twenty-four troopers in January. Lieutenant Maynard and two troops of the Fifth Missouri in September last year."

Dunn leaned forward in his saddle again, hands gripped together on the pommel as if for control. "Nobody knows about those patrols outside the Department. Who are you?"

"They haven't come back?" said Vidal. "What's going on up there, Captain? Up north. What happened to Maynard, and Wells?"

Dunn whirled sharply. "Arrest this man, Conners. I'll go back with you. Colonel Price'll hear this if we have to wake him up for it."

Conners had been standing on one leg, the other foot still in its stirrup. He tore it out and whirled toward Vidal, and two other troopers wheeled from the squadron and spurred their horses to cut off Vidal's escape toward the sheltering walls behind him. Vidal dodged the lunging Conners, throwing himself at the captain's bay. He caught the bridle and swung around with it.

The frightened horse reared up between Vidal and Conners, trying to jerk free. When the bay was pointed back into the line, Vidal shouted into its ear, throwing his weight on the bit. The startled animal broke free and plunged into the troops. The first pair tried to wheel their mounts away. The bay crashed through them, unhorsing one man. Trying desperately to keep from being thrown, Captain Dunn careened on through the ranks, sending them into wild confusion.

Vidal was already halfway to the high adobe walls on the opposite side of the *entrada* by the time Conners had gotten around the mill of frenzied horses and shouting men. He had a pistol out, and its first ball kicked at the red clay behind Vidal's feet.

The *haciendas* of New Mexico hid behind a solid wall fronting on the street. *Zaguáns* led through the walls into inner *placitas*, but the gates in these tunnel-like entrances were invariably closed. His violin and bow had disappeared into his voluminous coat, and there was a smooth flow to Vidal's movements, surprising in such a gaunt, ungainly man. He threw himself at the high mud wall, long hands striking the top. A red tile scraped off under his grip and he almost fell. Clutching the raw adobe in the space left by the tile, he jerked from one side to the other.

"Stop him, damn you!" bellowed Dunn still, fighting his big mare through the scattered squadron.

Conner's dragoon blared again, and the bullet took Vidal's chimney-pot hat off. But the *trovador* was swinging like a pendulum against the wall now, and he clawed far out to the side with one hand as he reached one end of his swing, heaving himself upward with a grunt. His leg went over the top, and he had that last view of the confusion of horses and men out in the street—of Conner's upturned face, twisted with frustrated anger—and then he dropped over into the *placita*. Conner's third shot clipped the adobe from the top of the wall where he had been a moment before.

Making hardly a sound in his buckskin boot moccasins, Vidal ran past the red-roofed well in the center of the patio, and through a small copse of willow trees. Light showed from an upstairs window, and someone stirred inside the house. The *trovador* rounded the adobe stables built on the flank of the house, running hard.

"¡*Madre de Dios*!"

Vidal couldn't get his arms clear around her,

but he managed to keep them from falling, and then let her sag against the wall. He caught a glimpse of soft black eyes in a fat face and black hair shot with gray pulled into a bun behind the plump neck.

"*Señor*," she said sharply, "what are you doing, running around and knocking down women in the middle of the night?"

The violin was suddenly in his slim hands. "How can you ask that, *Señorita* Liria, when I have come all the way from El Paso to sing beneath your window?"

"I am not *Señorita* Liria," she said angrily. I am going to call the *patrón* . . ."

"Ah, would you dare his wrath by waking him just because a poor ragged *trovador* has come to woo you," said Vidal, and the first trains of a plaintive *canción* floated from the Stradivarius. "Liria, *tu eres hermosa como los rayos del sol*, you are as beautiful as the rays of the sun. . . ."

Fat and ageing, the woman still retained the racial susceptibility of a New Mexican to love songs in the moonlight. She seemed to hesitate.

"*Pues*, I am not *Señorita* Liria, I tell you," she said in a pout. "And those shots. What happened in the *entrada*? What are you doing in here?"

"The American *soldados* are probably after some drunken peon," he said.

He could hear the faint sounds of shouting and the soldiers beating on the door of the *zaguán* on the other side of the stables, and he let the song swell to hide the noise. The Mexicans were used to the soft plunk of the *guitarra*, or the raucous sound of the Yankee trader's fiddle, but never such music as this. Vidal's own strange melancholy seemed to enter his violin, and the little *canción* rose to the soft moon, sad and sweet and heartrending, casting its subtle spell over the woman. When Vidal began backing toward the spindled doorway in the wall of the *placita* behind him, she followed, a rapt expression on her round face.

"*Dios*, *trovador*, how you play that violin," she murmured. "It takes me back to my youth. I was beautiful then. Many *galantes* sang beneath my window."

"You are still beautiful," he said. "You must be Liria Bazan."

She laughed softly, pleased despite herself. "What an atrocious liar you are, and how I love it! You know I'm not Liria Bazan. I am only Rosa. If you want *Señorita* Liria, go to La Fonda. She is stopping there on her way to Taos, with her uncle, *Don* Bernal Bazan."

"Oh," he said, "La Fonda." And, for a moment, a satisfaction showed in his eyes.

The noise outside grew louder than his song, and the woman frowned. "The *patrón* . . ."

"What do I want with *Señorita* Liria," he said swiftly, kicking open the door in the wall behind him. "I came to woo the most beautiful woman in Santa Fe, and I have found her. And not only *canciónes* do I bring, fair Rosa, but a gift for your beauty. A turquoise bracelet made by the Navajos, perhaps? A damask shawl from Sevilla? A silver necklace from Mexico City?"

As he spoke, the things appeared magically from beneath his coat, the damask spilling out from his hand in shimmering folds, the turquoise gleaming faintly in his other palm. A strange intent look crossed his pale face then, and he reached beneath the fool's coat once more.

"Or a ring, perhaps, from Spain, fair Rosa? A very old ring . . ."

Her eyes widened at the glittering array, and she followed him as he backed through the door into another smaller *placita*. With a foot, he shut the spindled gate, closing off the sounds from the outer *zaguán*. The woman's fascinated gaze rested on the ring for a moment. Perhaps she didn't recognize the pinpoints of light surrounding the heraldic crest as diamonds. She was only a simple peasant.

"*Dios*," she said, "where did you get all this? You must have traveled everywhere. The shawl?"

He tried to keep the disappointment from his voice. "You don't want the *anillo*, the ring? Only tell me what is inscribed on the inside, and it is yours."

"My husband would think I stole the *anillo*," she

said. "But I could say the *patrona* gave me the shawl."

He shrugged, and let the damask slip out of his hands into hers, and put the other things back into the myriad pockets inside his voluminous coat.

"Perhaps you could tell me how to get to La Fonda without going out of here the same way I came in," he said, and the subtle spell of his violin drew that rapt expression to her face again. "I would not want to be mistaken for that foolish, drunken, peon the *soldados* are after."

She pulled the shawl across her fat shoulders, stroking it with wide grateful eyes. "*Dios, Señor Trovador*, you are too kind. La Fonda? You go through that door behind you, and then another one beyond that, and find yourself in San Francisco Street. La Fonda is eastward on the *calle*, at the corner of the plaza. . . ."

She looked up suddenly, and he could see the surprise on her face as she realized he had backed clear across the *placita* while she was speaking.

"*Gracias*, Rosa *mía*," he murmured, and slipped through the door there, and let it shut softly behind him.

The door on the other side of this next *placita* led him into San Francisco Street; farther south, hidden from him by the turn the street took before it became the *entrada*, he could still hear the soldiers milling around the *zaguán*, and he couldn't help thinking about it again, as he always did, whenever he saw soldiers, or was reminded of anything connected with them. So they were sending the third patrol north, now. They didn't know what was going on up there. They just sent them, one after another, blindly. The stupid, narrow, bigoted . . . He stopped himself. He had promised himself he wouldn't feel like that any more. He really had no cause for bitterness. Why should they have listened to him or believed him, then, when nothing had started up here yet, when he could show them nothing concrete? And now, with it happening, what else could they do? Nothing. Nothing but send their futile patrols up there and watch them disappear and not know why, or when, or how.

"*Buenas noches, Señor Vidal.*" The man stood in the black shadows beneath an overhanging balcony. He was dressed in the white cotton shirt and pants of a peon, with a ragged serape over one stooped shoulder. From beneath the huge roll brim of his steeple sombrero, Vidal caught the intensely bitter eyes set in a pale, mordant face, and for a moment he was swept with the impression of having seen them before. He gestured vaguely with one hand.

"You . . . ?"

"Tomás," said the peon, and his voice held the same vibrant intensity as his eyes, "if you want a name. *Sí*, Tomás. I saw your escape from the soldiers. I didn't think you would come out the same way you went in. But then, your father was always a clever man, too, wasn't he? Jacques Vidal? Came to the Green River country from France to trap, about Eighteen Hundred Sixteen, wasn't it?"

"There are many Frenchmen among the trappers," said Vidal. "And many Vidals. A Black Vidal at Laramie in 'Thirty-Four. A Pierre Vidal in the Big Horns."

"This Jacques Vidal grew prosperous trapping the Green River," said the man with a soft insistence. "So prosperous, in fact, that he was able to send his son to West Point. That is a long way from Santa Fe, *Señor* Vidal. Did you walk the whole distance?"

— II —

It was La Fonda that next heard the haunting music of the *trovador*'s battered Stradivarius. The old inn stood on the southwest corner of the plaza, a sprawling structure of adobe, the hollow block of guest rooms surrounding an inner patio where gaming tables lined the walls and dances were held whenever the wagon trains came in off the Santa Fe Trail. The taproom, spacious and oak-paneled with round deal tables on one side, opened onto both this patio and the street outside.

The peon who called himself Tomás had left

Vidal there in San Francisco Street, with a last bitter glance skulking away into an alley. Still trying to recall the face, the latter slipped unobtrusively into La Fonda. There was a huge Yaqui Indian with a shaved head leaning both elbows on the bar in front of the barkeep. His buckskin leggings were belted with a string of silver bosses as big as teacups and into the belt was thrust a long-handled hatchet with a bright, polished blade of Yankee steel.

Beyond the bald Indian, a woman sat alone at one of the rear tables, apparently awaiting others, as the dinner service was set for three. A *criado* stood against the wall behind her, a Navajo retainer, his black cloak falling to the knees of buckskins, his black hat shadowing a sullen watchful face. Vidal knew it would be indiscreet to approach her, but he had come so far, and it had been so long. . . .

"May I sing for you, *Señorita* Bazan?" he said. "Dance? Joke?"

She tossed her dark head angrily. "Please go away. I am in no mood for your jokes."

The violin was in his hands, and the sweet strains floated through the room, causing the Yaqui with the shaved head to turn around. Vidal saw the sudden interest in the woman's big soft eyes. It was always that way. His music was magic.

"A love song, perhaps," murmured the *trovador*.

"Liria, *tu eres la flora de Nicaragua*, you are the flower of Nicaragua. . . ."

The *criado* moved away from the wall, and the woman half turned in her chair to halt him with an imperious wave of her bejeweled hand, speaking to Vidal: "Please. You play very beautifully, but you must know how improper this is. Even if I were with my *duenna* . . ."

"A gift, then," he said, and the things began appearing in his deft hands. "A parting gift to your rare beauty, *Señorita* Liria. Surely you can accept something as a compliment. A bracelet made by the Navajos. Pearl earrings from Barbados. A ring from Sevilla . . ."

She bent forward. "Where did you get that ring?"

His voice strained. "It is yours, *señorita*, if you will only tell me what is engraved on the inside."

His eyes took on a dark intensity, watching her, and the fingers around the ring were pale from the force of their grip. She tossed her head angrily.

"Fool. How would I know what is engraved on the inside?"

"Conchita! What are you doing?"

The voice stiffened Vidal. Slowly his melancholy face turned toward the elephantine figure pacing through the door leading from the inner patio. The man was the biggest Mexican Vidal had ever seen, standing close to seven feet tall in his high gray beaver. He had a girth to match his height, carrying a truly remarkable paunch in his white marseille waistcoat, and the skirts of his heavy double-breasted Inverness slapped at moleskin trousers threatening to burst with the pressure of thighs as big around as Vidal's own waist. His multitude of rather greasy chins were hidden somewhat by a black goatee, and a network of tiny, bluish veins patterned his quivering jowls, the rolls of sallow flesh puffing dissolutely beneath his small, bloodshot eyes.

"*Señor*"—his voice deafened Vidal—"are you molesting my daughter?"

Corday Vidal smiled, backing away in a shuffling two-step, drawing a few notes from his violin. "Ah, *señor*, how could I molest such a lovely creature? I only wished to sing a song for her. I am only a *pobre trovador*."

"*Bah!*" The stout oak chair almost collapsed beneath the huge man as he lowered himself prodigiously into it, turning to the woman. "I should have known better than to leave you alone, Conchita. Always getting into trouble with some man. Santiago, what a daughter"—he turned impatiently toward the door—"and you, come along, come along. We will have supper before leaving."

Vidal saw the other woman for the first time as she came in the door from where she had been standing in the shadows outside. She wore a dark blue *capisayo* that fell to the toes of her red satin slippers, its silk-lined hood hiding her face. The *trovador* caught a hint of delicately arched eyebrows as she glanced at him, and luminous black eyes. Then she had seated herself, face turned down. Two *criados* had come in behind her; they stood against the wall, ominous figures in their black cloaks and black, flat-topped hats.

"*Por supuesto, trovador,*" said the gross Mexican. "Play your songs, then. Perhaps it will entertain us, eh? But I warn you, I am a hard man to please. I am *Don* Bernal Bazan, and it goes badly with you if you don't amuse me. Eh?"

The *doncellita* came from the kitchen, a blowsy serving maid with pouting lips, and, while she served *huevas del rancho* and steaming mutton, Vidal began one of the local *decimas*, a parody that satirized famous people of the province. He puffed up and threw his stomach out, stomping around and blustering like Manuel Armijo, who had been the Mexican governor of Santa Fe when the Americans came, and who had been hated by the New Mexicans as heartily as the *gringos*.

"Armijo *es eso.*" Vidal patted his outthrust belly, and the violin mocked with a raucous laugh. "Armijo *es eso.*" He leered at the gold *peso* that had suddenly appeared in his hand, and the violin emitted a shrill catcall.

The gross *Don* Bazan began to chuckle, and his quivering paunch jiggled the table up and down, clattering the silver service. He took up a tankard of grape wine, still watching Vidal. The *trovador* postured around the room, imitating Armijo's well-known voice, roaring imprecations on the officials of Mexico for discovering his amazing system of graft, punctuating every move with bursts of almost human laughter from his violin.

The fat Mexican suddenly choked on his drink, unable to contain himself any longer. He spewed out the wine, almost upsetting the table as he leaned forward, breaking into uproarious laughter. "*¡En el nombre de Dios, señor!*" he bellowed, wiping his mouth, sputtering. "What an impersonation! I have never laughed so hard in all my life. You look more like Armijo than Armijo himself. Here"—he threw a buckskin bag of gold pieces on the floor—"tell me how you do it?"

Vidal bowed, and the bag disappeared somewhere into his outlandish coat. "Mimicry is one of a *trovador*'s accomplishments, *Don* Bazan. The Vidals have been mimes for centuries."

"You are French?"

"I am descended directly from Pierre Vidal," said the *trovador*, "the most famous *jongleur* France ever had. My family has kept the tradition alive ever since the Twelfth Century, when the fabulous Pierre played for the nobility of Provence, and even for the English King, Richard the Lionhearted. . . ."

"Play the *degüello!*"

It was a loud voice. It was a drunken voice. It was the voice of the Yaqui with the shaven skull who stood at the bar.

"But the *degüello* is for the bugle, *señor*," said Vidal.

"*Sí*," rumbled *Don* Bazan, "and it is Santa Anna's call for 'no quarter', if you recall. It would be indiscreet, would it not, *Señor* Yaqui, to play that here. New Mexico is an American territory now, after all."

The Indian lurched away from the bar. "We are still Mexicans here. Play the *degüello*."

Vidal smiled placatingly. "A *canción*, perhaps . . ."

The *trovador*'s coat ripped as the huge Indian caught it in one fist, jerking Vidal up against his sweaty torso. In the other fist glittered the axe.

"Play the *degüello* or I'll split your . . ."

The Indian's words ended in a gasp that contorted his face. Vidal's long fingers had closed around the fist holding the lapels of his vari-colored coat. The *trovador* was still smiling, and he didn't seem to be putting forth much effort with his probing fingers. But the huge bald-pated Yaqui cringed backward, releasing the coat. He forgot about his axe. Face stamped with that agony, he jerked spasmodically back and forth, trying desperately to release his fist from Vidal's grasp. The *trovador*'s long, pale fingers opened, and he took a step backward. With a strangled cry, the Yaqui lifted his axe again.

"*Señor*," said Vidal, and his soft voice emanated an ineffable threat that held the Indian there for that moment, "I am also a juggler."

The first knife appeared in Vidal's hand as if by magic, a wickedly gleaming stiletto with a blade as long as the Frenchman's forearm. It flipped into the air, and, before it descended into his hand again, another knife had appeared. A moment later, six stilettos were whirling through the air, forming a continuous flickering chain of gleaming steel in front of Vidal's faint smile. The Indian stood rigid, eyes fixed on the knives in a fascinated way. A playing card appeared in Vidal's fingers.

"The king of spades, *señor*," said Vidal. "Even emperors are not immune to a juggler's skill, you see."

Still juggling the knives in that continuous chain, he flipped the card into the air. The deft jerk of his right hand was hardly perceptible, but from it sped one of the stilettos. The blade caught the card while it was yet in mid-air. There was a solid *plunk*. The knife was quivering in the wall behind the bar, its blade piercing the playing card and holding it against the wood.

"*¡Por Dios!*" gasped the barkeep.

Without breaking that circle of flashing blades, Vidal threw another one, and its glittering path carried the Indian's eyes again to the wall, striking the center of the card just below the first blade.

Another knife plunked into the card, and yet another, and the fourth blade completed the work of the first three, cutting the cardboard completely in two, and before the first stiletto had stopped quivering, the two pieces of the king of spades fluttered to the floor. Vidal was still juggling the two remaining knives, and still smiling in that strange, melancholy way.

For a moment, no one made a sound. The two women were watching Vidal, wide-eyed; the barkeep's mouth hung open slightly. The Yaqui's face was flushed; he tried to speak, and his lips worked around words that wouldn't come out, and he shut his mouth again. Finally *Don* Bazan hoisted himself from the chair.

"Perhaps that will teach you, *Señor* Yaqui," he roared. "You bald coyote. You are incredible, Vidal. Six *cuchillos* at once!"

The Indian turned suddenly, lurched to the bar. He picked up the silver mug he had been drinking from, then slammed it down again. He was still holding the axe as he went to the door with heavy, angry stride. He turned around there, and seemed about to speak again. But his eyes were drawn to those two remaining stilettos, still curling in a lazy circle from Vidal's pale, deft hands in front of Vidal's pale, soft smile. A strangled snarl was all the Yaqui could get out. He whirled and shoved open the door, and it slammed shut violently behind him.

"I would like to see more of your singular repertoire," *Don* Bazan said, "but, unfortunately, we must be on our way."

The woman who had been at the table when Vidal first arrived went past him now, following the gross Bazan to the door. She threw a puzzled glance at the *trovador*, then went on. What had Bazan called her? Conchita?

The second woman seemed to hesitate in front of Vidal. Again he caught those wide, luminous eyes beneath the hood of her blue *capisayo*. This time he was close enough to make a query at what was in them. Fear?

"Liria!" called *Don* Bazan, waiting by the door. Vidal stood there looking at the *portal* a long time after it had swung shut behind them. Finally he heard the *clink* of steel on the bar.

"Your *cuchillos, señor*," said the barkeep. "Your knives."

Vidal turned and picked up the knives, slipping them one by one beneath his coat. "*Señorita* Liria is *muy bonita*."

"*Sí, sí*," agreed the barkeep. "Very beautiful."

"I would not want to be going to Taos with them tonight."

The barkeep swabbed angrily at the unpainted pine with a dirty cloth. "You, too? Why, *señor*? Why is everyone talking that way? Cheyennes in from Bent's Fort the other day. Winter six months off, and they head south already. What are they

242

afraid of? Nothing has happened. A few trappers disappeared there, a wagon train. That is nothing new."

"Perhaps, this time, it is," said Vidal.

"What about the soldiers?"

"Soldiers? What soldiers? What about them?"

Captain Dunn had been right, then, thought Vidal. Those patrols had ridden north under sealed orders, and the civilians didn't know they were missing yet. The Department must have begun to realize how serious this was, if they did the thing like that.

Vidal shrugged. "Never mind. You were speaking of the wagon train that disappeared."

The barkeep nodded. "Hagerman's spring wagon train, last April. The Indians've been doing that ever since Becknell opened the trail in 'Twenty-Two."

"There's talk it wasn't Indians this time," said Vidal.

"Talk, talk, talk," muttered the barman. "That's all I hear. That's all this whole thing is. Rumors. Stories. Talk. Nobody knows what they're afraid of. Nobody can put their finger on anything specific. What do you think it is?"

"*Dios* knows," said Vidal, flipping a coin onto the bar. "And perhaps a woman . . ."

The barkeep watched him walk to the door. Then he laughed, and took the gold piece. "*Que un loco*," he muttered.

Vidal stepped into the chill night and let the door close softly behind him. A *carroza* was rumbling away from him across the plaza, a black coach drawn by four midnight stallions surrounded by a party of outriders in cloaks and hats of the same hue.

"*Don* Bazan is leaving so soon," said a sibilantly intense voice from beside Vidal. "Too bad you couldn't see more of him."

Vidal whirled to meet the bitter black eyes of the peon who had called himself Tomás. Then, from the other side, Vidal caught a spasmodic grunt. He threw himself forward, ahead the blow, and the huge Yaqui with the shaved head crashed down across his body, his axe striking the ground on the other side. Vidal whipped over on his back beneath the Indian's great struggling weight. Tomás threw himself on them, clubbed gun gleaming. The butt struck Vidal's head and stunned him and sickened him and knocked all coherent thought from him in that moment. Yet some desperate animal instinct still forced his body into a spasmodic struggle, and he fought from beneath the Indian. One of his kicking feet caught the man on his shaven skull. The Yaqui howled with pain.

"Shut up," hissed Tomás, "you'll wake every American soldier in the palace. . . ."

His words ended with a harsh grunt as he struck again at Vidal. The *trovador* rolled from beneath the gun, gaining his feet with a surprising alacrity, and twisted to grab the Indian's arm. The Yaqui must have remembered those long fingers; he jerked away spasmodically. Vidal caught the long axe handle and wrenched it free. He shoved it back into the man's face almost with the same motion. As the Yaqui fell back against the adobe wall of La Fonda with a scream, the gun butt struck Vidal's head from behind. He went to his knees, his numb fingers dropping the axe, only dimly aware of the peon's shifting move behind him.

"*Espía*," gasped Tomás, and his gun whipped down again. "Spy!"

Still on his knees, Vidal lurched around, taking the blow on his shoulder. His whole right side paralyzed by pain; he caught his left arm around behind Tomás's jerking knees and threw his weight against him. Tomás fell backward with Vidal sprawling on top of him.

Dimly Vidal sensed the troopers running out of the Palace of the Governors across the plaza. One of them had a torch. Tomás saw it was no use trying to do it silently now, and he had the gun reversed by the time Vidal had clutched his wrist. The first shot deafened Vidal, hot lead whipping through his coat as he twisted the man's wrist desperately. Tomás writhed beneath him, trying to re-cock the gun. The Yaqui moaned from behind, trying to rise with the help of the wall. The light of the torch reached them dimly as the soldiers passed the sundial in the center of the square. Still moving in a sick haze of pain, Vidal struggled to one knee above the struggling peon. He ground a foot down on the man's wrist. Tomás gasped; his fingers opened spasmodically; the gun slipped from them.

Vidal was on his feet then, trying to kick free of Tomás's clawing hands. The peon hung on grimly, striving to pull himself up.

"What's going on over there?" shouted one of the soldiers.

Mouth twisting, Vidal raised a leg. Tomás saw his intent and tried to grab the foot, yelling hoarsely. Vidal stamped his boot hard into the man's face.

"Halt!" yelled one of the American soldiers. "Halt, or I'll fire!"

"Not right now, *compadre*," said Vidal, and he was already a stumbling shadow merging with the other shadows in San Francisco Street on the other side of La Fonda.

— **III** —

It was on July 24th that the ancient pueblo of San Fernando de Taos first heard the *trovador*'s sad Stradivarius. *Don* Bernal Bazan was giving his annual *fiesta* that celebrated San Juan Day, and the inner *placitas* of the huge Bazan house on Ojitos Lane were filled with the gay laughter of red-lipped women and the soft gallantry of black-haired *caballeros*. There were many entertainers, and even several other *trovadores* playing mandolins and *guitarras*, and Corday Vidal, moving through the crowds with the dust of the old Pecuris Trail still gray on his outlandish coat, did not attract undue attention.

"*Adiós, mi chaparrita,*" he sang, and his melancholy eyes roved constantly, seeking her. "*No llores por tu Pancho. . . .*"

A woman laughed. "Where do you come from, *trovador?*"

She wore a red satin gown cut low about her bosom, and her hair matched the black depths of her eyes. He looked at those eyes, wondering if this could be the one. Her face, down at La Fonda, had been shadowed by the hood of that *capisayo*, and all he had seen clearly had been her eyes.

"I am from Mexico City, *señorita*, and Durango, and El Paso." He bowed. "I come with a song for your beauty, and a gift. A turquoise bracelet, perhaps, from the Navajos? A pelisse from Paris, a ring from Sevilla . . ."

Her smile condescending, the woman felt the pelisse with a red-tipped forefinger, then the condescension left her lips, and she caught the cloth up with her whole hand, caressing it.

"*Dios,*" she said, "I didn't think you could find

material like this outside of Spain. Where did you get it?"

"The ring," said Vidal, studying her eyes, "is set with diamonds."

"Jewels." The woman pouted, still feeling the pelisse. "I can get jewels anytime. *Pues*, this *rebozo* . . ."

No, he decided, they were not deep enough, the eyes, or soft enough. He shrugged disappointedly, letting the pelisse slip from his hands into hers.

"It is yours, and, when you wear it, you wear the heart of a poor *trovador*. . . ." He wandered on through the laughing crowds, stopping here and there to sing a song, a tall, ragged figure in an outlandish coat who could alternately make the men laugh with his wonderful mimicry or make the women sigh with some strange, sad *canción* from his violin.

He saw *Don* Bernal Bazan in one of the inner patios, sitting in a huge throne-like chair, laughing drunkenly, and he slipped back into the crowd before the *don* saw him. Discouraged, he stopped finally at one of the long tables set beneath the adobe walls, and was reaching for some of the *abondigas* rolled in cornmeal and heaped up on a platter amid the other food that loaded the planks. His long-fingered hand stiffened suddenly above the steaming heaps.

She stood at the other end of the table, talking to a pair of sharp-faced *vaqueros* in buckskin leggings, split up the side in the traditional manner, to show the snowy drawers worn beneath. Her eyes were on Vidal for just that moment, and he wondered how he could even have considered the other eyes before. Suddenly she pulled her hand off one man's arm, and turned toward the house, disappearing into the gloom of a doorway without a backward glance.

Vidal took up his violin, and began singing a *canción*. He moved unhurriedly after her. He stopped beside the two men she had been talking with, singing a ribald verse for them; one laughed and tossed him a *peso*. Then Vidal was beyond them, and through the door.

The lower halls were filled with servants passing back and forth, carrying plates full of food outside, bringing back the empty ones, chattering incessantly. He didn't bother with the kitchens or serving rooms at the rear, and soon found she wasn't among the group of softly talking *duennas* in the front parlor. Then it was the upper halls, dark and empty and tomb-like in their echoing silence.

Thoughtfully, now, he began to play again. Not the sprightly songs he had been performing, or the popular ballads. When he was alone, he often played like this—music that rose almost inaudibly at first to the *viga* poles forming the rafters above, then swelling gradually to fill the hall with sound such as it had never heard before, and would probably never hear again. His face still wore that sad melancholy look, but his eyes were almost closed.

"I never heard a *trovador* play Schubert before, *señor*."

He showed no surprise, because it was what he had been waiting for, and he had not been lost as deeply in his playing as it had appeared. She stood in the doorway he had just passed. Her luxuriant hair was piled beneath a high comb, over which was thrown the delicate pattern of a snowy lace *mantilla*; her gown was some sort of dark brocade that brought out the startling white of her shoulders. He sensed the suppressed fear in the whole rigid line of her slim body, the taut huski-ness of her voice.

"*Señorita*." He bowed. "I am no ordinary *trovador*. I have seen the world, and from every place in which I stopped, I bring a gift for such as yourself. You wear no *rebozo*. A damask, perhaps, from the Orient? No jewelry. A ring, from Sevilla . . . ?"

Her small hand caught at his ragged sleeve, and he was inside the room, with her closing the heavy iron-bound door behind them and standing rigidly against it, palms pressed to the hand-carved paneling.

"Where did you get that ring?"

"The ring?" he said. "It is yours, *señorita*, if you but tell me what is inscribed on the inside of its golden band."

Her voice trembled slightly. *"Recibe mi corazón, recibe mi amor, recibe mi vida. . . ."*

"You have won my heart," he repeated, "you have won my love, you have won my life. *Sí*, that is the inscription."

Her breath ·made a harsh sound. "That's what you were doing at La Fonda, trying to reach me?"

He pressed the ring into her hand, surprised at how cold her fingers were. "I heard you were in Mexico City. That was last January. I missed you there. Your uncle had already taken you away from El Paso by the time I reached that town."

"I was south seeking word of my brother, Morales Bazan," she said, and her voice broke. "He was reported missing after the battle of Monterey in September of 'Forty-Six. I wouldn't believe he was dead without proof. And now, this ring . . ."

He had sensed how little time they would have here together, and how quickly it would have to be done, and he forced himself to tell her. "Your brother . . . died at the battle of Monterey."

She stiffened, and for a moment he thought she would fall. He reached out to her. She shook her head, blinking back tears.

"There's no time for that now, is there?" she choked. "I'm all right. Just the shock. I'm all right. You came here for more than just to tell me that. My brother gave you the ring. He must have told you what he was doing."

"The *revolucionarios*?" said Vidal.

Her mouth twisted with the effort of controlling her grief. "*Sí*, the revolutionists. Morales belonged to them. I do. They are the faction in Santa Fe that favored the Americans, the faction that has always opposed the tyranny of the Mexican government. For four centuries, *señor*, this northern province of New Mexico has been treated abominably by the mother government in Mexico City. At first, the revolutionist movement up here was only among the Indians, who had rebelled against the rule of Mexico ever since Spain conquered this country. Then, when Governor Armijo began his despotism in Eighteen Thirty-Six, as the Mexican governor in Santa Fe, even the *ricos*, like ourselves, began to join the *revolucionarios*. My brother received his military training at West Point. He graduated in Eighteen Forty-Four and came here to take a commission in the Mexican army. Nothing was suspected at that time, for many officers of the Mexican army were trained at your academy. But even then Morales belonged to the revolutionists. When the war broke out two years later, and he saw that the intention of the United States was to annex New Mexico, thus overthrowing the rule that he had rebelled against for so long, Morales contacted your Military Intelligence at once. It was his information that saved Quitman's corps from being wiped out at Cerro Gordo. He did other valuable work for your Army. The last word I had from him, he was with Ampudía's Second Mexican Dragoons at Monterey."

Vidal nodded. "General Ampudía was trying to stop the advance of the Missouri Volunteers down Saltillo Highway. I came across your brother in a ditch, pinned beneath his wounded horse. He said he'd been trying to contact our intelligence for some time. Told me something was starting up here in New Mexico, something that threatened Kearny's whole Western Army, something that meant we'd lose New Mexico and California right back to Mexico . . . doubly dangerous because it wouldn't come off until after the armistice had been signed, when the military had relaxed and withdrawn most of its forces from these territories. He said he didn't have many details, said the revolutionaries up here would know more, being closer to it. He gave me this ring. Whoever could tell me what was inscribed on the inside was all right. That other woman who was with you at La Fonda. Conchita?"

"She recognized the ring?" said Liria Bazan, then shook her head. "But she couldn't tell you the inscription, could she? Conchita is not a revolutionist. She is my cousin, the daughter of *Don* Bernal Bazan. The ring is a family heirloom, given to my great-grandmother by her husband many years ago, back in Sevilla. That's how Conchita recognized it. *Pues*, she has no aware-

253

ness of the intrigue that is going on around her all the time. The only thing she can concentrate on for over five minutes is a dance, or a man. I don't think she told her father about it."

"Morales was going to tell me what he knew," said Vidal, "but the battle was still going on around us, and all he'd gotten out was what I just told you, when a troop of Mexican dragoons passed by. One of them spotted us . . ." He trailed off, remembering the rearing horse looming up out of the shredding gunsmoke, the face of that dragoon, thin and bitter and haughty, the booming gun, and then Morales staggering.

"That's how . . ."—she faltered—"that's how it happened?"

Vidal nodded grimly. "The shot finished Morales. It almost seemed as if that Mexican officer had picked him out first."

"Probably," she said. "Morales was in contact with us. He said some of his brother officers were beginning to suspect him of spying for your Army. One especially. A Colonel Ugardes."

Vidal held out his hand in a helpless gesture. "I couldn't do anything for him, Liria. Morales, I mean. He . . ."

"I understand," she said. "And I'm glad you escaped. And I understand what you must have gone through trying to find us up here. The Mexicans loyal to the old government are known as Santanistas, after the party created by General

Santa Anna when he at last returned from exile to command the army. They are so bitter with the *revolucionarios* that even now, with New Mexico an American military territory, the Santanistas are still bent on stamping out my party. There are not many *revolucionarios* left."

"That's why it was so hard to contact you," he said. "What revolutionists I did come across, knew you only by name. I heard you were in Mexico City. Missed you there. At El Paso, I made the mistake of letting it be known I was hunting for you, got the Santanistas on my neck for that. It was the last time I asked for you openly. Even so, the Santanistas must have followed me. One down in Santa Fe. Called himself Tomás . . ." He broke off, caught her shoulders. "It's begun to happen already, hasn't it? Up north. Three patrols have been swallowed up there. The civilians don't know about that, but you must."

He saw that fear darken her eyes again. "*Sí*, the *revolucionarios* know of the missing troops. But we haven't been able to find out much. Many of us have disappeared trying to get to the bottom of it. I've been practically helpless. My uncle, *Don* Bernal, suspects me of belonging to the revolutionists. He's kept me a virtual prisoner."

"Prisoner?"

She saw the look in his face, spoke swiftly. "No, *señor*. You can't do that. I'm in no danger from *Don* Bernal as long as he only suspects. If you tried to help me escape, they'd know you were more than just a poor *trovador*. That would finish everything. You're one of the few remaining who isn't under suspicion, one of the last among us who can move with comparative freedom, who has a chance, at least, of finding out what is happening. And you must. I'm sorry I can't help you more. I can only send you farther north. Several revolutionists have disappeared up there, trying to find out. The last one I have been in contact with was trapping the country north of the Arkansas River. If he is still alive, you will be able to contact him near Bent's Fort. I've never seen him myself. You'll have to find him the way you found the others, and me. Here, the ring. He'll know the inscription on the inside."

She pressed the ring back into his hand, and for a moment her palm was soft against his fingers, and a strange searching look came into her great, luminous eyes as they met his. He felt dizzy suddenly, and wondered why, and then knew why. Her eyes were running over his face, as if to impress it in her memory; her hand seemed to tighten on his.

"*Señor*," she said, and there was a husky catch to her voice. "Before you go. Tell me . . . who are you, really?"

He was about to answer when he saw the glance go past his head, and her face go pale. She let go of his hand. He bowed swiftly, backing away, and the violin appeared from beneath his coat.

"I am a humble *trovador, señorita,* a poor ragged *juglar* who seeks only to amuse you. . . ."

"Are you now?" asked *Don* Bernal Bazan from behind him. "Eh? Are you now."

There was another man with the *don,* a slim foppish man in tight broadcloth trousers and a bottle-green coat trimmed with gilt. His blond hair was queued in the style still affected in this backward province, and his nose beaked haughtily over the supercilious, contemptuous smile with which he regarded Vidal.

"*Dios,* those stairs," panted *Don* Bazan, lowering himself into a chair by the door. He took out a purple handkerchief and mopped at his perspiring brow, then waved the cloth at the fop. "*Señor* Vidal, this is *Señor* Cray Lucas, the Santa Fe agent for Hagerman Shippers. We heard your violin, and followed the sound of it up here. Schubert, wasn't it? The *Konzertstück*?"

"The D Major." Vidal bowed.

"Isn't it rather odd," said Cray Lucas, tilting his nose slightly, "to find a . . . a minstrel playing such stuff."

"No," said *Don* Bazan. "No, not odd at all. *Señor* Vidal is no ordinary minstrel. He is descended from the fabulous Pierre Vidal who bewitched the fair ladies of Provence in the Twelfth Century. Eh, Vidal? *Sí.* And you should see him juggle, *Señor* Lucas. Knives. Eh?" There was something sly in his chuckle. "I am what you might call a lover of the arts, too. Do you play anything else, Vidal? Classic, I mean."

Vidal slipped the violin under his chin, and his strange dark eyes closed, and the faint tautness drawing his mouth thin relaxed, and he began to play. It was an eerie melody, soft at first, but insistent, holding them all in a strained, listening silence while it reached its *accelerando*, growing faster and faster and swelling to a wild shrill *crescendo* that ended with an abruptness that snapped *Don* Bazan up in his chair as if jerked from a trance.

He laughed shakily, dabbing perspiring jowls. "What a weird *canción*."

"The 'Dance of Death.'" Vidal smiled strangely.

Cray Lucas said: "Rather morbid, I say."

"My own . . . composition," Vidal said. "Perhaps also my own death."

"Eh?" said *Don* Bazan. "Ah, yes. Again. *Por supuesto*, you play masterfully. Your *pizzicati* are marvelous."

"A veritable Paganini," said Cray Lucas.

Sensing the mockery in the man's nasal voice, Vidal felt himself flush. His hand closed a little on his bow. Then he bowed stiffly. Bazan took a handful of *reales* from his pocket, tossing them to Vidal.

"That is for staying, *Señor* Vidal. I would hear more of your wonderful music. But hereafter I would advise you to confine your wanderings to the men's quarters, eh? After all"—he chuckled, shrugged gross shoulders, turned to Liria Bazan —"I would like to speak with you, my niece."

Vidal stooped to pick up the coins *Don* Bazan had thrown. He moved out the door, and heard the blond dandy follow him. From inside, *Don* Bazan's voice, speaking to the girl, covered whatever sound Cray Lucas made drawing Vidal over to the window of the hall.

"How many gold pieces did *Don* Bazan offer you to stay?" asked the fop.

"I think there were three or four," said Vidal.

Lucas took a handful of *reales* from his pocket and began counting them into Vidal's hand. "I'll give you twice as many . . . to leave."

"May I ask why?" said Vidal.

Lucas let the last coin *clink* into Vidal's hand; he had been looking out the window; now he inclined his head toward the hand-carved spindles forming the grille. Through the bars, Vidal could see down into one of the *placitas* that he had played in. A man had entered through the door set in a *zaguán*, and was making his way through the crowd toward the house. He was a huge Yaqui with head shaved perfectly clean and a big axe thrust into his belt.

"They call him El Hacho," said Cray Lucas. "Which means The Axe. Is that a good enough reason?"

— IV —

Many strange places heard the subtle music of the *trovador*'s violin after he played the "Dance of Death" at Taos, but the strangest of all, perhaps, was the row of graves. From early times, the troubadours of Europe had wandered about the country, accorded a singular immunity, welcomed wherever they went by evil men and good, for the entertainment they provided. In this new land, Vidal found himself accorded that same immunity, and had discovered that it was far safer for him, traveling alone as he did, to go openly, playing and singing all day long, whether passing through the comparative safety of a town, or the most dangerous Indian hunting grounds.

The white men who didn't welcome his songs and jokes were rare and left him alone, dismissing him as a ragged fool with no more harm in him than a fig, which not even the children bothered to knock off the branch unless they were hungry. The Indians, who would have killed any other man on the spot, thought Vidal crazy because no one in his right mind would walk around making so much noise in a country where even a heavy breath might bring instant death. So they left him scrupulously alone, as they let all crazy men alone.

Thus it was that Vidal was playing his *canción* as he came down the northern slope of Raton Pass, and thus it was that he came across the row of graves, a whole line of ominous mounds from which emanated the cloying scent of freshly turned earth. After a time, he realized how long he had stood there, and he lifted his violin and moved on down the hill, breaking into the song again. He had almost reached the bottom when he halted once more. The man standing in the shadows of the aspens beside the trail was slim and neat in fringed buckskins, a Paterson revolving carbine gleaming bluely in one hand.

"Well," he said, "a veritable Paganini."

Vidal didn't answer for a moment, because he had expected someone soon, but not this one, and he couldn't help his surprise. "I thought you'd be somewhere near," said the *trovador* finally. "The graves had been dug so recently."

Cray Lucas inclined his blond head over one shoulder. "My camp's back in the gully. I'm afraid I don't share your trust in our fellow man."

The man's horse was tethered near a smokeless fire, burning deep in the gorge cut by a river that had dried up eons ago, its light hidden by a bank of rocks and dead timber. Lucas hunkered down and gave his black-tail steaks a turn on their spit. Vidal lowered his tattered possible sack off one shoulder, watching the man narrowly, and squatted, too.

"You'll have to pardon me if I'm not the perfect host," said Lucas. "Those graves were rather tiring. That was Hagerman's summer train . . . at least it was the men from his spring train. I didn't find any trace of the wagons. Funny thing. The corpses still retained all their members, and they hadn't been scalped. Would that be Indians?"

"I take it you don't think so," said Vidal.

Lucas shifted the gurgling coffee pot on its rocks. "Hagerman lost another train last spring. I didn't see the remains of that one, but those who did claimed the bodies hadn't been mutilated, either, or scalped. Both trains hauling military supplies, a consignment of Springfield Yergers for Colonel Price on this one. My bet is you find the men who didn't scalp those teamsters and you find the Springfield Yergers with them."

Vidal tuned his violin, realizing what a consummate actor Cray Lucas was. He had been completely taken in by the man's supercilious foppery down at Taos. "I thought you were the Santa Fe agent for Hagerman Shippers," he said.

"I am," muttered Lucas, then looked up. "And you?"

"Don't you remember?" asked Vidal. "I'm a *trovador*. Jokes, songs, laughter . . . ," he trailed off, and a strange look crossed his face. He looked at Lucas with a sudden new intensity. "And wherever I go, Lucas, I pick up something. A shawl from Durango, a blade from Damascus, a ring from Sevilla . . ."

They had appeared in his hand, one by one, and Cray Lucas glanced at the golden ring, and spoke softly: "*Recibe mi corazón, recibe, mi amor, recibe mi vida.* You have won my heart, you have won my love . . ."

"You have won my life," finished Vidal, and sat there a long moment with the softly snapping fire the only sound. Finally he spoke again, unbelievingly. "You?"

Lucas shrugged. "Why not? If you can run around like a crazy *trovador*, I can play the fop, can't I? I'm Hagerman's agent all right, but not the kind everyone thinks. Hagerman sent me out last April when his first outfit disappeared. It's something bigger than just those trains, though. It's something connected with what these revolutionists are trying to find. That's how I got in with them. Found our interests all parallel. Since the Santanistas have been on their trail, though, the revolutionists make it a practice not to know one another by sight or name. That way they can't betray each other, even under torture. That's why the girl didn't know me . . . I take it she was the one who sent you. To all concerned, I'm just a fop, see, harmless, if disgusting. And, oh, how disgusting!"

"Why didn't you say something at Bazan's?" asked Vidal.

Lucas leaned toward him, drawing a breath. "If I'd told you who I was, it would have meant telling you what I know, and you'd have played the fool and tried to save the girl."

Vidal was across the fire, long fingers clutching Lucas's narrow shoulders. "You mean she's . . . ?"

"I knew you felt that way about her," Lucas gasped, wincing. "Let go, damn it. I saw it in your face down there when you looked at her. I knew you felt that way. I don't blame you . . . she's a beautiful woman. How do you think I feel? You only knew her a week. I've known her five months."

Vidal released him slowly, eyes widening. "You mean . . . you mean, you sacrificed her deliberately, you left her like that . . . knowing . . . ?"

"Shut up, damn you!" Lucas jumped to his feet. "Do you think I wanted it that way? How do you think I feel? No, you wouldn't know. Your conscience is clear. You didn't leave her deliberately like I did. She lied to you so you'd go, she told you she wasn't in any danger, and didn't tell you who I was, so you'd go, and you went. Maybe you think she didn't want you to get her out of there. Didn't you see the fear in her? Maybe you think I didn't want to tell her who I really was and get her out. A thousand times a day. A million!"

For the first time, Vidal saw the strength in that haughty beak of a nose, the lips that had lost their supercilious curl and were hard and adamant. It would take such a man to leave the woman he loved, deliberately like that. Vidal shook his head. "But why?"

"Can't you see," said Lucas harshly. "Anybody who tries to save her spoils it for himself and for all the rest of us. *Don* Bazan uses her as bait. He's already trapped five other *revolucionarios* who tried to reach her, or save her. Only reason you weren't nabbed is you played your part so well. Who'd suspect a damned fool *trovador*? Not *Don* Bazan . . . you pulled the wool even over his pig eyes. Not even me, till we found you in Liria's room there at Taos. Even then I wasn't sure. But if you'd tried to get Liria out of there, it would have given you away, and, if I'd tried to help her, it would have given me away, and that would have finished whatever chances we have left of finding out what the hell's happening up here. Morales must have told you. It's something that threatens the whole Army of the West. The girl, or every American from here to Los Angeles, take your choice. Can't you see? The girl saw. She made her choice. So did Morales, and all the others. She saw it was beyond personal feelings, Vidal, bigger than what you felt, or wanted, or what she felt or wanted, or what any of us felt or wanted. If she has the guts to play it that way, I guess we can."

Lucas lowered himself slowly, and hunkered

there over the gurgling coffee pot for a long moment, his face white. Finally he seemed to get himself under control. "Those wagon trains." He made a vague gesture with his hand. "Peanuts. They're hitched up with this somehow, but they're just peanuts. I don't know what the rest is, at least not the whole, but I've got enough pieces to make a good guess. Found a few things working up here, supposedly as a trapper. Both those trains hauled nothing but military supplies. The outfits working civilian contracts haven't been touched. All right. As Hagerman's agent in Santa Fe, I've had access to Military Intelligence down there. Through M.I., Colonel Price has been getting some odd reports from Mexico. You know how General Taylor started disbanding the Mexican forces below the border as soon as possible. He's been finding a discrepancy in the muster rolls. Killed and wounded don't half make up the difference."

"Over the hill?" said Vidal.

Lucas shook his head. "Would officers do that? No, ordinary desertion doesn't account for it, either. Too many rankers. M.I. gave me a list of names from Taylor's muster sheets. Captains Echero, Tecos, Salazar. Recognize any of them? No. Colonels, even. Tierra, Ugardes . . ."

"Ugardes." Vidal's voice was sharp. "Liria said Morales was suspected of being a spy by some of his brother officers. A Colonel Ugardes especially. She implied it might have been the colonel who shot Morales on the Saltillo Highway. That happened before Morales had told me enough of what he had found out to make sense. Maybe this was part of what he would've told me. But what could it mean?"

"Can't you guess?" said Lucas, and then his head turned slightly as he glanced past Vidal and he jumped up, shouting. "Watch it, watch it!"

His flailing moccasins scattered the fire in front of Vidal. There was a scuffle of running men through the darkness that settled after the shower of sparks. A man's hurtling weight struck Vidal and he jumped aside. There was a shot from somewhere beside him, a roar of pain.

"Get out!" shouted Lucas. "Get out!"

Vidal knew the man meant him, yelling at him that way without using his name so he could escape without being recognized, giving him the chance just as the girl had. But somehow Vidal couldn't leave him there. Maybe the game was bigger than he or Lucas or the girl, and Lucas might be strong enough to see it that way—but Vidal knew he wouldn't have left the girl if he had known her danger, and he couldn't leave Lucas now, even if he were being weak about it, or a fool. He threw himself into the struggling knot of men, one of the deadly stilettos flickering into his hand. He sank it hilt deep in the first body he met, and heard the agonized scream. The man twisted around with the blade still in him, grabbing for Vidal.

Vidal tried to free his blade. He staggered backward into an aspen, and with the man still hanging grimly to him went to the ground. They rolled over and over down the steep descent to the bottom of the gully. The man had a gun, but Vidal kept the hammer jammed with his thumb. He got his blade out of the man finally, and twisted for the lunge. The man sighed, and his grip on Vidal relaxed, and they rolled over for that last time with Vidal coming up on top of the relaxing body.

The second man must have followed the sound they made rolling down that gully, because Vidal hadn't yet risen when he heard the small avalanche of rocks and dirt *rattle* down from the bank above. He had the dead man's revolver in his hand as he whirled, still on his knees, straddling the body. The dim blur of a huge figure loomed directly above him, half sliding, half running down the sheer bank, some long-handled weapon raised above his head for the blow. Vidal's instinctive thought was that it should be a clubbed rifle, and, still twisted around on his knees, he fired.

He saw the shadowy bulk jerk, and crash on down. He shot again, and again, and saw the man jerk to each of those bullets, and then with the stunning weight of the tremendous body smashing into him and crushing him over on his back, he fired once more, and the sound was muffled against the man's chest, and the man jerked spasmodically to that one, too.

Vidal lay there for a moment, dazed, waiting for the stiffening of the body lying across him. It remained limp. He squirmed out from beneath, getting shakily to his feet, barely able to recognize the titan who had come down on him in the darkness. El Hacho's shaved head was strangely revolting, somehow, gleaming faintly pale, and dead, against the dark blot of ground. He held his arms still outthrust, his hatchet gripped in both hands. Its blade was buried in the sand just beside the imprint Vidal's head had made.

The Frenchman heard the movement up on the crest of the bank, and, realizing he had only two loads left in his gun, dropped on down the steep bottom of the gully in a swift silent run, then climbing up the bank and cutting into the scrub timber, heading back to circle around behind them and approach the camp from a direction that would at least give him the small advantage of surprise.

It took him longer than he had expected to find the camp again. Long enough for them to have found El Hacho and the other man there in the gully, and to hunt for Vidal, and to leave, when they couldn't find him. He squatted there in the aspens and looked out into the silent darkness covering the gulch Lucas had built his fire in. Even Lucas's tethered horse was gone. Finally

Vidal moved out into the open, soundlessly, in those Apache boot moccasins with their curled-up toes.

There were two bodies in the clearing. He felt mustaches on the face of one; still stooping, he found the other's head, and his fingers traced the haughty line of Cray Lucas's nose, and the thin strength of the lips. With a gasp, Vidal jerked his hand away. Then he forced himself to put it down again, below the chin, where the neck was damp and sticky. Cray Lucas's head had been severed completely from his body. El Hacho? El Hacho.

— V —

It was called Bent's Big Lodge by the Cheyennes, and Bent's Fort by the Yankees, and its square adobe walls seemed to huddle almost fearfully beneath the pall that had descended over the north country. Vidal had expected to discover something there, for it was the only outpost between Taos and Fort Bridger, and every trapper in the West struck it sooner or later. The enormous Mexican cook was famous for her ringing laugh and her biscuits, but sitting now in the parlor with the others at dinner, Vidal had yet to hear her laugh, and the biscuits were sour and soggy. He had told them of Hagerman's wagon train, and one of the hunters who had come north two days before spoke finally, looking dismally at his untouched salt pork.

"I was on my way here f'um Taos. When I passed 'em, they was all stretched out in a line on the trail like a bunch of Neds at chow call, and nary a scalp had been lifted."

"You didn't bury them?" said Vidal.

The man wiped his mouth. "A year ago, I would've. Now, anybody's a fool who stays at a place like that long enough to dig that many graves."

The *engagés* who worked inside the fort and ate pork three times a day were accorded the contemptuous appellation of "Ned" by the mountain men, and the Ned who leaned against the polished center pillar was cleaning his nails absently with a Barlow knife. "All right, so that accounts for Hagerman's train. But what about the trappers? Henry Wallace's party, for instance. He said he'd be in before summer. You been north, Blackeye. You see him?"

He wore a black patch over his right eye, and he finished with his pork, and wiped the grease off his fingers by the simple expedient of running them through his long hair. "Hell, no, I didn't see him. You think I would? If he ain't in by now, he won't ever be in. Just like Pinky Taylor and his bunch last winter. Indians had a ruckus with a party that size, we'd sure hear about it sooner or later, or come across the sign. We didn't hear, did we? No. And we didn't find sign, did we? Hell, no. Why you think I came down? Even the Indians are getting out. And when they get out, it's time for little Blackeye to lace up his possible sack and follow right along. Something I could fight, I'd stay and fight. The mama grizzlies . . . bare-handed! But it's nothing you can fight. It's nothing. Hell!"

Black Andrew shoved through the front door, jerking his wooly head over a stooped shoulder. "New gen'men outside. They got some trappers they found on the road. Want to see you, Mistah Chahles."

Charles Bent stalked to the door, a tall, angry man with a jaw like a jump trap and eyes like the business ends of two .44s. By the crude fur press in the courtyard were three riders who sat, tall and somber, in black hats that turned their faces to featureless shadow and black cloaks that draped in heavy folds over gold-mounted cantles. Something in their appearance struck at Vidal's memory. There were half a dozen others who didn't wear cloaks. They were lashed to their horses, dead heads dropping down on one side of the jaded nags, dead feet dangling on the other side.

"Our *patrón* is traveling north, *señor*," said one of the cloaked riders. "We found these bodies on the trail near Salt Bottoms. My *patrón* recognized two of them who had worked for you. He thought you would want them."

Bent didn't look long at the bodies. "Your *patrón*?"

The cloaked man tilted his head back toward the gate, and Bent and Vidal and the score of silent trappers followed them. The iron-bound doors were swung open, and the noise wakened the two eagles in their slatted cage atop the belfry of the gate house. Their raucous complaint echoed weirdly across the moonlit courtyard. Vidal shivered a little, passing through the chill of the tunnel in the wall. Then he was outside, and could see the cavalcade of horsemen, and the black *carroza* with its four midnight stallions, and it was too late to get back into the tunnel, because the man had already put his mat-gloved hand on the edge of the window, and leaned his head out.

"*Buenas noches*, *Señor* Bent. I am sorry to come with such a sad burden. My *criados* must have told you where we found them. All stretched out on the ground like. . . ." He stopped suddenly, and surprise rounded his little eyes in their pouches of fat. Then he began to chuckle, and it had a sibilant menace. "*A fe mía*, if it isn't *el trovador*! What a rare pleasure to see you so soon again, *Señor* Vidal. Eh? What a rare pleasure."

It was many days after this night at Bent's Big Lodge that El Hacienda Venganza heard the

273

haunting melody of Vidal's violin. Before the *hacienda*, of course, there was the trail. *Don* Bazan had insisted that Vidal accompany them. Whether Vidal would have accepted the chuckling invitation or not didn't matter now. It had been decided for him. It had been decided by that glimpse of the girl's face inside the *carroza*, tense and weary and pale against the rich dark velvet of the rear seat.

They headed westward from Bent's Fort, following a cutoff of the old Spanish Trail that led from Santa Fe to Los Angeles, keeping to the course of the Arkansas River as it wound into the mysterious Sangre de Cristos. Vidal had seen many ranges, from Yucatán to the British Territories, but never had he encountered the utter desolation of these majestic, unknown peaks, rising higher and higher on either side of the Arkansas gorge. He wondered if Lucas had gotten this far in his search; he wondered if any white man had seen these snow-capped *viejos* before.

"Play for us, Vidal. Why do you think I brought you along? Eh? I cannot understand why you left Taos so suddenly. I want you in my entourage, Vidal. You amuse me like no other *trovador* ever has. You shall become even more famous than your illustrious ancestor, Pierre Vidal. You shall be a mime in the court of an emperor greater than any King Richard the Lionhearted your Pierre entertained. *Sí*. Play for me!"

Vidal played. The coach *clattered*. The dusty days passed by in weary succession, leaving Vidal to sleep like a dead man at night, the cloaked figures huddled around him over the coals of a fire. Then they turned out of the gorge onto a narrow trail that looked as if it had been newly hewn from the rocks. They clung to the sheer side of the cut precariously, and topped the rimrock and *clattered* across a plateau and into the scrub timber, and beyond that the thick stands of pine that marked the beginning of the upper slopes. The riders had to hitch ropes to either side of the *carroza* and help pull it along.

"*¿Quién es?*"

The challenge startled Vidal out of a weariness approaching stupor. He stood there, staring blankly at the man who had appeared so suddenly ahead of them, from out of the trees. He was dressed in the red coat and white breeches of the Mexican soldier, with a rifle held at port arms. A bayoneted rifle. A Springfield Yerger.

"I am *Don* Bazan, you fool," said the gross Mexican from the coach. "Use your stupid eyes."

The sentry passed them, and farther on they went by a vedette of red-coated troopers, some lying in a row by a campfire, others watching them pass. On either flank of the slope, Vidal made out bastions built of boulders. "Howitzer emplacements." *Don* Bazan chuckled. "Twenty-four pounders, Vidal. It is not so much the inaccessibility of this place, you see, as it is the guard we keep. Eh?"

The trail dropped into the cañon, widening to a well-traveled road that wound, dusty and rutted, between frowning peaks. They passed several parties of troops working on the road, and every now and then on the upper slopes Vidal caught a glimpse of another battery of howitzers behind forbidding bastions. Finally they came to a stone breastworks laid across the road, with a heavy guard at its entrance. Beyond that was a broad meadow, lined on one side by log buildings laid out with the precision of barracks. There were several squads of infantry drilling at one end, beneath the banner that floated in a lazy breeze on its tall pole—the red and green flag of Mexico. Half a mile past the camp, they rounded a turn and came abruptly to a huge *hacienda*, sprawled out crookedly on a gentler rise of the slope. Vidal placed himself close to the door when Liria Bazan was helped from the *carroza*. Unloading the luggage from on top of the coach, one of the Indian *criados* faltered, almost dropping a heavy iron-bound trunk. Perhaps it was accident that *Don* Bazan got so far away from the girl when he stepped around in front of the *carroza* to shout at the servant, or perhaps it was intent; either way, Vidal took the chance.

"Did you know they were bringing you here?" Vidal asked the girl in low voice.

"You mean when I sent you away at Taos? Of course not. I've never been here before. All those soldiers, those barracks, what does it mean?"

"Can't you guess?" he said, and was still a little dazed by the obvious implications of what he had seen.

"Well," said the huge Bazan, coming back around the coach and chuckling, "shall we go in?"

It was a big somber house with heavy oak doors and chilly halls hung with gilt-framed mirrors from Spain, and finally the great dining hall with rich Brussels carpets on the floor and trophies pegged on the adobe wall. Above the huge stone fireplace at one end was hung the rusty armor of some *conquistador* who had helped conquer this land centuries before, and on either side of the door through which Vidal entered hung a pair of crossed swords.

A group of officers in red coats and Blucher boots were gathered around someone who sat in a high-backed chair at one end of the long table— one man stood apart from them, in civilian dress, white mane gleaming against the seamed leather of his face. His eyes held the vague, watery look that comes sometimes with great age.

"This is *Don* Veneno Panuela," Bazan introduced him. "He built El Hacienda Venganza when he was exiled by Manuel Armijo in Eighteen Thirty-Seven."

Don Veneno Panuela bowed to Vidal. "Being

one of us, *señor*, you can see why I called it The House of Vengeance. Many of my political enemies from Santa Fe have tasted the . . . ah . . . delights of our dungeons here. *Don* Bazan has promised to help me see that Armijo shall be next."

Vidal frowned. "But Armijo was overthrown. . . ."

"*Sí*, Armijo has been overthrown," said *Don* Bazan swiftly, and chuckled, "and *Don* Panuela shall rule Santa Fe, eh?"

The hubbub of talk by the table died, and, as the officers turned away from the man who sat in the chair, one of them stepped toward Bazan. In Santa Fe he had worn a steeple sombrero to mask the bitter intensity of his black eyes, and a peon's rags on his whiplash of a body; now it was a blue coat faced with red satin and bearing the insignia of the 2nd Mexican Dragoons, and the golden epaulets of a colonel. He was about to speak to Bazan, when he saw Vidal. He leaned forward, mouth still open. Then he began to laugh, and it had a thin, mordant sound.

"Well, *Don* Bazan. Let me congratulate you on catching our spy. How did he do it, Lieutenant Vidal?"

"Lieutenant . . . ?" blustered Bazan. "What are you talking about, Ugardes? He is a *trovador*."

"Colonel *Tomás* Ugardes, to be entirely correct," said the officer, bowing toward Vidal with a sardonic smile. "*Sí, Don* Bazan, he is a *trovador* . . . no one who had not been trained from childhood could have played such a part. But he is also Lieutenant Corday Vidal, of the Seventh United States Cavalry, who commanded the squadron that drove Ampudía's dragoons from the Saltillo Highway in September of 'Forty-Six . . . no, Lieutenant, I would hardly advise that!"

Vidal had controlled his instinct to run, knowing how futile any attempt at that was now, but he had been unable to stop the slight turning motion toward the door. It brought him face to face with the lowered bayonets of the guards; he turned back to look down the muzzle of Ugarde's Paterson Colt. Liria Bazan moaned softly. Her eyes were big and dark on Vidal.

"It was Lieutenant Vidal who found Morales Bazan unhorsed that day on the road to Saltillo," said Ugardes. "You remember, *Don* Bazan, even that far back I had sent you word that your nephew, Morales, was already under suspicion of being a *revolucionario*, working as a spy for the Americans. When I saw Vidal and Morales there on the road, the conclusion I reached was a logical one. I got Morales, but Vidal escaped in the confusion of battle. I didn't know who he was then, or even his name. But immediately after the armistice, we began hearing about a first lieutenant of cavalry who was causing a stir in

Washington, spreading rumors of some diabolical plot that threatened the Army of the West and the newly annexed territories of California and New Mexico. We got his name, finally, and I realized it must have been he who I had seen with Morales. Lieutenant Vidal tried to get the War Department to do something, but he had no proof of his claims, of course, and the officials in Washington laughed at him to begin with. Wouldn't even grant his request for an extended leave so he could work on it himself. But soon he brought such unfavorable attention to himself and the Department that they warned him to stop. He must have become obsessed with the idea by then. He didn't stop. Finally he caused so much trouble, trying to convince them, that they drummed him out for conduct unbecoming an officer. We lost track of him then. It must have been then he started on his travels as a *trovador*, hunting this by himself. You made a mistake, Lieutenant, using your own name."

Vidal shrugged. "I didn't think anyone would recognize me this far West. My father left the Green River country many, many years ago."

"You were right." Ugardes smiled. "No one would have recognized you, but for our chance meeting in Santa Fe. It was unfortunate El Hacho and I missed you there."

"El Hacho?" spluttered *Don* Bazan. "If he knew about Vidal, why didn't he tell me when you sent him to Taos for your orders?"

"I told him to," flamed Ugardes, jerking toward the *don*. Then he bit his lips, shrugging bitterly. "What can you expect from a stupid Yaqui? He couldn't keep anything in his mind five minutes. Even got the orders you sent me all mixed up."

"Didn't you get Lucas?" asked Bazan.

"We did that part all right," said Ugardes. "Your suspicions of Lucas were correct. We found a list of our names on him, obtained from the American M.I. down at Santa Fe. There was someone with him, but Lucas kicked the fire out before we could get a good look at the second man, and shouted for him to get out without using his name. The other man killed El Hacho and Pedro in the gully, and then got away. We hunted for him, but it was night, and we were in a hurry to reach here. I couldn't figure out which of the *revolucionarios* it was . . ." He trailed off and was looking at Vidal, and his voice was hardly audible when he spoke again. "You . . . ?"

Vidal nodded dully.

Don Bazan waved his fat arm in a sudden burst of rage. "Get him out, Ugardes!" shouted the huge Mexican. "I'm tired of all these *espías*. How can I trust anyone? He is a spy? Shoot him. Those are the articles of war, aren't they? A firing squad at dawn for spies. No. Not at dawn. Tonight. He is too dangerous to allow even that long. Shoot him tonight. In fact, I will go with you. I want to see him shot with my own eyes!"

Ugardes turned to the other officers, saying something to them, then to the man seated in the chair. This last rose. He was square and stocky in khaki shirt sleeves and blue trousers with the canary yellow stripe of the cavalry up their seams. He was short and red-headed with one arm in a bloody sling. He was Captain Dunn.

— VI —

The gloomy hallway echoed mutedly to the footfalls of the eight troopers comprising the firing squad for Corday Vidal. Colonel Tomás Ugardes led them in his blue dragoon's coat and his gold-trimmed dress cap; they were going to lock Captain Dunn up before they attended to Vidal, and the grizzled officer walked beside the *trovador*.

"*Lieutenant* Vidal." Dunn grinned wryly. "So that's how you knew where I was going when we met in Santa Fe."

"The *revolucionario* I contacted in El Paso told me about the missing patrols," said Vidal. "How did you get it?"

"I snooped too close to what Ugardes and Bazan have there," said Dunn. "Squadron of dragoons ambushed me. I lost five men before I ran out of ammo. We're prisoners of war, supposedly, my patrol and Maynard's and Wells's."

"Why didn't you just finish them off like you did Hagerman's teamsters and those six trappers?" Vidal asked Ugardes bitterly.

"Oh," said Ugardes, "did you find them?"

"At Salt Bottoms." *Don* Bazan was pleased. "I dropped them at Bent's Fort myself. The men there are already very upset. I thought another little hint wouldn't do our cause any harm."

Ugardes smiled faintly. "Those six trappers made night camp with me and my men. Perhaps they had found signs of our encounter with Cray Lucas the day before . . . they seemed suspicious. We backtracked on our trail after we had left them, and found two of them following us. We decided they had all better be stopped from following anybody any more." He turned to Vidal. "Civilians, you see, Lieutenant, have nothing of value to us besides a consignment of Springfield Yergers, perhaps, or a load of military supplies. There is no reason why we should burden ourselves with them. American troops, however, such as Captain Dunn and Lieutenant Maynard and their men, possess military information of the most extreme importance to our undertaking."

"Information which you haven't yet obtained, I take it." *Don* Bazan pouted as he glanced at Dunn's set face.

"Whoever wanders in here gets it," Dunn told Vidal. "That's what's scaring the Indians and trappers so, all these disappearances. I guess you're the only civilian that's gotten this far without being killed. The *trovador* business . . . ?"

"I'm really descended from Pierre Vidal," said the Frenchman. "My family's kept the tradition alive in France since the Twelfth Century. From early childhood, the eldest son is taught the *chansons*, juggling, mimicry. He doesn't necessarily have to take it up as a profession. Just a tradition with us. My father was Jacques Vidal, came here to trap when he was a young man. I was the eldest son. That's why I felt so concerned about this. Sort of my part of the country, up here."

"You were one of the few who didn't underestimate us," said *Don* Bazan, moving ponderously around the turn in the corridor with them. "You cannot dispense with us by merely putting your names to the Treaty of Guadalupe Hidalgo. We saw our defeat coming long before the battle of Monterey, and began our plans then. We secured this *hacienda* by promising to help *Don* Veneno revenge himself on his enemies in Santa Fe. You wonder why General Zachary Taylor found such a discrepancy in the muster rolls of the Mexican army? This is where they are coming, *Señor* Vidal. It is the way Colonel Ugardes came. He was on his way when he met you in Santa Fe. Already we have two companies formed here. In a week, a battalion. A month, an army. And General Santa Anna is coming to lead us."

"It's fantastic," said Vidal.

"Is it?" said Dunn bitterly. "The Mormon battalion left Santa Fe for Utah in May. That leaves Colonel Price with only a few hundred regulars to hold this whole end of New Mexico. Give Ugardes another month or two and he'll have enough men to crush Price. Give him a little longer and he'll have enough to match the whole Army of the West. You were in Mexico, Vidal, you know what a general like Santa Anna can do, given a chance. And unless somebody busts this thing, he'll have that chance. He'll smash Kearny and grab California and New Mexico right back again."

They halted a moment, and one of the guards got a torch from a bracket in the wall, lighting it. Then he unlocked the heavy door to one side, revealing a flight of stone steps disappearing down into the darkness beyond the light.

Don Bazan turned to Vidal. "One last request, *mi trovador*. Ever since you amazed me down at La Fonda, I have had a burning desire to see how on earth you carry so many things in that coat of yours. Now, as you won't be needing it much longer, I wonder if you would honor me. . . ."

Vidal flushed. "Look . . ."

"Give him the coat, if it pleases him," said Ugardes, and waved the Colt in his hand.

Vidal shrugged, slipped out of the voluminous garment. His fat face wreathed in smiles, like a child with a new toy, *Don* Bazan took the vari-colored garment and began to go through the myriad of inside pockets. He took out the violin and bow, then a silk shawl.

"¡*Caracoles*! Look, Ugardes! And the *cuchillos* he juggles, six at a time. And here, this necklace. Pearls. Vidal, you are a walking treasure house."

There was no reason for it, really, but somehow it irritated Vidal to see the gross man pawing through the things he had carried so long. He realized, too, that there wasn't much more time now. His head didn't move, but his eyes sought some chance of escape up and down the gloomy hall.

Bazan caught that and chuckled, still going through the coat. "Never mind, Vidal," he said. "In a few moments you won't have to worry about getting away. Nobody has escaped from The Hacienda Venganza anyway, ever. The dungeons in which Captain Dunn and his men languish are really remarkable."

"And they will continue to languish until they tell us what we wish," said Ugardes thinly. "The disposition of Price's forces in Santa Fe, the amount of his artillery, the condition of his cavalry mounts. We aren't going into this blindly."

"You know, Colonel," said Bazan, "maybe you are wrong about that, maybe we don't need Dunn and his lieutenants. Wasn't it you who always said if we found the leader of the *revolucionarios*, we'd have all the information we could wish. Maybe we have that leader. I am beginning to think I underestimated my niece. I thought she was just a pawn in this revolutionist movement. Maybe I was wrong. They all came to her, didn't they, sooner or later? Even Vidal, here. Of course, even if I had realized she was so important, I couldn't have done much to persuade her in Taos. So many neighbors and all. Hardly the appropriate place for such measures as we can take up here . . ."

"Bazan!" It was Vidal, and his strange melancholy eyes were blazing from a pale, set face, his fists clenched at his sides. "Harm that girl, and I'll come back. Living or dead, I swear, I'll come back and get you for it."

"Ugardes," roared Bazan apologetically, "take him away! Take this *cabrón* away. Take him down and stand him against the wall. I want to hear you shoot him. I want you to come back and tell me he is dead!"

The stairway leading down into the dungeon zigzagged back and forth, cutting back on itself so that the first landing was directly above the third, and the second landing was directly below the first, and over the fourth. As they reached the first level, and turned to take the next flight down to the second landing, a doorway on that second level opened, revealing a cell-like room lit faintly by the guttering torch held in the hand of a turnkey who came out, big and stoop-shouldered, with a ring of keys dangling from his belt. With him were two more guards with Springfield Yergers. Crossing that first landing, Vidal glanced over the edge; far beneath, he could see the dim plane of the third level.

"A long drop, eh, Vidal." Ugardes smiled sardonically.

But the *trovador* had made up his mind, and there were more ways than one of doing the thing. He was looking straight ahead when he stiffened his body and let his eyes widen, and his voice echoed through the dank place suddenly.

"That turnkey!" he shouted. "That turnkey!"

For just that instant, Ugarde's surprised attention was focused entirely on the turnkey below. "¿*Que esta* . . . ?"

Vidal grabbed him by one arm, spinning him around in front. Ugardes yelled and tried to jam a polished Blucher against the stairs to stop himself, but Vidal's weight was flung against him. They tottered together on the edge, and went off together, and Ugardes screamed.

It seemed an eternity of falling before they struck. Vidal had jerked the colonel beneath him, and it was Ugardes who took the full shock. Even then, Vidal's body seemed to explode with pain, and he heard his own involuntary gasp. The rock walls spun around him as he fought to rise to his hands and knees.

Ugardes moaned, stirred weakly, reached up to grab Vidal. The Frenchman caught his head and slammed it against the stone. Ugardes collapsed.

On the first landing, high above, Dunn was a raging figure in the midst of the eight troopers, holding them there as long as he could for Vidal. On the second landing, the two other guards and the turnkey had begun coming down toward Vidal, their slugs ricocheting off stone with wild screams as they opened fire. But it was pitch black down there, and their torch only made a small circle of light directly about them—they were shooting blindly. On the third landing, Vidal rose to his feet, panting, shaking, and began dragging the unconscious Ugardes down toward the fourth level.

There was another room leading off that fourth landing, and already two more sentries were plunging out the door, and up the steps toward Vidal. He fumbled for Ugarde's six-shooter, a Paterson Conversion model with heavy gold plating on its grips. His first shot rocked the dank walls, sending down the guard carrying the torch. Before the torch spluttered out, Vidal shot the other man, and, in the darkness that descended, heard him scream and fall.

He dragged Ugardes over their bodies, and stumbled into the dark guard room on the fourth landing. Outside, he heard the turnkey and his men coming down, but they showed a reluctance, natural under the circumstances, and he prayed for the time that would give him. Working with a swift desperation, he stripped off Ugarde's black Bluchers and silk-faced dragoon's coat and cream-colored breeches. Then he pulled off his own Apache *botas* with their curled-up toes, and greasy buckskins. He was about the same height as Ugardes, if slightly broader through the shoulders. The cream-colored pants fitted well enough; the boots cramped his toes slightly. His figure no longer looked lanky or ungainly; it had taken on the trim, compact military appearance that could come only from the academy.

"Colonel?" called the turnkey, and the torchlight wavered into the room as he reached the bottom of the stairs. "*¿Dónde está, mi coronel?* Where are you?"

Vidal had Ugarde's cravat torn off and whipped around his own neck, bunched up across the lower part of his face as if it had been torn out in the struggle. He jammed the colonel's dress cap down over his eyes, and stumbled out, shouting in an imitation of Ugarde's thin, bitter voice: "*¡Pendejos!* Are you cowards? After him!"

The turnkey stood on the bottom step, bending forward to peer through the flickering glow of torchlight, the two sentries behind him, gripping rifles nervously. "*Pues, mi colonel,* these two guards . . ."

"The *cabrón* had a gun!" shouted Vidal. "I tried to stop him after he shot those two men, but he wounded me and I fell into the guard room. He's gotten below somewhere. Are you going after him or do you want a court-martial?"

His ringing voice turned the turnkey pale. The man stumbled across the two bodies, passing Vidal with a scared glance. Vidal stool there, his lean body bent forward in the intense pose characteristic of Ugardes.

Captain Dunn had held those other guards on the second landing long enough, and must have accounted for one of them, even with his bare hands; there were only seven now, two hustling the battered, dazed Yankee officer down the stairs before the others. Dunn was doubled up, with his good arm held across a bleeding head, his wounded one torn from the sling, hanging limply. He stumbled by Vidal, hardly looking at him. One of the guards raised his torch, glancing closer. His face lit only faintly by the reddish light, Vidal whirled on the man.

"On down the stairs!" he screamed. "Two of you lock this fool *capitán* up now. The rest of you find him. ¡*Pronto*!"

Vidal bullied them down the last flight to the corridor where heavy iron-bound doors stood in a line on both sides of the hall, set with small barred windows at which haggard faces appeared. Vidal could hear the other guards he had sent down first, stumbling through the darkness farther on, hunting him.

"This one," he said, indicating the first door.

"*Pues, mi colonel*, this is not the *capitán*'s cell. . . ." It was the turnkey. He was there. He stopped when he saw the Colt in Vidal's fist.

"Open this one," snapped Vidal, "and then the next one, and the next. Just keep going till they're all open."

"Vidal," gasped Dunn, jerking straight.

"Mimicry is one of the *trovador*'s accomplishments, Captain." Vidal smiled, and his gun covered the two guards holding Dunn. "Did I do well?"

Dunn couldn't answer for a moment. Under the threat of the Colt, the astounded guards backed against the wall, relinquishing their rifles, and the turnkey opened the cells, one by one. From the first dank chamber came Lieutenant Maynard and three of his men. Wells was in the third. From the others came troopers of their squadrons, and of Dunn's, blinking in the guttering torchlight, staring at Vidal.

"Don't stand there like jackasses!" Dunn yelled, snapping out of his surprised daze. "Get those rifles. It's our chance . . ."

He broke off, whirling. The guards who had gone on down the stairs were coming back now. They reached the circle of light and realized too late how many men stood in the hall, and who they were. Vidal's Colt held them while the Yankees took their guns, too. Then Vidal locked the turnkey and all of the guards into a cell.

"Let's go," said Dunn. "They've got a lot of men on those howitzers, and working on the road. It doesn't leave many right here at camp. If we don't have to take them on all at once, we'll have a chance."

"Bazan's still up at that top door with the two guards," Vidal said. "They can hold you off and raise the alarm. The whole camp would be there before you could get through. Keep your men here."

"Vidal . . ." Dunn stopped there, because Vidal's slim, lithe figure was already halfway up the next flight of stairs. He moved without much sound in the darkness, passing the two guards he had shot on the third landing, and the turnkey's room on the second.

"¿Quién es?" called *Don* Bazan.

"Colonel Ugardes," said Vidal, halting on the stairs beyond the light cast by the torches. "Vidal got hold of a gun and shot some of my men. I'll need those two with you to help carry them up."

"I heard the shooting," said *Don* Bazan. "Vidal, he's . . . ?"

"Dead," said the Frenchman. "I had the honor myself."

"*Sacramento*, and he could play Schubert so beautifully." *Don* Bazan sighed. "Ah, well, the fortunes of war, eh? When you finish, you will find me in the main hall. We might as well begin with the girl."

The Frenchman heard him move ponderously

away down the hall. When the sound had died, Vidal ordered the guards to follow him down. He didn't want to risk anything up here, now that the end was so close. He led them past the third landing and was on the fourth flight himself, when one of them cursed behind him. The man carrying the torch had passed the half open door of that guard room on the third level, and the light must have fallen across Ugarde's stripped body inside. The guard turned down toward Vidal now, and the torchlight caught the surprise in his eyes, and the understanding.

"*¡Compadre!*" he shouted. "*¡Él no es Ugardes!*"

Vidal's shot drowned him out. He fell forward, dropping the torch. With a wild cry, the other man began firing, turning to stumble out of the circle of light cast by the torch sputtering in the stairway. Vidal fired again, missed. Then the man was a running blot in the gloom above him. He heard a wild, animal yell behind, and Captain Dunn and his men surged up from below, carrying Vidal with them.

They reached the upper hall, saw the guard who had escaped running toward the dining hall, shouting. A Mexican officer burst from the large room, followed by others. They began to run for the front door, following the guard.

"Halt, you *cobardes!*" bellowed the officer, hauling at his sidearm. "About face. Meet them like soldiers!"

But there was something terrifying about the haggard mob of American cavalrymen, charging madly down on the Mexicans, filling the hall with a din of crazed yells, eyes feverish in pale haggard faces, clothes tattered and bloody—a crowd of screaming devils from the bowels of hell. Two or three of the Mexicans stopped, and began firing, but they broke again. The enlisted man who had sounded the alarm dropped his rifle and ran for the door. The officer turned and shot him down. But a first lieutenant gave a hoarse sob, and turned and ran, and then others, and finally it was only the captain, standing there alone, above the body of the trooper he had shot. He emptied his revolver at the Americans.

Running in the first ranks, Vidal saw the flaming gun, and a stunning blow knocked his leg from beneath him. He went down with the boots pounding all around him and over him, and Captain Dunn's men took the door frame out with them as the press of their surging bodies went through. Sobbing, Vidal dragged himself to the wall, caught hold of the waist-high molding. The agony of putting weight on his wounded leg was almost unbearable. But Bazan had said . . .

Liria Bazan's white *mantilla* had caught on the table in that big dining hall, when she fell. It hung limply above her body, its lacy pattern marked by an ugly red stain. Vidal had to catch the table to keep from falling when he reached her. Her eyes opened at his touch.

"*Don* Bernal," she gasped weakly. "When he heard the shots . . . tried to take me with him. When I wouldn't go . . . shot me. Back door . . . leads to stairway. Hall above goes to rooms overlooking slope behind. Short drop to the ground. *Señor* . . . they said . . . Cray Lucas . . ."

He nodded. "I've got to tell you this, Liria. Lucas . . . Lucas loved you." He stopped, and then his voice came out choked. "You . . ."

"How could I," she said. "I thought he was just a disgusting dandy. Don't you know who I love, Corday Vidal? Didn't you see it . . . at Taos?"

For a moment he didn't understand, then it leaped up in him like a flame, and his words came out in a swift rush. "Why did you send me away, then? If you felt that . . . why?"

"You know why," she said. "For this. But if it hadn't been for this, and, if we had met, just like other people met . . . if I had lived . . . how would it have been?"

"Don't talk like that."

She shook her head weakly. "No . . . quickly . . . tell me . . . how would it have been . . . ?"

He saw how it was then, and a tortured look crossed his face. He tried to speak, but the words wouldn't come, somehow. Then she wouldn't have heard anyway, and he didn't try any more. There was a faint smile on her lips as he pulled the blue *capisayo* up over her closed eyes, and gently disengaged her small cold hand from his. His eyes were bleak and empty, and he stood up abruptly. For a moment he stood there, unable to think, stupefied by what had happened, unable to feel even his grief very clearly. Then something began working down inside him. Bazan? Yes, Bazan. The only thing left now.

As if in a daze, the *trovador* stumbled to where Bazan had dropped his vari-colored coat. He slipped out of Ugarde's blue dragoon's coat and into his own voluminous garment, and moved toward the door in the far wall without looking back, face pale and twisted with the pain it caused him to walk. The door opened on a stairway; he had to support himself against the wall going up. The corridor above was unlit, almost pitch black. *Don* Bazan was a singularly ponderous man, not used to moving about much, or fast, and it must have taken him that long to climb the stairs and reach the end of the hall. Coming from the blackness down there, Vidal caught a hollow, fumbling sound, such as a man might make trying to open unfamiliar shutters of the window that overlooked the slope behind the *hacienda*.

The *trovador* slipped the violin beneath his chin, and took the bow from another pocket in his coat, and drew the first strain from the battered instrument. *Pianissimo*, to begin with, soft and eerie in the sombrous hall. The movement at the other end stopped, and Vidal heard a sharply indrawn breath. He moved forward, biting his lips with every limping step. *Accelerando* now, swelling to fill the corridor with the bizarre melody.

"The 'Dance of Death,' " whispered the man at the other end.

"Yes, Bazan," said Vidal. "The 'Dance of Death.' I told you you'd hear it again, didn't I? Down at Taos. And I told you I'd come back if you harmed the girl, didn't I?"

"No!" *Don* Bazan's rising voice matched the *crescendo* of the violin. "Ugardes killed you. He told me himself. No, Vidal. You are dead. No, no, no . . ."

The sound of his gun drowned his shrill scream as he fired blindly in that darkness. The lead made a dull, *thudding* tattoo into adobe all around Vidal. Putting aside the violin, he began to slip the knives from his coat. The crazy blind shots of Bazan filled the hall with their thunder, and, every time the *don* fired, Vidal threw a stiletto, using the gun flash for his target. Through the crazy din, he could tell that his knives missed the Mexican by the muted, hollow *plunk* they made striking the wooden shutters down there. A slug whipped through his coat. He caught the flare of the next shot, and another blade left the deft fingers that could do so many deadly things at once. Then the bullet caught him. He felt the searing pain, his body jerked halfway around. He stumbled. He caught himself.

"No, Vidal, no, no . . ."

It finished in a mad bedlam of sound, the shrill yells of the gross Mexican and the roar of his gun, the dull *thud* of bullets striking around Vidal. The last shot echoed down the hall, and died. Vidal sent another stiletto where the gun flash had been. There was a moment of painful waiting. Then a heavy body shook the floor. Vidal had time to recall, abstractedly, that he hadn't heard his last knife make that hollow *plunking* sound down there, and realized that must have been the one that did it. Then he fell himself, and that was all, for a while. . . .

Someone was pulling off his ragged coat. He twisted around, fighting the hands. Other hands grabbed him, held him down.

"You got one in the ribs," growled the powder-grimed Captain Dunn. "We found you above, carried you down. Hold still. It's all over. We trapped those rankers before they could spread the alarm. When the enlisted men found we had the bulk of their officers, they made a deal with us. Only a few *vedettes* holding out on the road now. Lieutenant Maynard's mopping up. Hold still!"

Vidal didn't hold still, and Captain Dunn let him go when he saw why.

She sat very straight in a high-backed chair, with three ragged troopers hovering around her like nervous hens. Her dark eyes met Vidal's, and he seemed to be the only one she saw.

"I must have fainted when you were telling me how it would be," she said weakly.

"I thought . . ."—he stumbled—"I thought . . ."

"She'll be here as long as you will," said Dunn. "She'll be here to see them reinstate you in the Seventh, and hear the Department admit they were wrong for once, and maybe see them pin that brevet on your rank for conspicuous gallantry."

"I fainted when you were telling me how it would be," she repeated, eyes still on Vidal. "I didn't hear."

"I'll tell you again," he said, and reached for something inside his coat. Then he was kneeling beside her, and slipping the gold ring on her finger, and his voice was audible to her alone. "*Recibe mi corazón, recibe mi amor, recibe mi vida. . . .*"

— About the Author —

Les Savage, Jr. was born in Alhambra, California and grew up in Los Angeles. His first published story was "Bullets and Bullwhips" accepted by the prestigious magazine, Street & Smith's *Western Story*. Almost ninety more magazine stories followed, all set on the American frontier, many of them published in Fiction House magazines such as *Frontier Stories* and *Lariat Story Magazine* where Savage became a superstar with his name on many covers. His first novel, *Treasure of the Brasada*, appeared from Simon & Schuster in 1947. Due to his preference for historical accuracy, Savage often ran into problems with book editors in the 1950s who were concerned about marriages between his protagonists and women of different races—a commonplace on the real frontier but not in much Western fiction in that decade. Savage died young, at thirty-five, from complications arising out of hereditary diabetes and elevated cholesterol. However, as a result of the censorship imposed on many of his works, only now are they being fully restored by returning to the author's original manuscripts. Among Savage's finest Western stories are *Fire Dance at Spider Rock* (Five Star Westerns, 1995), *Medicine Wheel*

(Five Star Westerns, 1996), *Coffin Gap* (Five Star Westerns, 1997), *Phantoms in the Night* (Five Star Westerns, 1998), *The Bloody Quarter* (Five Star Westerns, 1999), *In The Land of Little Sticks* (Five Star Westerns, 2000), *The Cavan Breed* (Five Star Westerns, 2001), and *Danger Rides the River* (Five Star Westerns, 2002). Much as Stephen Crane before him, while he wrote, the shadow of his imminent death grew longer and longer across his young life, and he knew that, if he was going to do it at all, he would have to do it quickly. He did it well, and, now that his novels and stories are being restored to what he had intended them to be, his achievement irradiated by his powerful and profoundly sensitive imagination will be with us always, as he had wanted it to be, as he had so rushed against time and mortality that it might be.

Center Point Large Print
600 Brooks Road / PO Box 1
Thorndike, ME 04986-0001 USA

(207) 568-3717

US & Canada:
1 800 929-9108
www.centerpointlargeprint.com